FRIENDS
of the
FAMILY

Also by Camilla R. Bittle
in Thorndike Large Print ®

Dear Family

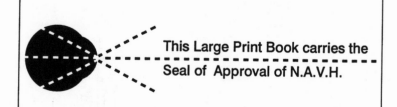

This Large Print Book carries the
Seal of Approval of N.A.V.H.

FRIENDS
of the
FAMILY

Camilla R. Bittle

Thorndike Press • Thorndike, Maine

Published in 1994 by arrangement with St. Martin's Press, Inc.

Thorndike Large Print ® General Series.

The tree indicium is a trademark of Thorndike Press.

The text of this Large Print edition is unabridged.
Other aspects of the book may vary from the original edition.

Set in 16 pt. News Plantin by Rick Gundberg.

Printed in the United States on acid-free paper.

Library of Congress Cataloging in Publication Data

Bittle, Camilla.
    Friends of the family / Camilla R. Bittle.
      p.   cm.
    ISBN 0-7862-0260-2 (alk. paper : lg. print)
    1. History teachers — Massachusetts — Fiction. 2. Family
— Massachusetts — Fiction. 3. Massachusetts — Fiction.
4. Large type books. I. Title.
[PS3552.I7739F75 1994b]
813'.54—dc20   94-13821

For Claude, Elizabeth, Robert, and Rebecca with love

1

When they were growing up, Eleanor and her sister, Jane, had the mistaken notion that Aunt Alice was rich. They used to talk about "the Dwires" with undisguised envy — the Dwires being Aunt Alice, who was a widow, Harold, who was older than their brother, Wilson, and Cornelia (called Sissy), who was Jane's age. Eleanor was the youngest. Sissy actually spent two summers at a dude ranch in Wyoming (it escaped their notice that her uncle owned it) and later, when Sissy was at Vassar, she spent her summers on Cape Cod with the Barringers, who were old-money rich. There again, they overlooked the fact that while Sissy was treated like one of the family, she was actually there to baby-sit the Barringers' two small children.

Jane and Eleanor were impressed by Aunt Alice's house in Cambridge, by Aunt Alice's Packard car, and impressed by Sissy's hand-me-downs (Sissy wore things like jodhpurs and angora sweaters), and although they realized later that Sissy's things may have come to her as hand-me-downs from Aunt Alice's old friends before they ever found their way out to Harrison, they didn't think of that then. As a matter of fact, Eleanor wasn't sure when it was that she had realized Aunt Alice lived on the thin edge of genteel poverty, which was exactly what she did.

Aunt Alice was not actually a relative at all. She was a courtesy aunt and the wife of a fine man who had befriended their father at a time when he needed such a friend. Aunt Alice's husband, Elliot Dwire, was a stockbroker with a North Shore background, and Aunt Alice was from Philadelphia. Her family, prior to her father's misfortune, which was another way of describing his squandering of a large inheritance, had been wealthy. Aunt Alice understood the management of a large house and presided graciously at tables on which there were silver bowls of fresh flowers. She liked to think of herself as a patron of the arts, although after 1929 all she could offer in patronage was her name and by 1935 her name didn't count for much. Charming ladies of pedigree were not revered in 1935 as they had been in gentler times, but in Aunt Alice's case there was one exception, Eleanor's father, in whom gratitude to Elliot Dwire survived a multitude of services and snubs.

"If it hadn't been for Elliot Dwire," their father would say, "I'd never have gone to Harvard," and going to Harvard had opened the door to an academic life for their father, who was more suited to the scrutiny of history than to the dairy farm of his boyhood. He spent his life at the Harrison School, thanks to Elliot Dwire. Jane and Wilson and Eleanor grew up on its campus, and their father always gave the credit for this to Elliot, although it was his own dedication to the principles of Harrison that held him there year after year.

Elliot Dwire was the youngest trustee on the board of the Harrison School near Northridge, Massachusetts, when their father was a student there. At that time Harrison was a school for disadvantaged boys who, but for its generous financial aid policy, would not have been educated at all. In 1913, boys of fourteen were as apt to be down in a coal mine or milking thirty cows twice a day as sitting in school learning algebra; the Harrison School was founded for those among them who had noticed that, indeed, the corn was green and had had the good fortune to attract the attention of anyone who was connected with the school and knew of its mission to educate the promising young of the poor.

So it was that John Richards, fresh from

a New Hampshire farm, arrived with his trunk at the Northridge railway station one day in 1913 and four years later graduated with honors and a vast discontent for the rocky pastures of New Hampshire.

It was at that point that Elliot Dwire, a young man himself although already established in a brokerage firm in Boston, singled out several boys from the graduating class for a noble experiment. With persuasive zeal, Elliot established the Dwire Fund, a scholarship pool from which to award grants to graduates of Harrison who qualified for admittance to universities of distinction. Other men of vision and compassion who had the means to educate their own sons and saw the wisdom in extending the same benefits to less fortunate boys of promise joined in the effort, and thanks to Elliot Dwire their father went to Harvard and graduated in 1921.

During his years in Cambridge he did odd jobs to support himself and found time to express his gratitude to the Dwires by making himself useful to them as a sort of houseboy-handyman. Aunt Alice, despite her own father's profligate ways, retained her conviction that past distinction entitled one to present oblation and had no trouble finding things for John to do on his Saturday afternoons during the four years he was in Cambridge. By the time he got his degree one bright June day in 1921, he had washed every window in the Dwire house on Fresh Pond Park a dozen times, served at countless dinner parties wearing a borrowed black coat and tie, and shoveled the walks and drive at Number 24 through four long winters of heavy snow. Besides all of that, he had found time somehow to meet and court a girl named Grace, who sang solos in the choir of the School Street Congregational Church and taught third grade at the Madison Park School. As soon as he graduated they were married, and it was only shortly before this that it occurred to him that a diploma was no guarantee of a job. Inasmuch as he didn't like to admit to this small oversight, he rarely spoke of it, but Grace used to tell the story with such feeling one would have thought she had been there herself.

"It was only a month or two before commencement," (it was actually three) their mother said, "that Aunt Alice's husband called your father into his library and said, 'I hear you're getting married, John. Congratulations.' "

They could all imagine it. Following their mother's energetic dramatization carefully, they saw the revered Elliot rise and come around his desk to shake their father's hand and pound him on the back. As their mother

11

talked on, conjuring up the Dwire library, a dark, paneled room with shelves to the ceiling and a stepladder on wheels, the children visualized lamps with parchment shades casting a glow on Oriental rugs and shining warmly on mahogany furniture. Outside a stiff March wind whipped forsythia bushes into frenzies of lemon froth and sun struck bright swords of light into the room, where a fire crackled behind a brass screen. They shuddered in anticipation as Grace quoted the great man.

"Well," said Elliot, "sit down, John, and tell me your plans."

"Plans," laughed their mother, "can you believe that we didn't have any plans? Can you imagine your poor father sitting there with nothing to say?"

One might have thought the story would be humiliating to their father, but he sat back with an air of diffidence, demonstrating his belief that women were to be humored in the matter of romantic tales. He was, after all, a professor, he had provided his family with a comfortable home and the campus of the Harrison School had proved a singularly pleasant place to spend the Depression.

Jane and Wilson waited patiently for the familiar story to unfold, polite and bored, but Eleanor, whose imagination often ran wild

12

with anxiety, could see her father in that splendid room, sitting bolt upright in a chair that he probably wished would swallow him, and could actually feel her father's embarrassment as he croaked, "Plans? I plan to get a job, of course."

"History, isn't it?" said Elliot.

"That's right."

"That means teaching, I suppose. Have you thought of going back to Harrison?"

He hadn't. All he had thought about was approaching organizations where a Harvard diploma would have meaning . . . banks, perhaps. "I hadn't thought of Harrison," he confessed.

"Think about it," said Elliot. "I'll inquire next week when I'm up for trustees' meeting. I think you'd make a good teacher, John."

The story ended there. They all knew the rest and accepted the fact of Harrison gratefully, although sometimes John himself wondered if there might not be some sort of life somewhere else, beyond the protective walls of the sheltered society of the Harrison campus. "If Elliot Dwire had lived . . ." he often said, but Elliot had died quite suddenly and when, not too long afterwards, penicillin removed the terror and tragedy of pneumonia, they lamented Elliot's death even more, for the loss it was to them all and the bitterness

13

of knowing it was needless.

Anyway, John and Grace went back to Harrison and moved into one of the cottages in the woods reserved for junior faculty, and for eight years, during which time the three children were born, they were relatively happy. By the time of the crash in 1929 the family had outgrown the cottage and been moved to Drury House across from the chapel. This was the house Eleanor remembered, and this was the house that Aunt Alice used like a way station in a foreign land for as long as they lived there.

Drury house was a large, white New England house with a side porch, an attic, a dining room separated from the living room by wide double doors, and a deep backyard behind a hedge of lilacs. There were four bedrooms and one bathroom on the second floor. Eleanor, being the youngest, was put in the smallest room, but by the time she was twelve Wilson was in college and she moved into his room. Their mother then made her room into a sewing room.

Grace was delighted to have a sewing room, although she did say wistfully, "What a difference it would have made to have a sewing room when you girls were wearing dresses. Now it's nothing but sweaters and skirts and dungarees."

14

Or she might remark, "I wish we'd had that room when Mother Richards was alive." What she meant was that she wished it could have been used for a sewing room then to accommodate the boxes of quilt pieces her husband's mother had saved from a lifetime of making aprons and housedresses, but, of course, when she was with them they had needed space for beds.

Grace was a sweet, pretty woman, tireless in her devotion to family, and if she had a failing it was simply that she never saw life for what it was. When the children were small she focused on the future and when she was finally old she focused on the past. In between she canned more tomatoes, baked more bread, and read more books than anybody else they ever knew.

Gradually Eleanor began to think of this as the main difference between her mother and Aunt Alice because Aunt Alice never canned a tomato in her life, never baked a loaf of bread, and if she read at all it did nothing to broaden her understanding of her fellow-man. Caught in the great flood she would have emerged bedraggled but triumphant, and when the log that had borne her over the water touched land she would have stepped off, looked around, and found someone to make her a lean-to and crack her a coconut.

Eleanor never realized how her mother resented this until it was all over and done with. Mostly she remembered looking out of an upstairs window to see Aunt Alice's black Packard parked beside the spruce trees that lined the drive and hearing Jane shout, "They're here again!"

In the summer of 1935 when Eleanor was seven the family experienced two invasions, one was the usual and expected, though unannounced, arrival of Aunt Alice with Sissy and Harold, and the other was the appearance of a troop of Gypsies who rattled up the state road in wagons and two ancient black Ford trucks to camp in the Purple Meadow for over a month and to change the family's life forever afterwards.

Aunt Alice came first.

Eleanor was at the bedroom window looking up the hill to see if the headmaster's children were riding their pony in the circular drive in front of Colton House, where they lived, when Aunt Alice's Packard appeared, nosing like a sleek seal along the sinuous road from the chapel to Drury House.

"They're here again," she said to her sister, Jane, who was lying on her stomach on the bed, reading.

"I suppose that means Sissy is going to be

here for a month," said Jane in disgust. "Look and see if Harold's with them."

Harold was sixteen and her tone suggested he would be more welcome than his sister, perhaps even sufficiently to entice her to put down her book.

Eleanor pulled aside the curtain to get a good view as the car turned in and drew up beside the spruce and hemlocks that lined the drive.

"Yes," she said, as Harold, wearing khaki shorts and a white shirt, opened the door on the driver's side. She added excitedly, "He was driving!"

Aunt Alice and Sissy emerged from the other side of the car, and suddenly there was their father, crossing the lawn with his arms out, saying heartily, "Hello, hello," because, once again, Aunt Alice was providing him an opportunity to demonstrate his gratitude to her husband, Elliot, who had delivered him from a life of spreading manure. Behind him their mother, who had torn off her apron and dropped it on a kitchen chair, came forward to meet the Dwires.

"Alice," she said warmly, "how nice to see you. Come in. I'll call the girls."

One would have thought that the Dwires' arrival was the nicest thing that could have happened on that sultry July day in 1935, and as they all came up the front steps together there was a pleasant babbling as Aunt Alice said, as she always did, that the campus looked beautiful.

"Every time I come I think how much it would mean to Elliot to see the new buildings and the grounds," she said.

"A great loss," murmured their father, meaning that Elliot's death ten years ago was a tragedy, which it was, and that Elliot's worth would never be equaled by anyone now living or to be born. Their father felt this sincerely.

"How about some tea or lemonade?" said their mother. "It won't take a minute," and as she passed the stairs she called, "Jane . . . Eleanor, come down, girls. Aunt Alice is here."

In the kitchen Grandmother Richards was shelling beans. It would be another two months before she left to go to her daughter's in Florida for the winter. She knew all about the Dwires, and what it meant to have one of these unexpected visits from Alice and the children, and when she saw Grace's mouth set in a grim line she said, "Well, what is it this time?"

"We'll see," said Grace.

In the living room Aunt Alice sat down with a sigh and said offhandedly, "Why don't you girls run along out and find the boys. I think they've gone over to the chapel."

18

Climbing the chapel tower was something people did. It was something everybody but Eleanor seemed to enjoy. Sometimes Sissy teased her, but usually they all took it for granted and thought nothing of leaving Eleanor in the balcony, alone and trembling at the thought of the chapel tower. In her nightmares she crawled, clinging to an open railing, up the steep wood steps from loft to loft, past the gigantic dark bells that shook the stairway when they pealed the hours as she struggled to reach the top, and then, having succeeded, she crouched in terror against the stone parapet while others admired the view of the valley below.

As Jane and Sissy bolted for the door, Eleanor sank down on the stairs and Aunt Alice, noticing her there, waved and smiled.

Aunt Alice wore a tan linen skirt and had a lavender scarf around her neck. Her stockings were so sheer they looked like her skin and she wore alligator pumps with high heels. She was sleek and elegant and it was clear that she made Grace feel dowdy. Grace brushed nervously at her hair, which was escaping the bun at the back of her neck in wisps and strands. Alice's abundant hair, the color of molasses, was wound in a neat french twist. Stretching out her long, slim legs, she said with a sigh, "I wish I could stay, Grace, but

I can't. Something's come up and I haven't had time to think."

What had come up was an invitation for Alice to spend a month at Lake Champlain, where her friends the McAllisters had a summer house. Harold and Sissy weren't invited, she said, and she'd brought them along to Harrison in the hope she could leave them there.

This had happened before.

"I should have called," said Alice, "but it all came up so suddenly. Of course if it's not convenient I can take them along to Rita Forbes's in Burlington, but they'd so much rather be here with the children."

"Of course," said John, "glad to have them." He turned to Grace, "Aren't we, dear?" he said.

Grace smiled. She would have smiled if he had said, "I've brought home a wildcat for the children to play with." A smile was her first reaction to everything, but she said, "You know your mother's here, John. How will we sleep?"

"Oh, heavens," said Alice, "put Harold in a tent in the yard and Sissy on a cot. It's summer."

"Harold can go in with Wilson and Sissy with the girls," John added cheerfully, "and how are you, Alice?"

Grace went to the kitchen and filled the tea-kettle, and then she called to Eleanor. "Fix a plate of cookies, dear," she said. She pulled out the tea cart and reached for the good china, but she was not smiling.

"Are they staying?" Eleanor asked.

"Yes," her mother replied.

Sissy and Harold spent a month with them that time. From blueberries to peaches, from peas to summer squash. They batted tennis balls with old rackets and swam in the pool when it was open to the faculty. It was better here than at the dude ranch, Sissy said, and Jane, who discovered an interest in Harold she had not suspected before, wondered why she had dreaded their coming.

Jane and Sissy spent hours that month poring over Jane's movie-star scrapbook. At the table they whispered and giggled. Sissy pushed at Wilson whenever she encountered him, and Jane made a point of ignoring Harold. As for Eleanor, there was always Marmalade, offspring of the cat that came with Drury House when they'd first moved in. Eleanor thought Jane and Sissy were silly. Hearing them whisper, she would say scornfully, "What's so funny about that?" and she would pick up Marmalade and carry her out to the swing and put her face down and whisper that they were silly girls. "I love you best, you darling cat," she said softly. They sat there until Marmalade grew tired and stalked off. It was hot and she was bored. If they would behave themselves her father would take them to the pool after supper. *All* of them, she thought happily.

Grace thought to herself that the noise and the meals and the wash were going to kill her, and Grandmother Richards, sitting and observing as she shelled beans or peeled potatoes or sliced cucumbers, asked, "Why do you put up with it, Grace?" in an indignant voice that failed to penetrate the frantic exhaustion that rendered Grace speechless. Since Grandmother Richards usually answered her own questions, her daughter-in-law's silence didn't trouble her.

"I know," she said, "you do it for John. Men don't realize."

"Elliot was very good to John."

"That was a long time ago."

"Things have been hard for Alice."

Grandmother Richards snorted.

Everyone knew Alice was rich. If she weren't rich why did she drive a Packard? She lived in a big house, her clothes came from Jordan Marsh, and Sissy and Harold went to private schools.

"Why have things been so hard for Alice?"

22

asked Grandmother Richards, and Grace couldn't answer.

The truth was that even in those days Grace suspected Alice's clothes had been given to her by old friends, that Sissy's and Harold's tuition was taken care of by educators who remembered and revered their father, that the house in Cambridge hadn't been painted or redecorated since Elliot's death, and that in spots the mortar was crumbling and interior walls that had once been ivory were gradually turning to beige and would eventually achieve the dull brown of bronze.

Alice managed, of course, by simply keeping up appearances. Her manner was the beautiful assurance that goes with money, her address was correct, she knew the right people, at least she conversed knowingly of them because she continued to be invited to their tea parties and summer houses. Elliot had left her with a portfolio of good investments and when, after the crash, the certificates became as worthless as wrapping paper and the broker and banker tried to explain this to Alice, she simply held up her hands in helpless horror.

"Don't tell me," she cried, "I don't want to know. Elliot said everything was in order and he trusted you implicitly. He said I'd never have to worry about money because the most honorable men in the world looked after his affairs, so I leave it all to you."

Grace and John never inquired, but they suspected Elliot's friends did what they could for Alice and, in all likelihood, supplied Alice from their own pockets as they could and spared her the truth, which was that most of Elliot's holdings were valueless.

Grace said privately to John, "Of course she must know. You can think what you want to, but Alice isn't stupid. I think she decided long ago that helplessness is her only chance for survival. As long as her friends think she doesn't know how badly off she is, the farce will go on."

"That's very uncharitable, Grace."

"That may be, but she's played her little game for years. She knows it isn't convenient for us to have Sissy and Harold right now. That's why she didn't call. She knew if they just appeared we'd say yes."

Somehow or other that interminable visit came to an end. Alice returned from Lake Champlain with a beautiful tan and a big box of maple sugar for Grace. She collected Harold and Sissy and drove home to Cambridge, and they didn't hear from her again until it was time for Christmas cards. The cot in Wilson's room was folded up and put in the attic, the cushions from the hammock that had been used to make a bed for Eleanor were taken down to the porch again, and Eleanor went back into the double bed with Jane.

By then it was already the middle of August and Grandmother Richards, with her steamer trunk, was ready to take the train to Florida. The garden was full of tomatoes and cucumbers. Squash bugs crawled lazily up furry squash vines to sleep on the broad, flat undersides of the leaves. The sultry heat of early August gave way to the dry heat of late August, and pumpkins, like oranges, appeared in the garden, tight, hard fists that would swell to become the lurid faces of Halloween. And then one day their father came home from town and said, "The Gypsies are back in Purple Meadow."

In the old days, he told them, the Gypsies came every summer, but times were changing and it had been some time since they'd last appeared. They roamed in wider circles now, moving farther and farther south to escape the cold, forced by snow and hard times to seek new campgrounds. When the Gypsies came, he said, people locked up their chickens and their houses, kept their daughters inside and their sons busy in the garden.

Wilson and Jane and Eleanor were wild to go down to Purple Meadow to see the Gypsy camp, but their mother said, "Certainly not!

25

I don't want to hear of any of you going near that place." And she looked hard at Wilson and said, "And I mean you too, Wilson."

"Now, Grace," said their father, "I don't see the harm in riding by there one day. These are the nomads of the world, a people without a history, with no culture and no art, a spectacle to remember. One of these days they'll disappear."

"It can't be too soon for me," she said, "they're dirty and sly. Only fools trust them. I'm going to put what little silver I have in the attic."

"I want to see them," said Jane. "I've read about them and seen pictures of them, Mother. They dance around bonfires and tell fortunes."

"It's all rubbish, Jane," she said, looking sternly at their father, who replied, "Your mother's right, children. They'll move on in a day or two and I doubt they appreciate being stared at."

They didn't move on in a day or two. They settled down to stay. Besides pitching their tents, they made lean-tos of wood scraps and flattened-out cardboard boxes and tar paper. From a distance the camp looked like a dump, but at early dusk when the place was veiled in the smoke of their fires and a faint whine

26

of violins drifted over the meadow, passersby pulled up in the shadows, irresistibly drawn by the air of mystery and romance.

This was what Jane and Eleanor suspected and longed to see, but the closest they came to seeing the Gypsy camp was when their father drove past on their way into town one afternoon. From the road they couldn't miss seeing the ropes that went from tent to tent and from which strips of vivid material hung like battle pennants marking a medieval camp. In the still heat of late August these small banners dangled motionless, giving the camp a poor and dispirited look. One wondered if these Gypsies danced with tambourines or if they, like the limp rags that hung around them, had surrendered to the heat and the dirt and the cruelty of hard times.

"Slow down," begged Eleanor, and their father took his foot off the gas pedal so that they could gawk as the car inched along the dirt road.

Beyond the camp, horses grazed in the middle of the meadow, moving in slow motion over the field and hardly disturbing the tall grass that nodded like a gold sea around them. Around the tents and shacks the grass had been worn to dirt, and dust rose as small children and chickens and dogs ran shrieking and laughing and cackling and yipping through it.

A strange ringing, clanging, howling sound floated constantly across the meadow, except during the hottest part of the day, when nothing stirred. Then, in the distance, could be heard a dull pounding as men stood over fires, beating red-hot iron and shoeing the horses of local farmers. Late in the day when the trees along the banks of the muddy creek that ran through the meadow threw out their thin shadows, the occasional jangling of cowbells tied to the Gypsies' three or four bony cows could be heard as the animals moved from the dense thickets to graze on the stubble of the open field.

"Satisfied?" asked their father, for he had stopped both on the way to town and going home. "Now you've seen it," and he put in the clutch, shifted gears, and headed home.

When they drove into the yard their mother was at the clothesline, and the minute she saw the car she came rushing across the grass.

"They've been here," she said breathlessly, "they were here an hour ago, they came up on to the porch and they wouldn't leave."

"Who, Grace?"

"Gypsies!" she cried in exasperation. "They wanted food. They wanted to work in the garden. They wanted knives to sharpen. They wanted old clothes. They wanted to cut the grass. They wanted to know when the apples would be ready to pick. They wanted to tell my fortune," she said indignantly, and, shaking a towel she had taken off the line, she said fiercely, "I'm short a towel, John. They took it right off the line."

"Now, Mother," he said, "calm yourself. They'll be moving on in a few days. They're childlike people, but I don't think they mean any real harm. If they took something I doubt they'll be back."

But he was wrong. They were back the next day and the next. Sometimes the man came alone, but more often there was a small boy with him.

"That poor child," sputtered Grace, "he looks half starved. He can't be eight; he looks more like five."

Apparently she had asked his age and then rejected the answer given. To Grace, all Gypsies were dark, stunted, dirty, and ageless. They had no identity of their own and, like garments marked "small," "medium," or "large," they might simply have been labeled "young," "grown-up," or "old." Her contempt was evident in all she said, and their father replied mildly, "It's hard to tell about them, but of course, considering the diversity of their origins, how could it be otherwise?"

"What does that mean?" asked Eleanor.

"It means they have no distinctive characteristics from which to draw logical conclusions as to their physical appearance or mental processes. They cannot be readily cataloged, as, for example, one makes generalities about the Italians or the Irish. Gypsies emerged so to speak, from India, Persia, Armenia, Syria, Egypt, the Balkans, Austria, Bohemia, Germany —"

"Don't bother your father with questions," said their mother. "They don't come from anywhere. They move from place to place. They are wanderers, shiftless people who never settle down or accomplish anything."

"I wouldn't say that," replied their father.

"It's true," she said, "You've said so yourself. They have no art, no literature, no written history. . . ." and she looked at him triumphantly as though to say, Deny that if you can.

He gave her a little bow of acknowledgment, but, as though in this instance he had decided to abandon history for the sake of humanity, he said grandly, "But they are blacksmiths, farriers, kettle smiths, tinkers, and the makers of wood spoons, baskets, mats, and clothespins. They are bear trainers and dealers in wool and cattle. They are fortune-tellers —"

"Rubbish," said Grace.

Eleanor wondered if there were bears in their camp, and one day when the man appeared, asking for work in the hope of receiving charity, as he always did, she sidled up to the boy and asked if there were bears at Purple Meadow.

He regarded her strangely, as blank as though she'd spoken in Greek, and watched with no interest when she spread her arms and staggered across the porch, growling and shaking her grizzly head.

"He don't speak," said his father, shifting from one foot to another, his eyes darting over the porch furniture for anything someone might have left there, a book, a pair of glasses, a handkerchief, anything small enough to pocket.

Their mother was in the kitchen getting something to give him, for she had begun to hand things through the door almost as soon as they appeared on the porch, then she would watch until they disappeared down the road. She said she had decided a little Christian charity never hurt anyone, the giver or the receiver, and besides, it was the only way to get rid of them. In a minute she returned with a jar of peaches still hot from the canner, and when he backed away, bowing and smiling as he retreated down the steps with the boy beside him, she opened the door and pulled Eleanor inside.

"Don't try to be friendly, Eleanor," she said firmly, "they're not like us. They'll be moving on soon."

But they didn't move on. They were there through the sweltering dog days of August and into September. Grace continued to dole out food until after Labor Day when the children went back to school, and then she sorted through Eleanor's clothes, which had once been Jane's or Sissy's, and gave away the things she'd never wear again. Pretty soon they saw the little boy wearing Eleanor's shorts and overalls.

Although she had only given them things to get rid of them, these small acts of charity seemed to prompt proprietary feelings in Grace, and she sputtered, "It's a crime those children aren't in school."

Of course she would have been alarmed if the Gypsy children had appeared in the North Lane School, since she was convinced they were all troublemakers and probably lousy. When she saw the boy in Eleanor's things she declared that if "he" ever put one of Eleanor's dresses on "that child" she would never give him another thing, and for a while it almost seemed that the Gypsies were to be a con- tinuing part of their life, which, in a terrible and unforeseen way, was exactly what happened.

Campus children went to public school in the village, and after Labor Day Jane and Eleanor took their lunch boxes and set off across the field behind their house every morning, heading for the state road, which they walked along for half a mile until they came to the North Lane School. The school was a two-room frame building with two outhouses, a playground in the back, and thickets beyond this. The lower grades were taught in one room, and the upper four in another. Campus people called it the North Lane University, and campus children usually skipped at least one grade as their village counterparts labored slowly through the names of the presidents and the multiplication tables. It was unlikely that Gypsy children would have known what to do with pencils and lined paper, but now and then people caught glimpses of them skulking at the far end of the playground or peering with the frozen eyes of startled rabbits from the thickets beyond. Who could doubt that they would have known what to do with a jump rope or a ball or a full lunch box?

As Jane and Eleanor walked along at the edge of the tar road one morning, kicking gravel and swinging their lunch boxes, they caught sight of the girl whom Eleanor came to think of afterwards as "Jane's Gypsy." Eleanor reached out and grabbed Jane's arm and pointed.

"She's one of the Gypsies," Jane hissed. "Don't stare, Eleanor. You'll scare her away."

"I'm not staring," said Eleanor, fixing her eyes on her new brown shoes that were already gray with dust, determined not to stare, although her heart was pounding with excitement.

"There," said Jane, "she's gone. I knew it!"

"I didn't stare."

"Never mind," said Jane, "they're like that."

The next morning they began to walk more and more slowly as they approached the spot, for if she was there they were determined to see her. Suddenly Jane whispered, "There she is. Behind that bush. Stop, Eleanor, and pretend you're tying your shoes. I'm going to say something."

Eleanor scooched down obediently and untied and retied her shoelaces while Jane said in a loud voice, "I wish we'd see that girl again. I'd like to talk to her."

She put her hand on Eleanor's shoulder and pressed hard. "Don't move," she whispered,

"I can see her looking at us. I'm going to give her an apple."

"How?"

"Just watch."

Jane opened her lunch box and took out an apple.

"I think I'll leave this apple here," she said in a loud voice. "I don't need it and somebody might come along who would want it. See, Eleanor," she shouted, "it's a nice big one." And she put it down in the grass beside the road, then she pulled Eleanor to her feet and they walked slowly along toward school.

The trees were full of apples then, and the Gypsies could slip in and out of a dozen orchards, which undoubtedly they did, picking as many apples as they could carry away, but Jane and Eleanor weren't very far along before they saw the girl emerge from the bushes, and then Jane clutched Eleanor's arm in excitement. "She's taking it," said Jane, "I knew she would."

On the following morning the girl had moved to a stone wall, where she sat in the sunshine, swinging her bare feet with their stubby toes and black, broken nails and showing her ankles, which were swollen with bug bites and streaked with dirt. Her skirt was made of curtain material, a coarse fabric printed with faded red and blue flowers. She wore a blouse from which the sleeves had been ripped. The frayed edges of the seams made a fringe against the brown of her upper arms. Her black hair, stiff and tangled, stood out around her face in a snarled mass, and under this the eyes in her pointed face darted around feverishly. When she saw Jane and Eleanor she smiled boldly and Jane said, "Want to come to school?"

She shook her head no.

By the beginning of the following week, however, Jane had coaxed her down to the thicket bordering the playground where, hidden from view, they shared Jane's lunch.

"I think she's starved," said Jane. "I doubt they ever get enough to eat."

"She can have half of mine," said Eleanor.

"No," said Jane, "she's afraid of people."

Jane's tone was smug. It was an accomplishment, after all, to have captured one of the Gypsies, and Eleanor took her lunch and settled down under a tree to eat alone. On the other side of the playground where the grass was worn to dirt, the boys were playing ball, while most of the girls sat in little clumps in the shade with their lunches, trading sandwiches and cookies and whispering and giggling.

After a while, when she saw that nobody was watching her, Eleanor moved silently toward the thicket, slipping into the bushes and crawling on her hands and knees toward the sound of voices. Sticks and small stones dug into her knees and twigs and thorns caught at her dress. The midday sun was hot overhead, and it burned through the drying underbrush that crackled all around her. She paused, panting and anxious. And then she saw them, sitting together cross-legged, face-to-face, the girl drinking from Jane's Thermos cup, holding it to her lips as though it were a chalice. The exchange bonded them in some mystic way. Eleanor sat back on her knees and waited. Something wonderful was about to happen, she was sure of it.

"Now," said the girl to Jane, "I will tell your fortune."

Her voice was husky and filled with promise. She tossed her head, whipping her hair away from her face as she prepared for her performance with the guile of the ages. Reaching out, she took Jane's hand in her own and then, as though she were mixing a potion drawn from the air and sun and the secrecy of the place, she passed her fingers over Jane's open palm. She might have been concocting a witches' brew in the hollow of that upturned hand and Eleanor shivered, pressing her hand to her mouth to keep from crying out.

As the girl continued she hummed and

moaned, her small body swayed, her eyes closed, her lips parted, and then, suddenly, without warning, she clapped her hands to her head and Jane gasped. "What is it, what do you see?"

"Ah," sighed the girl, "I see a handsome man, tall as a tree, strong as an ox, brave as a lion, and I see chains of gold around your neck and earrings down to your shoulders. I see a big house on a hill and a church with a tower."

It's our house, thought Eleanor in amazement. She can see our house and the chapel, and her heart began to thud, pounding against the narrow cage of her ribs. What might the girl see in *her* hand, she wondered, and she wanted to burst through the bushes and into that charmed circle, but at that moment she heard the bell.

Jane withdrew her hand slowly and screwed the top on her Thermos and gathered up her things. "I've got to go," she said, "Will you come again tomorrow?"

The girl nodded yes.

Turning away, Jane stumbled through the bushes, and as she passed Eleanor she hissed, "You were spying, Eleanor."

"I wasn't spying. I was just looking."

"It's the same thing."

"Do you think it's true?"

"How do I know," said Jane, who, nevertheless, could already feel the weight of gold earrings dangling from her ears. She put out her hand and said, "Come on. We're going to be late."

They woke to rain, a slow, cold September rain that lasted for almost a week and then, overnight, the temperature dropped and in the morning there was frost on the fields. That night their father came in and said the Gypsies were gone.

"Without a trace," he said, as though they had blown away, disappeared, or had been dissolved as the leaden skies poured rain over the parched meadow. It was as if they had evaporated, had been drawn up by the sun to be absorbed by the clouds overhead, crystallized, and scattered to the ends of the earth. Gone.

Jane and Eleanor looked up in dismay. Now they would never see the Gypsy girl again. They would never know her secrets. "She wouldn't have told you anything much, anyway," said Eleanor. "Mother says it's all just superstition," but she didn't say it with conviction. Was it possible for anyone to look into the future and see things that might happen to you then? Jane tossed her head and made a face. "I don't believe all that anyway," she said. But Eleanor wasn't so sure.

"Now we can forget them," said Grace in relief, but she was wrong. It wasn't long before they knew that the Gypsies had struck camp and moved away because with the coming of the rain something terrible had been unleashed in the meadow and half the children in camp were sick.

"It's no wonder they were sick," said Grace, "living in hovels and filth."

She was sorry, of course, but who could fail to be glad that these dreadful people had vanished from their lives? No one suspected then that they had left something behind, for there was nothing in the meadow to testify to their presence there, no tent, shack, tar paper, cow, chicken, pennant, fire. Even the flattened-out cardboard boxes had been whisked away, and when the grass grew in the spring it covered the great circle of dirt where they had camped and then there was nothing left. Nothing, that is, except the terrible unseen thing they left behind, something the Gypsy girl had not seen in Jane's palm, for she was nothing but a child imitating her elders, but something bequeathed in those days of shared lunches, for Jane was sick. Her head ached, her throat was sore, she had a fever and diarrhea, and she was throwing up. Grace moved a cot into Jane's room and slept there for the next six months because Jane had infantile paralysis, and things were never the same again.

For weeks Drury House was in quarantine. Neighbors left boxes of groceries on the front steps, their father's classes were taken by colleagues, Miss Gee brought the second-grade readers home for Eleanor, and Wilson, who was then a freshman at Harrison, had his assignments dropped by once a week. Grandmother Richards wrote long letters from Florida offering to come home to help and John read these aloud to Grace as she stood at the stove stirring custard or cereal for Jane. When he finished reading, Grace shook her head.

"Why not, dear? Wouldn't it be a help to you?"

"No," said Grace.

"I should think that with the meals and —"

"No!" asserted Grace, and she lifted the double boiler off the burner. Then she took a knife and began to peel potatoes, whacking away more than the skin. After this she sank the corer into six apples with deadly precision.

John watched her silently. "Why not, Grace?" he asked again.

"No."

"Oh, come —"

"I couldn't stand it!" she cried. "She'll stand

in the hall and wring her hands. She'll talk. Whenever I come downstairs she'll be here in the kitchen, and she'll want to know how Jane is. I'll have to hear about the time you had mastoid. She'll tell me how she boiled onions and slipped the hearts into your ear, and tied on hot poultices. She'll tell me they were so hot all the skin on that side of your face blistered and peeled off like tissue paper, and how scared she was you'd be scarred for life."

"That's only her way of trying to make you feel better."

"Feel better!" cried Grace. "Dear God, how would that make me feel better?"

"Well," he said gently, "I wasn't scarred for life, was I?"

Sitting on her bed upstairs, Eleanor watched the world outside. In the distance she could see boys crossing the campus and through fluttering red and gold leaves the chapel took on the appearance of a castle. It was easy to imagine occupants in the tower gazing down across the fields to the river as they watched for the approach of friends or enemies. The house was silent. Her father was in his study working on notes for a book he wanted to write. Wilson was in the garden pulling up dead cornstalks and squash vines and raking them into a heap for burning. Her mother was across the hall in Jane's room reading her *The Wind in the Willows*, her voice droning on monotonously through the long, still afternoon. Eleanor knew it was *The Wind in the Willows* because when she stood outside the door to listen she heard the word "Ratty," and then "Toad." There were special inflections in her mother's voice when she spoke those names. One would have thought from her mother's tone of voice that Ratty was a valued friend who brought comfort and strength while Toad elicited only amusement and scorn.

I am like the mole, thought Eleanor sadly, wishing she could do a brave thing, although she had no idea what it might be. If only she could make Jane well, but of course she couldn't. When she went to bed at night she prayed hard for Jane. Her mother or father, whoever happened to be tucking her in, would lean down and say, "Just be a good girl, dear. That's the best way you can help." But it wasn't enough. She wanted desperately to *do* something.

That afternoon as she lay on her bed she heard voices in the distance as the football team scrimmaged on the athletic field. Wilson stood in the garden watching his bonfire. The smoke drifted up in a pungent cloud that smelled like Halloween.

Wilson had gathered the pumpkins and

lined them up on the porch and from Eleanor's window she could see the orange stripe they made along the side of the porch. Wilson's fire was orange, the pumpkins were orange, the leaves were orange, and when Eleanor squeezed her eyes together and squinted through her lashes, she saw all the orange streak and shimmer and fuse to become gold. The whole world had turned to gold. The lawn was gold and the trees and the chapel. Her room was a cave, but through the opening that was her window the outer world shone in glorious perfection, and she began to pray that they could all go back into that perfect shining world again. She forgot that she wanted to do a brave thing. There was no need to be brave, actually, she decided. What bravery did it take to pray? she wondered, and she found herself praying fervently, re-membering all of the miracle Bible stories she had ever heard in Sunday school, and as she prayed, it suddenly occurred to her that per-haps prayers were like money. They were heavenly exchange, what you gave for what you got, and she was ready to spend her lifetime's share of prayers for what she wanted now because she wanted things to stay the same. She wanted Jane to be well again, for her parents to return to her, for Wilson to cross the campus and join the other boys, for everything to be all right.

Grace sat on the kitchen stool scribbling a shopping list on the back of an envelope. While she wrote she drank a cup of coffee and ate a piece of cake. On the counter in front of her there was a notebook, in which she wrote *Edith Maddern — sponge cake.* Above Edith's name was written *Ruth Harris — apple pie,* and above that *Alma Van Valkenburg — chicken and rice.*

Grace looked up with a dazed expression when she saw Eleanor and then she smiled and stretched out her arm to reach around Eleanor and pull her closer.

"Are you all right?" she asked.

Eleanor nodded.

Grace put her hand on the back of Eleanor's head and pushed down until Eleanor's chin touched her chest.

"Does that hurt?" asked Grace.

"No."

She stroked Eleanor's throat and forehead. "Sore throat?" she asked. "Headache?"

Eleanor shook her head.

Grace sighed. "Are you helping Daddy?"

"Yes."

"Good girl," said her mother.

She rose from the stool and crossed to the stove where the canner, filled with water and strips torn from old sheets, sent clouds of steam toward the ceiling. The boiling cloths rolled like swells on a gray sea. Towels hung in rows on a rack behind the stove. Grace filled a basin with wet cloths, took up a pile of hot towels, and started for the back stairs with Eleanor at her heels.

"What are you going to do now?" asked Eleanor.

"I've told you, dear. These are bandages for Jane's legs," said her mother, "just turn the doorknob for me, Eleanor, and then go back downstairs."

Eleanor opened the door to Jane's room, and as it closed she heard her mother say in a bright, ordinary tone of voice, "Here we are, dear."

Eleanor paused to listen and for a while there was no sound at all, then Jane began to cry.

"There, there, dear," murmured her mother, "I know it hurts, but it will help. Try to be brave."

One day a crate of oranges was delivered by Railway Express, set down on the front porch by a delivery man who saw the quarantine sign and didn't even stop to ring the bell. Besides the oranges, the box contained kumquats and orange-blossom honey and a card with the Dwires' names on it.

Eleanor watched as her father drew the card from its envelope and said, "It's from Alice and Harold and Sissy. Isn't that nice?" and he stood there nodding and smiling as though he didn't quite know what to do about this nice thing that had happened to them in the midst of all their trouble. Then he washed his hands and pulled open the drawers of the kitchen cabinets until he found the orange juicer and he cut and squeezed two oranges, poured the juice through a strainer, and took the glass upstairs to Jane.

"Look at this, Jane," he said, "all the way from Florida and there are a hundred more oranges just for you from Aunt Alice."

Grace looked up in surprise and he said, "That's right, Grace," as if to tell her that she shouldn't be surprised. After all, hadn't he always maintained that Alice was basically good and generous?

"Try it, Jane," he urged, "it's good."

His voice sounded as though they were at the dining table having breakfast. One would have thought to hear him that this was an ordinary day, that things were as they should be, and to confirm this Grace said cheerfully, "I'll just run down and see about supper, dear. I'll be right back."

She walked briskly down the hall to the back stairs, knowing that Jane could hear the sound of her feet going *tap, tap, tap.* See, her feet seemed to say, everything is all right.

When she came to the stairs she put her hand on the rail and started down, and then suddenly the stairwell began to revolve slowly until it was spinning dizzily, like an eddy in a river. She clutched the rail with both hands and closed her eyes. I'm so tired, Grace thought, breathing heavily and waiting for the feeling to pass, willing it to pass so that she could go back to stirring custard and wringing out hot cloths and massaging Jane's limp legs.

After a minute she opened her eyes and looked down, expecting to see the stairs again, but there were no stairs there, only a dark, narrow tunnel leading nowhere. Her good sense told her that if she proceeded she would find the kitchen at the bottom of the stairs and that in the kitchen she would find a crate of oranges. It was nice of Alice to send oranges, she thought. Alice would have had to *pay* for oranges, which indicated how very nice it was, unless, of course . . . and she paused to think about it, for suddenly it seemed likely that if Alice had sent oranges it was because Elliot had had a classmate with an orange grove, in which case . . .

She couldn't go beyond this. She couldn't think another word, or take a step, or wonder what there was for supper. All she wanted to do was stay there forever, halfway between the upstairs and the downstairs of the house, where she might hope to remain suspended and safe from the crushing weight of a cruel truth, for she knew by then that Jane would never walk again, that Alice was never going to change, and that all the hot cloths and orange juice in the world weren't going to make any difference at all.

The following summer the Dwires appeared as usual, unannounced and ready to stay. By then Jane was able to sit up for most of the day. She had braces on both legs and John and Grace said confidently to anyone who came to see them that it was only a matter of time before Jane would be walking again. No one asked how much time.

It was a hot day in July when Alice, with Harold and Sissy, drove into the yard. Grace was in the kitchen canning tomatoes, Wilson, who was working with the school grounds-crew, was somewhere on campus clipping grass, and Jane and Eleanor were playing Parcheesi. An ordinary day.

It had begun as every day now began, with a sponge bath for Jane and then family breakfast. Following this, Eleanor cleared the table and did the dishes, while Grace and Jane decided how Jane would spend the day. Grace was teaching Jane to darn, and while Eleanor cleared the table she could hear her mother's pleasant voice saying, "See, dear, you just slip the darning egg into the sock and then you weave over the hole like this."

Darning sounded like fun. In no time at all Jane would be taking over the darning basket, said Grace, and her father remarked, "I'll have to wear holes twice as fast, Jane, just for the pleasure of seeing your perfect darns."

Eleanor turned the water on full and watched the soap bubble up. She didn't see that darning socks was something to joke about, but Jane laughed. It had begun to seem to Eleanor that everything her father said was said to make Jane laugh. When he said there were more bugs than roses on the bushes, it struck Jane funny. At least she laughed. If he said it was raining cats and dogs, Jane laughed.

Eleanor filled the rinse pan with hot water, then she went to the dining room door and looked through and into the living room. Her mother was now brushing Jane's hair. From where Eleanor stood Jane, propped up by pillows on the sofa, looked doll-like. She was white and thin and small, and so pale one could imagine she had been washed and washed until she had faded and shrunk. Her shoulders were as narrow as the space between the stair rails, and her arms and legs were spindly. Above her frail body her face was framed by a crown of short curls. Eleanor watched as her mother bent down to rearrange the pillows and heard her say, "What shall we read today, Jane? Would you like to try poetry this morning?"

When Aunt Alice arrived that afternoon she went right across the room to Jane's chair and bent down and kissed her and said, "Darling Jane, what a terrible time you've given us, and how glad we are to see you better."

Then she turned to Grace and said, "I didn't know she had such beautiful hair, Grace. You'd better keep it short, Jane. It's very becoming."

Alice talked as though Jane were perfectly well, even though she could see how changed Jane was, and see her braces, and see Jane's bones, like white straws, shining through the skin on the backs of Jane's hands.

Then Harold went straight across to Jane and sat down beside her. Reaching out, he touched one of her braces, the way he might have reached to touch her hand, as though he were making a get-acquainted overture, and he said simply, "I'm sorry, Jane."

Then Grace said, "Isn't it hot? I can't think when we've had a hotter July. Who would like some iced tea? It seems hot enough to me for iced tea."

"Heavenly," said Alice. "I would love a glass of iced tea," and then, turning to John, she said, "Well, John, you're looking very fit."

John wasn't feeling particularly fit. None of them were. He wasn't inclined to say, "Thank you, Alice"; he was more inclined to say, "Oh, shut up, Alice." But years of dedication to Elliot Dwire prevented this.

He said, "Where are you headed, Alice?"

"Lenox," she said, "do you think I'll make it by dinnertime?"

"I should think so," he replied.

"What about the children?" asked Grace.

"My dear Grace," said Alice firmly, "I wouldn't dream of asking you to keep them. I'm planning to leave them with the Hubbards in Pittsfield. I haven't been able to get in touch with Ruth, but I feel sure they're there, and it's been a long time since the children have seen each other."

"I expect she's there," said John.

"Leave them here," Grace said. "It wouldn't be any trouble."

John shot her a look of amazement. "Now Grace," he said gently, "Alice has her plans made and you know how tired you are."

"It would be good for Jane," said Grace. "Let them stay, Alice, we'd love to have them."

Of course they stayed. The Hubbards were

in Europe that summer and they all suspected Alice knew it. Who could tell what Alice knew, or didn't know? She might even have thought it would be a welcome change to the family to have Sissy and Harold there for a visit, but if she did she was wrong. It wasn't the change that was welcome, it was getting back to normal that helped. When, after all, had there been a summer without them?

2

As soon as Alice let herself be persuaded that they really did want Harold and Sissy to stay, she jumped up and, kissing Harold, told him to bring in their bags. Then she kissed Sissy and told her to be good.

"Now, darlings," she said, addressing the whole group as though they were little children, "don't be a bother. Don't let them be a bother, Grace. They can pick strawberries and things. Harold has his license, if that's any help. Sissy, you and Eleanor can do dishes, and for heaven's sake make your own beds. I'll only be gone a month."

Then, heading for the door, she paused to embrace Grace. "You are an angel," she said. "I'd hate to have had to refuse the Barringers. We've known them for years. Ned, their youngest, the one I sent you a photo of, with his polo pony, you remember. Anyway, he's just been married, and . . ." Alice rambled on while Grace tried to place Ned Barringer.

She did have a faint recollection of a young man and a horse cut out of the rotogravure section of the Sunday paper, a soft brown image of money on the hoof, but the name hadn't meant anything to her then and it didn't now. Anyone who could afford to play polo in depressed times like these was someone she would never particularly have cared to know, but Alice was quite the opposite. Whatever she actually knew, Alice would have been inclined to act as though these were not depressed times.

This infuriated Grace, who knew all about depressed times. Faculty salaries were in the neighborhood of two thousand a year. But there were bonuses: housing, milk from the school's herd, produce from the gardens, free tuition for the children of staff and faculty. Grace could understand why Alice wanted to hang on to her "good connections," but she almost pitied Alice, for whom position depended on money. At least they were all in the same boat here at Harrison. As all of this flashed through her mind, Grace almost lost track of what Alice was saying. "Wait a minute," Grace said, "you've lost me."

"They're in Paris for their honeymoon, the young Barringers. Not that it matters, I'm going to see Violet and Alex. What does matter is how you can manage all this. May I really leave you alone with these children?"

"Of course," said Grace, who was ready for Alice to leave so that she could start supper. "You ought to get going," she said, "Lenox is over fifty miles. Are you sure you don't want to spend the night and start off in the morning?"

"Heavens," said Alice, "it's only two. I'll be there by six-thirty." And then she looked around to see if she'd forgotten anything and realized she hadn't seen John's mother. "I must just speak to Mrs. Richards," she said.

But Mrs. Richards was still in Florida suffering from dizzy spells, according to John's sister. When Alice heard this, she said, "Oh, well then, perhaps it won't be so hard to squeeze in my two."

And then she was gone. With a great scraping of gears and a strange squawk as her car grazed the stone wall that surrounded Grace's rock garden, she was off. Her blue chiffon scarf blew and her hand waved as she shot down the drive and disappeared over the hill.

Among other things, Harold had brought a chessboard. Will looked at it and decided it was just another form of checkers. Now that he was fifteen and old enough to work on campus, he refused to pick vegetables or mow the lawn at home. He came in from work every day dog tired, he said, sweating and bare-chested, his shirt balled up and dropped into the laundry basket as he headed for the shower. When he came in that day and discovered Harold and Sissy in residence he barely spoke. It must be nice to be rich, he thought grimly.

Harold had wanted to get a job this summer, but his mother wouldn't let him mow lawns or caddy or do any of the things he might have done to earn a little money. The neighbors along Fresh Pond Park probably would have been glad to have him mow their lawns or rake their leaves in the fall, but Alice didn't want them to know how desperate she always was for money. There was hardly a one who wouldn't have been delighted to take advantage of Harold's age and pay him half what they had to eke out for a real gardener, but Alice didn't know this.

When Harold had been there a few days and sized up the situation and saw how many things there were for him to do, he gladly picked peas and strawberries and mowed the lawn and taught Jane to play chess. He would have played with Will too, but Will was entertaining himself with Sissy, who was just twelve but looked older. He liked to tease her. No matter what she said, he growled an answer and sat, grinning sardonically as she began her insistent begging for something to do. Everyone was surprised when Sissy finally persuaded him to meet her every day at four (when he finished his day's work) at the tennis courts for an hour of play before it was time to get ready for supper.

Grace was glad to see Sissy start off with rackets and balls. Sissy wasn't the kind who would settle down with a book when there was nothing better to do. Sissy wandered from room to room, picking up this and that, a magazine, a photograph album, a piece of china, and when Grace asked her if she didn't feel like picking strawberries with Eleanor, Sissy said, "Oh, sure," and she took a basket and went out to the garden with shoulders sagging and feet dragging.

"You would think," said Grace to John, "that I had asked her to go to the well and bring in ten pails of water."

"We don't have a well," said John.

"If we did," she replied. "You know perfectly well what I mean."

Just then they heard Jane laugh and they looked up in alarm. Had she laughed or was there something wrong? Grace, who was shelling peas, stood up and started toward the door.

"Don't," said John. "It's all right, Harold's there."

And then they heard Jane say, "Checkmate," her voice strong, almost natural again.

"No you don't," said Harold, "you missed this big fellow over here."

"Oh, rats," said Jane, "so I did."

Eleanor liked to watch them play. She was learning right along with Jane and she wished Harold would ask her to play. She knew what checkmate meant. She could name all the pieces, follow the moves of the knights, view the thin red line of the pawns for what it was. She didn't dare ask to play — it wouldn't have been fair to Jane — but someday Harold would ask her and when he did she'd be ready.

That afternoon Eleanor missed the game because she was in the garden with Sissy, who had filled one basket of strawberries and was now eating them. Red juice bled down Sissy's fingers and trickled over her hands. When Sissy picked one that had been bored into by a bird she said, "Ugh," and threw it over her shoulder to land in the grass, where it would mold and eventually be devoured by hundreds of crawling creatures that lived out their uneventful lives in such places as the undersides of geranium leaves. But Grace used the damaged berries for jam, and Eleanor scolded, "You shouldn't do that. You're supposed to put those in another basket for Mother to make jam."

"It was rotten all over," said Sissy, taking another and looking at it very carefully before popping it into her mouth. Then she said, "I've got to go. It's almost four."

"I know," said Eleanor. "You're going to play tennis."

"What's wrong with that?"

"Nothing. I didn't say anything."

"You are a child, Eleanor," said Sissy, who was old enough to think about things that almost made her shiver with excitement, even though she didn't know why. At that moment she was visualizing Will, his chest bare and sweaty, his body tanned, his hair curly and wet after he let faucet water pour over his head.

"I am not," said Eleanor.

"Have you ever been in love, then? You don't even know what love is."

"I do so."

"I am in love with your brother," said Sissy, tossing her head and shaking her hair away from her face, "and if you tell anybody I said that I'll say you're a liar."

"I think you're silly," said Eleanor.

"That's what you think," said Sissy, and, jumping up, she went quickly across the lawn and into the house.

I *am so* in love, thought Eleanor, who was indeed in love with Harold and wouldn't have told him for anything. Never.

★ ★ ★

That evening at supper John said, "Who knows what happens day after tomorrow?" He made it sound mysterious and Grace had a dreadful sinking feeling as she thought, Who's coming now? She immediately imagined John's mother, whose room was being occupied by Harold. They hadn't heard from Florida for some time. It was possible.

"The Fourth of July," said John. "Don't tell me I'm the only patriotic soul in this house?"

"Fireworks!" shrieked Eleanor. "When can we go for fireworks?"

"Tomorrow," said her father. "Who wants to come?"

Everyone, except Grace, wanted to drive across the river to Northridge, where the fireworks man pitched his tent on the green and set up shop on a table of boards lying across the empty crates that had been packed with the sparklers, firecrackers, roman candles, and skyrockets of his trade.

As everyone else decided what they should buy, Grace sat there wondering how she could have forgotten the Fourth and the Barbers' picnic, which was an annual event, one of the traditions of campus life, a community effort begun some years ago by Clive Barber when he and his wife, Mildred, first came to Harrison from a military school in the South. Everyone brought food: beans and hot dogs, cabbage salad, rolls and cake, and fresh things from the garden. The Barbers provided paper plates and fireworks. Why hadn't anyone mentioned the Barbers' picnic to her? Usually somebody called and told her what to bring.

Suddenly they all stopped talking and she said, "The Barbers' picnic. No one's called me about the Barbers' picnic."

"I didn't know they ever called," said John. "I thought we just went."

"We do, but usually someone calls. Maybe they aren't having it this year. We've been so out of things. . . ."

Here she stopped, because all of them knew why they had been out of things, and Grace said briskly, "I'll just call Alma after supper. Don't worry about it. We'll be going, don't worry."

Nobody was worried, except perhaps Eleanor, who was still young enough to put the Fourth of July on a par with Halloween or Thanksgiving. But she didn't say anything. Last year when they crossed the river, they had found the man packing up, ready to head over the hill to Winchester, until her father got out of the car and called out, "Wait a minute there, don't pack those sparklers and firecrackers!"

She didn't want that to happen again this year. Last summer Jane had said, "You're not getting enough, Daddy. I want some roman candles. The Barbers never have enough." Jane liked to dance on the lawn in her bare feet, and when the sky was almost dark and all you could see of the trees were their huge lollipop shadows against the gray black of the sky, her father would light a roman candle. She would hold it up like a torch, spinning it around and around until all the colors of the rainbow surged up, up, and burst in round balls of red, white, and blue overhead.

Jane wouldn't dance on the lawn this summer and Eleanor knew it. Eleanor had never had her own roman candle and had even thought about asking her father if she could have one this year. If Jane was old enough, so was she.

Thinking about it now, Eleanor knew she wouldn't ask, and if her father said anything to her about roman candles, she would say in an offhand sort of way that all she wanted was sparklers because she knew Jane could sit in her chair and hold a sparkler and that was at least something.

"Make a list, Jane," their father said, "we better catch that fellow in the morning before he skips out."

He made it sound exciting. As if the Gypsies

had come again and he wanted to be sure no one missed the spectacle of these ancient nomads making their careless way across the face of an indifferent world.

Harold handed Jane a pad of paper and a pencil and John said, "Good boy, Harold. See that she doesn't forget anything. Better put down roman candles, Jane. We all know how the Barbers are."

Jane looked up and smiled, but Sissy said, "How can Jane do a roman candle? That's silly. You don't sit in a chair and —"

Harold turned and said in a savage undertone, "Shut up, Sissy."

But John said to Sissy, "Why not? A chair's as good a launching pad as any other. We'll show them," and then, lifting his hand in a sort of dismissing wave, he left them and retreated to the sanctuary of his study.

When the dishes were done and the younger generation was listening to Fibber McGee and Molly, Grace went into the front hall and picked up the telephone and rang for the operator. It didn't seem possible that she might have overlooked the picnic entirely if John hadn't remembered what day it was. When she heard Alma's voice, she said, "Alma, this is Grace. How are you?"

"Fine. I've been thinking about you. I don't

see how you do it, Grace. It must be impossible having those children there."

What children? thought Grace, and then she realized that Alma meant Sissy and Harold. She said, "It's really all right and it helps keep Jane entertained."

"I suppose so."

"I called to ask about the Barbers' picnic. Are they having it this year?"

"Of course," said Alma. "Don't you remember my speaking to you about it after church two Sundays ago?"

"No," said Grace. "Did you?"

"I feel sure I did. I remember saying that you were lucky because there weren't going to be enough desserts and you could bring a cake. Cakes are easy, at least I think so. Don't you remember?"

Grace didn't but she said, "That begins to sound familiar. Half the time I'm not sure who I am or where I am. Well, thanks. A cake it is. Same time, same place?"

"Yes," said Alma. "See you there."

Grace hung up the phone and leaned back in the chair. It was dark in the front hall, except for the light on the stair landing. The screen door was hooked for the night and she could feel cool air stirring outside and drifting in through the screen. She was tired. She was always tired. Alma was right. She should have remembered, but she didn't. It didn't really matter, of course. It wouldn't take more than thirty minutes to get a cake in the oven and they could have arrived on time if she'd waited until the Fourth to check on things. The cake didn't bother her. To be late wouldn't have bothered her. To miss it entirely wouldn't be a tragedy. But something did bother her, something that seemed to be happening more and more often lately. She couldn't seem to remember things. If Alma had spoken to her after church, why couldn't she remember? Alma always wore the same thing to church in the summer. The same white-and-blue-print dress with the lace-edged jacket of the same material and the same white straw hat with a navy ribbon around the crown. If Alma had spoken to her, why couldn't she remember?

3

Although they didn't know it at the time, that was the last summer Sissy and Harold would spend an extended vacation at Harrison. Harold graduated from Choate the following June, 1937, and went to Amherst that fall. Even though he didn't come often, Harold appeared now and then, always with something for Jane, always content to sit in the living room with her, even managing to persuade her to show him her paintings, which were good, he thought, despite her insistence that they were nothing, hardly worth looking at.

During the summers he worked as a counselor at Camp Sea Grove on Cape Cod. He wrote letters occasionally and there were one or two times when he and Sissy and Alice actually came together and spent a night at Drury House. But it was time carved out of the few holidays Harold was allowed by Sea Grove, in between the house parties Alice was invited to, and the week or two Sissy escaped from her life as a dude rancher in Wyoming with her uncle and his family.

Eleanor thought the most exciting thing anyone could possibly do was visit a dude ranch or a real ranch — anywhere with horses. She envied Sissy, who was never satisfied and never seemed to appreciate things. All Sissy seemed to care about was Will. She teased him to climb the chapel tower with her. She begged him to ask for the car and take her to Northridge to the movies, and, of course, now that Will was going to Dartmouth she needled him constantly about the winter carnival. "If you would only ask me once," she said, "I would die happy." This was a lie because she would always want more of everything. She's dumb, thought Eleanor, whose wants were still reasonable and predictable.

Where did the time go? wondered Grace, whose nights and days were so similar she almost forgot what year it was. She knew the seasons by the things she canned. She knew which day of the week she changed the sheets. She went to bed on Saturday knowing that in the morning it would be Sunday. But when it came to the years, she could only relate to Jane, and she knew almost to the hour how long Jane had been sick.

During those years Grace prayed that something good would happen. A treatment for victims of polio, a serum that would work miracles with shrinking muscles. She read everything about infantile paralysis that she could find in the library. She tried to talk about it to John and he would listen patiently, shaking his head slowly and reaching for her hand, or touching her shoulder as he said, "Someday. One of these days, who knows when, there will be an inoculation of some sort. Our grandchildren, perhaps. Don't torture yourself, dear."

"Sometimes I think I can't bear it," she said, tightening her hand on his, her tears ready to fall.

"Be thankful we have friends," he said. "Think how often your friends drop in. How alone we would feel if there weren't people who recognized suffering and did what they could to alleviate it."

"I know, I know," said Grace in a voice close to breaking. "Even Alice and Harold stop in when they can. I couldn't manage the long visits anymore, but just to have Harold surprise us with a visit means so much. He is so good with Jane, but, oh, John —" and she stopped and tried to breathe more slowly and talk more sensibly.

"What is it?" he asked.

"She's in love with Harold."

"She's too young to be in love with anybody," he said. "How do you know?"

"I just know," said Grace, thinking of the way Jane reacted when Harold thumped up the back steps and came into the house, calling out, "Anybody here? Jane? Aunt Grace? I've got an hour. What's up?"

"I'm here," Jane would call out. "In here, Harold," and as Grace came down the stairs or into the living room, she could see a radiance in Jane's face that she could scarcely bear.

The time did pass. Harold advanced through the ranks of junior counselor and senior counselor to become an instructor at Camp Sea Grove. Will was at Dartmouth and, as far as Grace and John knew, Sissy had yet to persuade him to invite her up for the winter carnival. John told Grace that he thought Sissy was a little hussy. "Thank God Eleanor is still too young to be interested in boys," he said, but Grace, who knew when Eleanor had had her first period, was of another opinion. She tried desperately not to think about Jane, for whom she could see only unrequited love.

But Grace didn't know about Jane's thoughts. She didn't know that Jane was determined to walk again. Sometimes Jane lay awake, crying softly, but at other times she seemed to see herself rising from her wheelchair. She could feel her legs growing stronger. She would wake up in the morning and it seemed to her that she was moving, sitting up, putting her feet down on the floor. And then something happened to change even this.

It was on one of the days when Harold arrived unexpectedly. He was still a boy, even though he was a senior counselor in camp and had his driver's license. He was indeed a boy, and he still thought like a child. There was no other way to reconcile what he did with the hard truth of Jane's infirmity.

Afterward Jane could recall every moment of that visit. She had sat in her wheelchair under the trees, talking to Harold and trying not to hear Sissy's remarks to Eleanor and Will. Sissy had come along for the ride, she said, and she teased and flirted with Will, who seemed indifferent to her. Only a deep flush at the back of his neck and spreading upwards to his face indicated his true feelings.

Jane had turned to Harold and said, "Sometimes I think I could walk if I tried. I can actually feel my legs and I seem to be standing on them."

"Someday maybe you will," said Harold.

"They say I can't," she had said. "I've asked the doctor and he says I can't, but he doesn't know how I feel. Nobody can know who hasn't been this way. I wonder if I could hold on to a rope or something and just pull . . . you know."

Harold glanced at the clothes reel and the coiled rope that Grace used when she hung sheets and needed extra line. He suddenly visualized Jane with rope under her arms and knotted in the middle of her chest. He could see them hoisting Jane up from the chair, the four of them pulling and supporting her with their strong arms and, caught up in his hopeless vision, he jumped up and looped the two ropes together. "Come on, you guys!" he called out. "Give us a hand."

And then, suddenly, they had pulled Jane to her feet and, putting their hands under her arms, they dragged her toward the reel. Without warning Jane gave a small shriek of pain, and she gasped, "I can't. I can't."

At once the back door had burst open, and Grace came out, waving a dish towel at them and screaming, "No, no, no! You'll hurt her. Stop. Carefully, now," she said, as she came panting up to them. "Oh, darling," Grace cried, putting her face down and trying to embrace her. "Are you all right?"

"I'm fine," said Jane. "Really, Mother. It's my fault."

"It's my fault," said Harold bitterly. What

ever persuaded me to do such a damn fool thing? he thought. "Oh, God, I'm sorry, Jane."

"It's all right," said Jane. "I asked for it." And she had smiled up at him and said, "Forget it."

They never mentioned it again, but Harold never forgot that day, and neither did Jane. She would never think again that she could walk, or that someday she would walk. After that it seemed to Jane that on that day one life had ended and another had begun. Gone were the memories that tortured her, memories of running after fireflies, walking to school, going upstairs to go to the bathroom. All of that ordinary life gone, a book closed forever.

In June 1941, when Harold graduated from Amherst, Alice and Sissy drove from Cambridge to Amherst and then, instead of going home, drove up the Connecticut Valley, passing farms with acres and acres of tented tobacco, and Sugar Loaf Mountain, meandering through Deerfield and arriving just in time for dinner. For once Alice had had the foresight to call ahead and Grace was ready for them with a cold supper of chicken and ham, potato salad, fresh peas, and strawberry shortcake.

Inasmuch as all of this was ready before they arrived, Grace took a bath, and, when she was dry, drenched herself with Yardley cologne, redid her hair, touched her lips with Tangee lipstick, and went downstairs to wait.

Jane was in her wheelchair in the living room reading a book. She had experimented with her hair. According to the *Ladies' Home Journal*, a french knot was a becoming and sophisticated hairstyle for girls of all ages, but Jane hadn't quite managed it, and the curls that had escaped her efforts framed her face with delicate waves. She wore a blue dress with a white collar and had draped a crocheted afghan over her legs. If it weren't for her legs, Jane could have endured all the rest that living in a wheelchair entailed. She hated her legs, which were useless sticks of curved bone, small, shrunken, and ugly. How many times had her mother and father told her that her body was not important, that she would always be loved for her courage and goodness and cheerfulness? They thought this would help her, but it didn't. Sometimes she thought she would start to scream and never be able to stop.

When Grace sat down near her, Jane said, "You smell wonderful, Mother. It's Yardleys, isn't it?"

"Yes," said Grace. "Want me to get you some?"

Jane shook her head. "I'd rather smell it than wear it," she said, and her mother smiled and touched her hand and said, "Silly," in a soft and loving voice.

At four o'clock the Dwires had still not appeared, so Grace fixed the tea tray and she and Jane and Eleanor sat with their teacups and gingersnaps. Grace said, "Where on earth can they be?"

"Probably Harold has lots of friends to say good-bye to," said Jane.

"I suppose so," replied Grace, but Eleanor retorted, "Pooh to that. Probably Sissy has gone off to play tennis with somebody. *She* never thinks of anybody but herself. I've heard you and Daddy talking about her and how she is about Will so you can't deny it."

Grace knew better than to be drawn into such a conversation, and at that moment they heard a car in the drive. Jane set her cup on the table beside her; no one noticed how the spoon rattled on the saucer.

"At last," murmured Grace. "Just in time to spoil tea."

Eleanor ran straight out the front door and down the steps and into Harold's arms. "You're here," she gasped. "You're here."

"Of course we're here," said Harold,

"where else would we be? How's Jane?"

"Fine," said Eleanor.

"Come in, come in," said Grace, "and congratulations, Harold. Hello, Alice," and she kissed Alice and then Sissy, who said, "Where's Will? Is he home yet?"

"Hush, dear," said Aunt Alice. "He's here somewhere, just be quiet," and turning to Grace, she said, "Ah, Grace, how lovely it is to be here, where nothing ever seems to change." Then she crossed the room and took Jane's two hands in hers and said, "And our darling Jane, pretty as ever."

"Thank you, Aunt Alice," said Jane. She looked around until she saw Harold. When their eyes met, it seemed to Eleanor, who was watching, that Jane had really reached across the room and touched Harold. She wished that she could look at Harold the same way, but she wasn't sure how to manage it. Besides, Harold and Jane were probably in love, and he wouldn't care how she looked.

"We're just having tea," said Grace. "I'll make a fresh pot."

"Don't bother, darling," said Alice. "It's too hot for tea."

"How about some root beer?"

"I don't suppose you have a drink?" asked Alice.

"I could make iced tea, or lemonade."

Alice laughed. "I always forget about campus life. I hoped you might have some gin, but I don't suppose you do."

"No gin," said Grace. "Sorry."

"Well then root beer," conceded Alice. "Sissy, go out and help Aunt Grace and ask Harold if he wants some root beer."

Then she stretched out her lovely long legs in front of her and lifted her arms up over her head and moaned. "It has been a frightfully hot day. The campus was covered with tents. People everywhere looking for the right tent. I don't see how the men bear it, suits and then robes. Where's John?"

And then suddenly she remembered that Grandmother Richards had died in January and that Grace and John had taken the train to Florida for the funeral. "I was so sorry to hear about Mrs. Richards. I meant to write. I should have. I am so sorry. It's no wonder Sissy hasn't any manners and I don't think Harold even knows. What a hectic life we lead and yet I don't seem to accomplish much."

"Everyone's busy," observed Grace.

"But what's the point unless you take time for old friends? And that reminds me, I had no idea so many of my friends had boys at Amherst. Being in Cambridge, I tend to feel that everyone's sons are at Harvard. Which reminds me, how does John feel about having

Will at Dartmouth?"

"Well enough," answered Grace. "He was a little disappointed, but Will has to ski. It was either Dartmouth or Williams."

Sissy absorbed this and filed it away in one of the priority slots of her mind. Where was he, anyway? she wondered as she loosened ice cubes from the tray and dropped them into glasses. Sissy could remember when she'd had to get ice by chipping at a block of ice with an ice pick. That ice was cut from Peatry Pond and stored in the icehouse here. It had been Harrison's only ice supply in those days. She hadn't thought about it before, but it was pond water. It was a miracle they hadn't all had typhoid.

Grace heard John's voice in the living room and said, "Another glass, Sissy, and be careful when you pour it, it's pretty fizzy this time."

"Did you make it?" asked Sissy, "really put it in the bottles and put on the caps? Really?"

"Yes," said Grace, "and it's pretty good, even if I do say so myself."

Sissy lifted the tray and went carefully through the door Grace was holding. From where Grace stood she could hear Alice's voice.

"You'll never guess who I saw at Amherst, John. The Pingrees. Remember Ellis Pingree? That strange little man has made something that goes in airplanes. He's given Amherst a small fortune. He was there with his son, a nice-looking boy, I must say."

Did Alice, by any chance, think that that nice-looking boy would make a suitable husband for Sissy? "Well," said John, "I'm glad Ellis is doing well," and then he said, as he took a glass of root beer from Sissy's tray, "Just what I need." He smiled up at Sissy and said, "I suppose you're off to the wild west pretty soon."

"No," replied Sissy, "I have a job."

"Wonderful," he said. "Doing what?"

"You must hear this," said Alice, turning to Grace. "You remember the Barringers. I sent you a newspaper picture from the rotogravure. You can't have forgotten. It was Ned Barringer — the Lenox and Boston Barringers."

"Yes, I guess I do," said Grace.

"He was engaged then, about to be married. He was such an old bachelor they thought he would never marry, but he did, and has two small children now. They have a place in Chatham and Sissy's been hired to be a nannie's helper for the two children. She's very excited about it. Aren't you, Sissy?"

"Yes, Mother," said Sissy. Then she turned her back and made a terrible face at Jane and Eleanor, as though to say she loathed the thought.

"Summer at the Cape," said Grace. "That should be lovely, Sissy. And I suppose you'll be going back to Sea Grove again this summer, Harold?"

"As a matter of fact, no," said Harold. "I'm thinking of —"

"He's thinking of the navy," said Alice. "You have got to do something about it, John. He values your judgment. He won't listen to me. Can you imagine? The navy."

"There was a retired naval man on the faculty here about five years ago," said John. "He was a fine fellow, well qualified to teach and, even though he was somewhat long in the tooth, he was as good a soccer coach as we've ever had. There's nothing wrong with the navy."

"I don't like it," said Alice. "Suppose there were a war. What then?"

"There's not going to be a war," said John.

Harold felt differently. He had majored in Government and his knowledge and understanding of the situation told him that things were desperate in England. It seemed unlikely that the United States wouldn't be pulled in eventually. Aside from that, he didn't have the money for graduate school. He wasn't even sure how he had had the money for college.

"War or not," he said, "I've signed up for the naval reserve."

Alice looked stunned. "When?" she asked. "When did you do it? Oh, Harold, why didn't you ask me?"

"I knew you wouldn't like it," said Harold.

"But I know people who might have been able to change your mind. I could get in touch with Bill James, you remember him, John. He came to the house so often when you were there. He's an admiral. He could do something. I'm sure of it."

"No," said Harold.

"You don't know what you're doing," said Alice. "The navy may sound romantic to you now, but it's either dangerous or deadly dull. What a waste. You tell him, John. He won't listen to me."

John didn't tell Harold anything except to keep his powder dry, and in the spring of 1942 Harold went to the Great Lakes Training Station and disappeared for six months. By then the Japanese had all but sunk the navy at Pearl Harbor and Alice went around and around inside the house at Fresh Pond Park like a mouse in a maze, wringing her hands and saying to anybody who would listen, "I knew it. I told him. They sank the *Arizona*. All of those boys, those fine young men, gone. Gone. What's going to happen to him? What can I do? Who do I know? Isn't there somebody with influence? The Websters, the Adamses, the Salt-onstalls." But what was the use? Lev Salt-onstall was already preaching war bonds and enlistment. People were mad, she decided.

While Alice was agonizing, John was reading the *New York Times* and the *Wall Street Journal* and the *Christian Science Monitor* and writing frantic letters to Will because it was evident that the draft was coming. Coming? It was here, in every town and village in the country, and if Will didn't sign up for the navy or the air force he would be drafted or sent off to OCS to become a ninety-day wonder, with a gold bar on his blouse and orders in his pocket that would throw him up on the green grass of England or the sandy shores of the Philippines.

Will, who should have been in the ski patrol, didn't know there was such a thing, and when his father's pleas began to annoy him he enlisted in the Air Corps reserve. When that was accomplished, his enlistment orders were stamped in purple ink with the words *Deferred until June 1944*, his graduation date. Unfortunately, despite the deferment, Will's group was called up in May 1943, and by August of that year Will was an aviation cadet stationed at Maxwell Field in Montgomery, Alabama.

He wrote to his family only occasionally because he was swamped with classwork and exhausted from marching, drilling, and PT. The life of an aviation cadet was frustrating and infuriating. Wilson had never known weather could be so hot, and when he was free he had no desire to do anything but lie on his bunk in his shorts and try to sleep. The heat of Hades couldn't be worse than the humid heat of Alabama in August, and he thought longingly of home.

At home Jane sat in her wheelchair on the porch sketching a hummingbird that darted and spun among the peonies. Jane's room was now on the first floor of the house in the room that had once been her father's study. She spent her days in her studio, which had been made by enclosing a portion of the porch and was reached by a ramp from the living room. Another ramp led from the front door onto the remainder of the porch, and in nice weather Jane sat outside, sketching or reading.

Eleanor was in the kitchen with her mother. They were canning peaches. Sometimes Jane helped. Peeling fruit and vegetables were jobs she could manage — like darning — but even a little of this sort of work tired her and, besides that, it was hot. Eleanor took a strainer and fished peaches out of the pan of hot water in which they had been scalded. The peach skins slipped off easily, leaving the fruit glistening. Quickly she halved and pitted them and dropped them into sterile jars.

Grace stirred sugar syrup in a saucepan on the stove. She had measured the sugar carefully because she wanted to save enough for a birthday cake for Jane. The next batch of peaches would be done with cloves and cinnamon and molasses. When the telephone rang she moved the saucepan off the burner and went into the hall to answer it.

"Harold!" cried Grace. "Where are you?"

Eleanor looked up quickly, her face burning and her heart pounding with her secret love for Harold. She had always been in love with Harold. There were boys in her life, but no one in particular, except him. Now she knew that he was going off to be killed and she would never see him again. Either that or he would marry someone else. She knew Harold had a special love for Jane and he would say, "You're only sixteen, Eleanor." Which was true, but her great-grandmother had been married at sixteen and crossed from Missouri to Oregon in a covered wagon and had her first baby on the way west.

Grace was saying, "Come for lunch, Harold," and "We'll see you in a few minutes." There wasn't much time. This time Eleanor was going to tell Harold how she felt and, dropping her knife, she tore off her apron and ran up the back stairs to her room. Jerking off her dress, she pulled on a pair of shorts. Snatching her hairbrush, she brushed out her hair furiously and then she raced down the hall to the bathroom and grabbed her lipstick. As she ran through the kitchen Grace called out sharply, "Eleanor!"

"I'll be back, Mother."

She streaked past the garage, through the garden, and across the field to the state road. When she reached the North Lane School, she stopped and sat down on a bench under the trees that shaded the front of the building. It was hot and hazy and as she sat there panting and slapping at the gnats that swarmed in the heat, it occurred to her that if Harold was driving a strange car she might miss him. She looked up and down the road and since the road was straight and flat she could see almost to the Purple Meadow and decided she couldn't miss him because she knew what the car looked like. There was no such thing as a new car anymore, or new tires, or enough gas. It was true, however, that if anybody could get tires and gas in wartime, Aunt Alice might be able to manipulate someone into providing her with a new car. The thought made her anxious, but suddenly she saw the familiar black Packard and she ran toward it, waving and calling, "Stop, Harold. Stop!"

She climbed in beside him, saw his troubled expression, and gasped, "It's all right. Nothing's wrong. I just wanted to see you alone. I had to see you alone."

He leaned over and kissed her and with a little moan she collapsed against him. "Oh, Harold," she gasped, "hold me. Please hold me."

"Hey," he said gently, "something *is* wrong. What's up?"

"Nothing."

With her face pressed to his chest, she could hear his heart pounding, and to be almost a part of his heartbeat filled her with joy. She couldn't imagine ever wanting more.

"I couldn't bear not to see you alone," she said. "I love you so much, Harold."

"I love you too, Eleanor."

She pulled back in amazement, saw the thin line of his jaw and the shadow of his beard, like smoke, on his face. The sexual feelings she was suddenly aware of startled her and she said, "You do?"

"Of course I do. I love you and Jane. I love all your family."

"That's not what I mean," she said. "I love *you*, Harold. It's different from family."

Harold was in love with a girl named Marilyn who was a junior at Smith and lived in

Northampton. When he left Harrison he was going to drive down the valley to spend the night with her. He hoped she'd been able to take care of the question of privacy. Eleanor was as familiar to him as his sister, and in her earnestness she seemed even younger than she actually was. He said gently, "I love you too, Eleanor, but I love you the way I love Sissy and Jane."

"No," she said, jerking away from him. "You love me differently. You kissed me, Harold."

He smiled and grabbed her arms and shook her. "I kiss all pretty girls," he said, and then, seeing her look of disappointment, he said, "Look, Eleanor, there are all kinds of love. You and I have family love. It's the best kind."

After lunch Harold wheeled Jane outside, and Eleanor, who stood at the sink washing dishes, watched them enviously as they settled down under the trees.

"Harold seems tired," said her mother, "I wish he'd try to get a little nap," and then, as though they had heard her, Harold stretched out on the grass with a pillow under his head and Jane took up her sketch pad.

Hot August sun splashing through the leaves scattered patches of light across Harold's body. A breeze stirred in the tops of the trees and later, when Jane had finished the painting she made from the sketches she did that day, Harold's body seemed to have become a reflection in a pool where gold leaves drifted on the surface of dark water. No one would have known it was Harold, except Eleanor and her mother, who had watched with different feelings while Harold slept away that drowsy August afternoon.

A year later, in August 1944, Eleanor walked across campus to the post office for the mail. She had done this regularly since Wilson graduated from navigation school. His APO was San Francisco, which meant he was somewhere in the Pacific and since he'd left only a few weeks ago Grace kept hoping for something more specific. She watched the clock, and by three in the afternoon she was sure the mail must be in and sorted, and then either she or Eleanor went for it.

"Anything from Wilson?" she asked that day, and Eleanor shook her head.

"Just something from Aunt Alice and a letter from Harold for Jane."

"Oh, good," said Grace, turning the shirt she was ironing and going carefully up and down the front panel because it was double thick and she wanted to be sure the starch was dry. Harold's letters were like a tonic to

Jane and Grace was always glad when one turned up in the mail.

"Put on the teakettle," she said to Eleanor, hanging up the shirt and unplugging the iron, "and set the tray, dear." She reached across the kitchen table for the mail.

Alice's letters are all alike, she thought as she tore it open. Alice rolled bandages at church, helped at the USO, and worried about Harold. Grace pulled out the letter and began to read and then, abruptly, put it down. Her hand flew to her face and she looked up with a dazed expression, glancing around the kitchen as though to reassure herself that she was still there. After a moment she folded the letter carefully and slid it back into the envelope where it belonged.

"It's Harold," she said to Eleanor.

Harold, thought Eleanor, not taking in the significance of those two words as she followed her mother through the hall to Jane's room and watched Grace take Jane's hands, saying gently, "We've had a letter from Aunt Alice with some very sad news, dear."

When her mother said, "Harold was killed a month ago," Eleanor began to shake. She clamped her teeth together and, turning quickly, ran through the kitchen and down the back steps. As she crossed the garden she remembered Harold's last visit and, closing her eyes and clenching her fists, she thought, He's not dead, he's not. He can't be. They've got him mixed up with someone else.

Her throat ached and her heart pounded heavily in her chest. She sat down on a stump, gasping and choking, and even though she tried to believe that in the house Jane and her mother were having tea, she couldn't.

Later that fall Aunt Alice sent Jane Harold's diary, in which he had kept a record of the mail he'd had from home. *This is for Jane,* wrote Alice, *because he mentions her so often and she wrote so faithfully.*

Over and over Harold had scribbled *Letter from Jane. Letter from Jane* on a page that had got wet so that now the words ran over the paper like a watermark. *Letter from Jane* until it must have seemed to him that Jane was there beside him.

When Jane unwrapped it and saw what it was, she put it in her lap under the crocheted afghan. "I'll look at it later," she said and went back to her painting. She was painting birds at the feeder that her father had fastened to the porch rail. A pile of pictures was growing rapidly and half filled a dress box.

Grace said, "One of these days you'll have enough to illustrate a book, even more than that." After nine long years of her daughter's illness, even after Harold's death, Grace's voice was still the strong, cheerful voice she used when someone was sick, but Jane didn't respond. What did she care about a book? What did she care about birds, for that matter? She gripped the brush tightly, her hand trembling, and she daubed feathers with swift, stabbing strokes. The cardinal she was painting became a torch of small leaping red flames erupting in little bursts of blood.

That night Eleanor heard Jane crying. She stood in the hall outside Jane's door and wondered whether or not to go in. Jane never cried. She hadn't cried when Aunt Alice's letter came, but she was crying now, a hopeless, tired crying. It was the kind of crying that purges and purifies as it washes through the body, drawing away passion to make room for grief, but Eleanor didn't know this. To stand there in the hall listening was like watching someone bleed to death, and when she was able to control herself she opened the door and sat down on Jane's bed. Putting her arm tightly around Jane's shoulders, she handed her a Kleenex. "Blow," she said.

Jane mopped her eyes and blew her nose and said firmly, "It's all right, Eleanor. Not for Harold because he had so much to look forward to, but it's all right for me because I've already had as much from Harold as I could ever hope for."

What about me? thought Eleanor. She grabbed a Kleenex and blew her own nose and wiped her own eyes. Then she said, "Oh Jane, you were such a good friend to him and he cared about you so much."

"He was a good friend to all of us," said Jane. "We will all miss him."

Tears ran down her cheeks and she reached out and patted Eleanor's arm. Jane couldn't bring herself to say any of the things she felt. The unborn babies that might have been hers and Harold's if things had been different. If she had been able to walk. The house they might have lived in together. A house with front and back stairs where she would run up and down. Not a one-level house.

And then she thought of living on the fringes of life as she did now, knowing that someday Harold would come through the door, presumably for a visit. Before he left he would tell her that he had found someone to marry, to have his children, to live in his house and become his wife. And he would say, "I wanted you to be the first to know, Jane. We have been friends for such a long time. You will like her. I want you to like her."

And Jane knew that she would smile and say that it was lovely news and ask him to tell her about this phantom person whom she would like.

But she wouldn't like her and when she saw their children, as she surely would, she would ache with self-pity.

Now she said, "I'm all right, Eleanor. This is what war is all about. It's like this for everybody who loses someone. Everyone suffers. I'll be all right."

4

When Jane had first begun to get well after being so sick, and she was well enough for her father to carry her downstairs and put her on the sofa, first for an hour or two and then for all afternoon, she had been nothing but skin and bones. No one said this. People frequently described others that way. "So and so is nothing but skin and bones," but inasmuch as it was true of Jane, no one said it.

Polio had turned Jane into a miniature person, as delicate as glass. Only her hair was the same, brown with springy curls. All the rest of her had been diminished by illness. Even her mouth and the teeth in her mouth seemed larger than they were in contrast to the rest of her. Seeing her from across the room, one might have wondered what Jane had found to grin about.

Gradually through the years, however, there had been an improvement of sorts, but after Harold was killed Jane's eyes grew enormous.

Circled as though smudged black-and-blue, they were like stones in her face. Sometimes it seemed to Eleanor that Jane had become an old-fashioned rag doll to which white porcelain hands and feet had been attached and from whose slender neck a large and perfect white porcelain head bobbed, its sweet face showing perpetual approval for whatever it was that its eyes, opening and shutting without conscious effort, could discern. The horror of Jane's dependence appeared to Eleanor in her sister's every act, and Eleanor would jump up to furnish a book or a paintbrush or a glass of water, for it seemed to Eleanor that if she was quick enough to supply Jane with whatever she needed before she realized she needed it, perhaps Jane's feelings of helplessness would subside. It never occurred to her that Jane had come to terms with her body long ago and that Harold's death had, curiously, liberated her from a life of helpless longing and regret.

In March of 1946 another of Alice's startling letters appeared and when Grace read it, sitting at the kitchen table before supper and taking in every word, she sputtered, "The idea!" and put it down. Then she mashed potatoes and made gravy and arranged carrots and onions around the pot roast they were having for dinner. When they had eaten and were drinking coffee, she brought it out and read it aloud to Jane and John.

In it Alice announced that she wanted to come in April and bring Sissy because Sissy was engaged and going to be married right away and Alice couldn't think of anything nicer than having a wedding in the chapel at Harrison.

"Well," said Grace indignantly, putting down the letter, "there it is. Sissy's going to be married and Alice wants the wedding here. Of all things! She wants *me* to plan a small reception. She wants flowers in the chapel. 'Whatever is blooming,' " snorted Grace in fury. "What blooms in April? All sorts of things bloom in May, but what about April?"

John said in his maddening way, "Forsythia, perhaps," and Grace turned to Jane for support, saying, "This is too much. When will Eleanor be home? Was it the fourteenth? It seems to me that Smith must have spring break then."

It was hard for Grace to think of Eleanor as a "college girl," even though she had been away from home for almost a year now. "Will she be home?" she asked again, and Jane, who missed Eleanor greatly and kept careful account of the days, said, "Yes."

"I honestly think, John," said Grace, "that enough's enough."

"Who is she marrying?"

Grace snapped open Alice's letter and said, "Read it yourself. Edmund Barringer. Weren't they the people Sissy went to the Cape with? The one whose wife divorced him a year ago?"

"Ah," said John, "*that* Barringer," and he turned to Jane and said with a wink, "it would appear our Sissy is well on her way to becoming rich."

Grace continued to sputter and he said, "Now, Grace, Alice doesn't mean to impose. She has real ties here. Elliot was a trustee, and I think we might be a little charitable this time."

"This time!" exclaimed Grace, but it was possible to see that she was already resigned to the inevitable because she left the table to find a pencil and began to make a list on the back of Alice's envelope.

"I suppose I could manage something for about fifty," she muttered, "and I can't imagine many will come way out here on such short notice. I should think he was too old for Sissy. How old is he?"

"Midforties, I'd say."

"Oh, dear," sighed Grace, "and two children."

"At least she knows the children," said Jane.

"Summer baby-sitting isn't the same as having children full time," said her mother, "but I suppose they're away at school. I thought Sissy was fond of Wilson," and she turned abruptly to Jane again. "Wasn't Wilson writing Sissy when he was overseas, and didn't he go to see her when he was discharged? Even before he came home?"

"I think you're right," said Jane. "Didn't Aunt Alice mention that Sissy had heard from Will?"

"And another thing," said Grace. "They met in New York before he was sent overseas. I seem to remember his telling us, but things were so confused then."

Grace had put away the war. Packed up letters and photographs. Put Wilson's uniforms in mothballs. Put his air medal in her jewel box. He didn't seem to want any of it, but the time would come, she supposed, when it wouldn't be so painful.

She looked up and realized that Jane was speaking and she said, "What were you saying, darling?"

"I was thinking of that awful time," said Jane, "when his friends were killed. He didn't want to talk about it, but . . ." Jane didn't go on because she had been about to say that her crippled condition seemed to invite others to reveal things to her that they would not have told anyone else. Someone who was whole and could walk. Someone who might understand. But Grace knew and she said, "Oh, yes. That was a terrible thing. They wanted him to identify the bodies."

And then she stopped because you couldn't put such things in jewelry boxes or mothballs. The happenings that horrified. The words that cut so deep.

"And another thing," said Jane. "Before he was sent overseas he was stationed at Mitchell Field, and he had to stand roll call every morning. We wanted him to come home, but he couldn't and somehow Sissy seemed to know this. Maybe they just bumped into each other and had fun together. She wrote about it afterwards and we were glad to know that even if he couldn't get home he had someone to be with. Surely you remember that, Mother?"

"Ah yes," said Grace. "I can remember now. It never occurred to me that there might have been something romantic about it."

"Probably you're right," said Jane, "but Sissy's always had her eye on Wilson. All he would have had to do to encourage her was to shake her hand or give her a brotherly kiss on the cheek. I could see that years ago. Couldn't you?"

"No," said Grace, "but we were always so

busy and there was so much confusion and we were so worried."

"Yes," said Jane.

"Oh well, it doesn't matter," said Grace wearily. "It's the same old story. If Sissy's married here Alice won't have to entertain in Cambridge. She won't have to have a church wedding. She won't have to pay for flowers or a caterer."

"The crime of poverty," said John wryly. "Alice has borne up fairly well, I think."

"Alice floats on the top," said Grace. "Alice is borne up by everybody else. She could have sold the house and lived sensibly. She could have gone to work. She's spent her life sponging."

"Well," said John, "the end's in sight. From what I hear Ned Barringer is worth the Vanderbilts and the Rockefellers put together."

Sissy and Alice arrived three days before the wedding. The car, a Buick Electra that Alice had acquired in a trade too good to turn down (the Buick dealership in Cambridge happened to be owned by one of Elliot's friends and nobody drove Packards anymore) was crammed with luggage, and by the time Sissy's trousseau, in glossy Jordan Marsh boxes and all charged, was unpacked, the sewing room looked like a fitting room. Even Grace gasped and there was a wistful look on her face as she examined the satin and chiffon of Sissy's new wardrobe. The good tweeds of fall would come later when Sissy could sign *Mrs. E. W. Barringer IV* on the sales slips, but all the froth of spring and summer, the soft silks and smooth linens, the simple dresses with their small round collars and covered buttons, were there, displayed on hangers next to Grace's old dress form that stood like a stodgy and disapproving matron beside them. The clothes were Aunt Alice's grand send-off for her daughter's maiden voyage into the sea of matrimony, which, in her opinion, thanks to Barringer money, was not the terrifying uncharted passage that faced most girls.

Sissy seemed remarkably unconcerned for a bride-to-be and hung up her things carelessly. She arrived in an old cashmere pullover and brown slacks, and when everything was unpacked she plunked herself down on the double bed where she and Eleanor would sleep until the big day. The ring her future husband had given her flashed like a traffic light on her small brown hand, but she seemed indifferent to it as she sat there cross-legged and morose.

"Is Wilson coming?" she asked.

"Friday," said Eleanor.

After rummaging through a bag, Sissy

pulled out her hairbrush and began to brush her beautiful hair. It rippled and shone, but Sissy took no pleasure in it and after a minute she twisted a rubber band around it and pulled it away from the perfect oval of her face. Her face looked thin then, her eyes lacked life, and, sitting there biting her lips, she seemed intent on diminishing herself.

Eleanor, who was wildly curious about Ned Barringer, waited for Sissy to confess her love and excitement, but Sissy had nothing to say. Eleanor thought the impending marriage was incredibly romantic. She wondered if, during the summers when Sissy was in Chatham with the family, she had flirted with Ned, and she conjured up little scenes in which Sissy, lissome and tanned, looked up to discover Ned Barringer looking at her hungrily, saying nothing, of course. Perhaps he had even made small overtures, nothing improper, just tiny indications of his own feelings so that once he was divorced it didn't come as a total surprise to Sissy to find him on her doorstep.

After all, during those summers at the Cape with the Barringers, Sissy had been free to do what she wanted to, except for mornings and some evenings. Once a week she had a day off and went into Boston to an art studio where she was taking painting lessons. Perhaps, thought Eleanor, she had driven into town with Mr. Barringer on those days and maybe they had fallen in love sitting in the backseat of his limousine, sneaking small covert glances at each other as they flashed through Harwich and Dennis on the way north.

When Mrs. Barringer divorced her husband and left for Paris, Alice said, everyone who was anyone in Boston was shocked, although not very surprised. People who knew Edith Barringer knew that she was odd and didn't pay any attention when she said in her deadly way, "But of course Ned is 'nice,' that isn't the point." No one seemed to know, however, exactly what the point *was*.

"I thought you liked being at the Cape with the Barringers," said Eleanor. "You said you went into Boston every week on your day off and that he paid for your art lessons."

"He did. He was very nice."

"When did you know he was falling in love with you? What did he actually do?"

Sissy looked up in surprise. "Don't be a ninny, Eleanor. He didn't do anything. He just talked about painting and what a good sort of thing it was for a woman to do."

"I didn't know you liked to paint."

"I didn't either," said Sissy, "but . . . oh, God," she said, "it was so boring in Chatham. Mother was always showing up and sleeping in the guest room when they were away and she would meet her friends and drag me from one place to another where she thought she might find somebody marriageable."

"And did she find anybody? What exactly was she looking for?"

"People with money, of course. You are so naïve, Eleanor. Haven't you learned anything yet?"

"I am not naïve," said Eleanor indignantly, stifling the impulse to remind Sissy that she was almost through her freshman year at Smith and was no longer naïve. "I just wonder what happened," she said. "I always thought you were in love with Will and were going to marry him."

"Who told you that? Did he tell you that?"

"No," said Eleanor, "and I wouldn't have asked him, but he did write to you when he was overseas and there were all those times here," she said vaguely. "I just thought —"

"Don't think," said Sissy. "You are still a child, Eleanor. Just don't think."

It was true that she had expected Will to marry her, anytime, immediately if necessary. She had written him and he had gone straight from Devens when he was discharged to Cambridge to see her. But more importantly they had met in New York, half by chance and half by design, before he shipped out for California and the Pacific. The memory of the two days they had spent in the Commodore in New York, registered as Mr. and Mrs. Allen Freeman, was a time she would never forget. "Who is Allen Freeman?" she had asked Will as they entered the elevator, and Will laughed. "Just somebody from Dartmouth," said Will, and, kissing her as they shot up to the tenth floor, he added, "lucky bastard."

Sissy was a virgin then and didn't care if he was or not. They lived like nudists for two days and two nights. They were so desperate for each other they were like wild pups pulling greedily at the teats of Mother Wolf, terrified their sustenance would vanish and leave them alone to starve. Of course she expected Will to marry her.

Abruptly Sissy said, "I'm going for a walk, and I want to go alone."

Downstairs in the kitchen Alice was coming to grips with reality and stood at the table unpacking a cardboard box that took up half the floor. First she unpacked a cut-glass punch bowl and set it on the table, then she began to unwrap the cups.

"I was afraid you wouldn't have a punch set, Grace. This was my mother's. Be careful when you wash it. Rachel Dorman, you remember my speaking of her, is bringing the champagne. Punch is easier than poured un-

105

less you have good help. What do you think?"

Grace knew what Alice meant by "good help" and smoldered silently. "Yes," she said, "punch is easier, but you'll have to ask John about the champagne. Alcohol isn't allowed on campus."

"Oh, dear," said Alice, "I never thought of that, but I ought to have remembered. I never think of champagne as alcohol, do you?"

Grace never thought of champagne at all, but she was relieved when John said that, inasmuch as the only campus people invited were two young instructors who had known Harold at Amherst, he saw no objection to champagne punch. "After all," he said, "by no stretch of the imagination could this wedding be thought of as a school function." And that settled it.

Even the minister was coming from Cambridge and, being Episcopalian, was certainly accustomed to alcoholic receptions. Alice had ordered the cake in Boston and once again her friend Rachel was standing by.

Meanwhile Sissy was walking through the woods that separated the campus from the state road and trying not to think at all. It was Friday. Will was coming on Friday. Why wasn't he here? Why had he stayed away for so long? She turned and started down the hill to the orchard and then across to the gymnasium. Boys on the soccer field ran and shouted and bounced balls off their heads. They could have been Indians tossing the bloody head of a captive and screaming in horrified glee and Sissy wouldn't have noticed.

As she dragged back toward the chapel she wondered what to do next. How had this dreadful thing happened? She didn't love Ned. She had even stopped enjoying the extravagant things he did for her. She would rather have had a cigar band from Will on her finger than Ned's two-carat diamond.

Sinking down on a granite bench, memorial gift from the class of 1912, she glanced across to Drury House and saw a car and there was Will. Suddenly she was like a prisoner reprieved just as the executioner raised his ax. Tearing the rubber band off her hair, she raced down the hill, across the road, and through the budding lilacs and threw herself into his arms. With her arms around his neck she cried, "I thought you'd never come. Oh, darling. We've been waiting for you."

Inside the house Grace was trying to make order in the midst of chaos. "Dinner's ready," she said two or three times. "Fill the glasses, Eleanor. We'll need another chair, John. Take the one in the study."

And there they were, in one of the whirls that always seemed to occur around mealtime. One would think the occasion had nothing to do with me, thought Sissy, trying to remain calm as she made her way slowly through ham and scalloped potatoes.

When it was over at last she stretched her hand out to Will and said, "Let's go see the sunset from the chapel tower."

"Don't be silly, dear," said her mother. "It's getting dark."

"It won't be dark for ages," argued Sissy.

"It's chilly," said Alice, "you'll get cold, Sissy. Don't be foolish."

"I'm fine, Mother," said Sissy. "Come on, Will."

"Why don't you go too, Eleanor," said Aunt Alice. "I'll help with the dishes."

"Yes, Eleanor," said Sissy, "we need a chaperone. After all these years mother thinks we need a chaperone."

"Shut up," growled Will, standing there like a post until it became apparent that Sissy would have her way, and then he opened the door.

They went rapidly across the lawn in the fading light of early evening, Sissy dancing along with excitement, pulling at Will's hand, then running ahead of him like a child playing tag. Finally she turned to Eleanor and said,

"I know you hate the tower. Mother is such a dunce. Stay here and wait for us if you'd rather."

The sound of their voices faded and the noise of their feet on the wooden steps grew faint until suddenly there was Eleanor alone in the silence of the chapel, with long straight rows of empty pews under the vaulted ceiling spread out below her. In the growing darkness Eleanor imagined she could see the pews filled with boys sitting in their assigned seats. It was a scene so familiar it seemed almost to breathe. She could see herself with the family, sitting in the balcony and, in the gathering shadows, it seemed to her she could actually see the backs of the assembled congregation, see the thin lines of white collars edging jacket collars, see the scrubbed necks, the short haircuts, and hear a scraping sound like dozens of bows being drawn across the strings of dozens of reluctant violins, as the boys rose in a body to sing.

How many of them had been killed in the war, she wondered, and how long would it be before she would be reading those names on a plaque in the vestibule? As dusk deepened she could almost imagine that she was standing in a company of ghosts and that at any minute Harold would step out of the shadows to confront her. "Still afraid of the tower?" he would chide, smiling and holding out his hand.

A lump rose in her throat, the awful ache of it bringing tears, and, turning abruptly, she tugged open the heavy oak door that led from the balcony to the tower and started up the steps.

It had grown too dark in the tower to see the terrifying drops from one loft to another, but when she reached the top of the first flight she could sense the drop below her, and, pulling herself onto the wooden platform, she huddled, her arms locked around her knees, shivering with fear. She thought then that Harold was right, she was still afraid of the climb, the open stair railings, the bells above her waiting to strike the hour.

Suddenly she heard Sissy's voice clearly.

"But Will," Sissy pleaded, "you love me. I know you do. Your letters said you did. Please, Will, please hold me. Please, Will."

"Now, Sissy," Will said, "now, Sissy, you're getting married tomorrow."

"Oh, my God," she cried. "I'm not married now. I only said I would because of you. I thought if you heard I was getting married you'd see how wrong you were."

"Please don't, Sissy," groaned Will.

"You loved me, Will. I never stop thinking about how it was before you went overseas. I can see the room we had. Whenever I go to New York I stay in that hotel. Oh God, Will, please."

Wilson moaned and said in a strangled voice, "It's too late, Sissy. There's a girl. I've already asked her. I never thought it meant that much to you . . . before the war. I thought it was just something that happened, something good that happened before I shipped out, that's all."

Sissy began to cry and suddenly the bell rang, shattering the silence and shaking the loft. Eleanor clamped her hands over her ears and closed her eyes and waited. When the bell had struck seven times she inched toward the top of the steps and began her descent, clinging to the rail and collapsing at last into the blackness of the chapel.

Outside the sun was setting in a band of red that shone along the tops of the hills. Red seemed to boil up into the sky, as though it came from the center of a volcano, as though the whole world were about to go up in flames.

By the time Wilson and Sissy came down from the tower it was pitch black and Eleanor was nearly frozen.

That night Sissy hummed cheerfully as they got ready for bed. She had washed her hair and sat at the dressing table rolling it up. To Eleanor it seemed incredible that Sissy would be married the next day. How could she sit there, humming and unconcerned, after what she'd said to Wilson in the tower?

"You're not in love with Ned, are you?" asked Eleanor. "I don't understand. How can you think about marrying him? How can you sit there as if nothing had happened?"

"Simple," said Sissy. "I'm not going to marry him."

She put down her comb and smiled knowingly, as though Eleanor were a simpleton, a child unable to grasp the obvious. Then she took another roller and wound a long strand of hair around it with steady fingers. "You'll understand one day," she said.

"What about all the people? What about the food, and the minister? What about *him?*" she asked, unable to call the poor deluded Ned by name.

"I'm sorry about that," said Sissy, "but it's not really my fault. I was only trying to show Wilson . . . who is too dense for words . . . anyway, Eleanor, I am not getting married."

"What about Will?"

"Oh, him," she said with a sigh. "He thinks he's in love with somebody named Valerie, but he's not. He thinks he has to get his CPA before he gets married, but he doesn't. To be perfectly honest, I don't think Wilson has any idea what he really wants, but he'll come around. You'll see."

"What will your mother say?"

"She'll get over it."

Sissy pulled down the bedspread and thumped the pillows. She looked happy, really happy, for the first time since she'd come, but all Eleanor could think about was Sissy's beautiful clothes, especially the nightgowns. What would happen to them? she wondered.

Even at breakfast it was easy to see that it was going to be a beautiful day. Forsythia and Japanese quince, just off the porch, were nodding pink and yellow bouquets. A light breeze rustled in the birches, where small, tight curls of green stood out like french knots embroidered on a blue sky.

"A beautiful day," said Alice, as though she had arranged it, then she turned to Sissy and said, "Feeling better, dear?" as though Sissy might have complained of a headache, when she was actually on the edge of a breakdown.

"I feel fine," said Sissy.

"Well," said Grace, passing the muffins, "we won't be eating again for a long time so don't hold back," and then she turned to Sissy and said, "if there's anything you need as you get ready, just ask Eleanor."

"Get ready for what, Aunt Grace?" asked Sissy.

"To be married," said Alice with alarm in her voice.

"But I'm not going to be married," said Sissy, and she went right on spreading jam on her toast, not even bothering to look up. It didn't seem to matter to her that Mrs. Ware was already in the kitchen counting plates; that the house was decorated with sprays of forsythia and pussy willows; that Will, rising and mumbling "excuse me," had left the table abruptly. None of this seemed to bother Sissy, and she scarcely turned her head when her mother gasped, "Don't be silly, Cornelia," as she smiled the stiff smile of concealed terror.

"I mean it, Mother," said Sissy. "I'm sorry if it upsets you and I'm sorry about all the bother, Aunt Grace. I didn't mean to let it go on this long, but I couldn't seem to stop it and you were so determined, Mother."

"*I* was so determined?" said Alice.

"It certainly wasn't me," said Sissy.

"But Sissy, you agreed. You accepted his proposal. You encouraged him."

Sissy shrugged. "If I did, I'm sorry, and it doesn't make any difference now. I'm not going to marry him."

"Now, dear," said Alice quietly, "all brides are nervous. I understand. You'll feel differently later."

"I will not feel differently later," said Sissy,

raising her voice. She whipped around and glared at Eleanor as though she had no business sitting there in silence and she said, "You tell her, Eleanor. Tell her I told you last night and that I am not nervous. I was nervous last week, but I am not nervous now."

"There, now," soothed Alice, "let's talk about something else."

"Certainly, Mother," said Sissy. "Let's talk about something pleasant. Let's talk about how much money Ned has. Let's talk about the Barringer paper mill in Chicopee and that Barringer house in Chatham, and the Barringer estate in Wellesley, and the Barringer finishing plant in North Carolina, or is it South Carolina? Wherever. Down there somewhere."

"Stop it, Sissy," said Alice. She turned abruptly to John and appealed to him. "Can't you do something?" she said.

"I'm afraid this is out of my line, Alice," he said, putting his hands on the arms of the chair he had pushed back from the table. Then, taking the handles of Jane's wheelchair, he said cheerfully, just as though it was an ordinary day, "Come on, Janie. Let's you and me take a walk."

"Here we are," said Grace, coming through the door with the coffeepot. Then, taking in the disintegration of the group, she asked,

"Where's everybody going? Doesn't anybody want another cup of coffee?"

No one bothered to answer. Alice crumpled up her napkin and said, "Please excuse us, Grace," and then in a flat, cold voice, "Come upstairs with me, Sissy. Right now."

As they disappeared up the stairs, Grace turned to Eleanor with a little smile. "Weddings are like this sometimes," she said, as though it was important to maintain the appearance of controlled joy even in the face of impending disaster. "Clear the table, dear, and then go into the pantry and start taking down the good cups and saucers."

A heat register in the pantry opened into the sewing room overhead, and as Eleanor climbed onto a stool and reached for the Richards china, she could hear footsteps and then Aunt Alice's voice pleading with Sissy.

"What is it, dear? What's wrong? I thought you wanted to marry Ned."

"When have you ever cared what I've wanted?" demanded Sissy hatefully. "You've known all along I didn't want to marry him."

"How could I have known that? If you weren't interested you should have discouraged him."

"It never occurred to me he'd want to marry me," said Sissy. "I didn't dislike him. He always seemed nice enough at the Cape. I never

116

thought of him in that way. He's old enough to be my father."

"Age is relative," said her mother, "and you aren't a child. What could you possibly have thought when he took you out, and don't tell me you haven't enjoyed it. How many girls your age have the kind of chance you have now? You must have guessed he wanted a wife."

"He won't have any trouble finding someone else."

"You're being childish," said her mother. "I'm not going to listen to any more of this."

"Then don't," said Sissy, "but I'm telling you, Mother. I'm not going to be there this afternoon."

"Where are you going to be?"

"On a bus going home."

"Oh," said Alice, "and where is home?"

"You know perfectly well where home is."

"I know where my home is," said her mother, "and I thought I knew where yours would be, but if you don't get married, dear, where will your home be?"

There was a long silence and then Sissy said, "If my father were alive he'd understand."

"If your father were living we wouldn't be in the position we're in," said her mother.

"I don't know what you're talking about. What position? I'm not talking about positions. I'm talking about my life."

"Come, now," said her mother, "or are you blind? How much longer do you think I can keep the house?"

"What do you mean, keep it? Isn't it paid for?"

"That's only the beginning," said Alice. "After that come taxes and insurance. The roof leaks. What do you think it cost to put in the new furnace and how do you think I've managed to pay your tuition at Vassar?"

"I don't know. How have you paid the bills before this? Good Lord, Mother, an imbecile could see we haven't any money, but we're not paupers."

"I don't know what you mean by paupers, Sissy, but you don't know the first thing about money. What do you think I did with Harold's insurance money? We wouldn't have the Buick if it weren't for Mr. Forbes. How do you think I managed to send you out to Wyoming to Uncle Fred's? You wouldn't have been in Vassar if it weren't for Rachel Dorman and the Cambridge Vassar Club. How do you think I managed credit at Jordan Marsh? Even the people there knew who you were marrying without my having to tell them."

"That makes me sick," said Sissy.

"I'm sorry it makes you sick, dear," said her mother. "I didn't choose to live this way.

If your father had lived and if my own father hadn't squandered his money — but that's beside the point. I've only done what I had to. Harold was on full scholarship at Amherst. It's through the generosity of your father's friends who happen to be on the boards of corporations that survived that both of you have had the opportunities you've had. What do you think will happen to you if you don't marry well?"

"I'll get a job."

"Where? Doing what? You paint very prettily, Sissy, but you'd be lucky to get a job dressing windows or selling stockings at Filene's."

"I don't love him."

"He's a good man," said her mother. "People respect him. His wife was a silly woman, but she has money of her own and that makes all the difference. You do like the children. You always said you did, and, besides that, they're away at school most of the time."

"Oh, God, Mother," she said, "he's old and his teeth are yellow. I think about getting into bed with him and I want to throw up."

"It will work out," said Alice urgently, "you'll see."

"*You* marry him," said Sissy. "*You* marry him. He's nearer your age than mine, and then you'll have all that nice money and you can roll around in bed with him and let him paw at you."

"Sissy!"

Sissy was silent.

"If he disgusts you so much perhaps you'd better not marry him, but, believe me, all men are alike once the lights are out. They all behave the same way and it's over in a minute. Eventually they leave you alone. They're all alike, even the best of them. The only thing that matters is money because there's no other way to live well."

Eleanor heard Sissy on the back stairs and saw her streak out and across the yard. She's looking for Wilson, thought Eleanor, and as she counted cups she imagined them out in the woods somewhere, sitting on a log, holding each other and crying and kissing until Sissy had persuaded Wilson to marry her. Then the cups would all have to be put up again, no one would come, and the family would sit around in gloomy silence eating up nuts and sandwiches.

Eventually Sissy came back to the house. Her eyes were red and she went up the back stairs and into the bathroom without saying a word to anyone.

A half hour later Wilson slipped through the kitchen and disappeared into Jane's room, and at exactly one o'clock Sissy was married with her hair pinned up and her eyes two black smudges in her white face. She looked beautiful and sacrificial, which seemed to suit everybody who took it for granted that all brides were troubled by delicate uncertainties and bound to show the effects. People murmured "so sweet," "tears to my eyes," and "lucky Ned." All except Eleanor, who watched in misery and knew that something terrible was happening.

In the dining room people milled around with plates of chicken salad and sandwiches, accepting cups of punch as Aunt Alice ladled with regal composure. Pretty soon everyone was talking loudly and happily and flash bulbs were popping. Wilson and his friends huddled in a corner of the living room and, drinking champagne out of bottles, they were getting progressively more tipsy. After a while they began to sing songs. Following this, they moved to toasts. They drank to Harold and to everybody else who had been killed in the war. They drank to the bride and groom, to the president of the United States, and to the king of England. If there had been a swimming pool they would have looked for a victim, but the only pool on campus was locked up in the gym and, far gone as he was, Wilson knew it was inaccessible.

Now and then he looked up, scanning the

crowd, looking for Sissy. He could see her moving in and out among the guests, smiling and kissing people. She kissed all the men in the living room, going from one to another, saving Wilson for last, as though he were dessert, and when she finally came to him she put her arms tightly around him and kissed him as though she'd never stop. It seemed to go on forever, until people stopped talking entirely; until Ned walked into the living room and said in a hearty voice, "It would appear I have arrived just in time." Then everyone laughed. Conversation resumed. Sissy pushed Wilson away and ran up the stairs, throwing her bouquet over her shoulder without a glance at anyone.

By then Wilson was blubbering and at that point Grace pushed through the mob and hissed, "You're a disgrace, Wilson. Go out to the kitchen and get some coffee." Then, seeing Eleanor, she snapped, "Go upstairs and see if you can help Sissy."

Sissy was crying. Her dress was in a heap on the floor and now she was tearing at her veil. When she saw Eleanor she gasped, "Why did he let me? Why didn't he stop me? I counted on him stopping me," and she jerked savagely at her veil, tearing it off and throwing it on the bed.

Eleanor picked up the gown and took Sissy's

suit off the hanger. She knew that Wilson was "he," and that he was now in the kitchen drinking coffee. What could "he" have done, she wondered, except marry Sissy, and, after all, how was that possible when he'd already proposed to somebody named Val?

When Sissy was ready she looked as though she'd stepped out of *Vogue*, her makeup so perfect that no one would have known she'd been crying. Smiling bleakly, she went down the stairs to make the rounds, thanking Mrs. Dorman, who had brought the cake, and even Mrs. Ware in the kitchen. She said, "Thank you, Aunt Grace, for everything," and then put up her arms and hugged Eleanor's father, murmuring, "Thank you, Uncle John. You're the closest to a father I've ever had."

He couldn't have asked for more.

And then, turning to Ned, she smiled sweetly and took his arm and they went down the walk to his limousine. Giving a quick little wave, Sissy stepped inside.

5

After Sissy's wedding, things settled down. The following spring Eleanor finished her sophomore year at Smith, and Will, who had graduated from Dartmouth, continued at Harvard Business, where he was halfway toward becoming a CPA. He had lined up a job with a bank for the summer. Grace had ceased to think he was seriously interested in a girl named Val, whom he had met in California when he returned from overseas, because he rarely mentioned her. Whatever he had told Sissy about her had yet to surface in the family. If they were engaged he hadn't announced it to them, and Grace hoped privately that it would be a long engagement.

And then, just as summer became official, Will called and asked if he could bring Valerie home to meet the family. Long-distance calls were always treated as emergencies at Harrison, particularly if they came at mealtimes. At the phone's ring, John rose and stepped into the front hall and they heard him say, "Fine. . . . Yes, fine. . . . Let me get your mother." He came back into the dining room and said, "Grace, it's Wilson. He wants to come home this weekend and bring Valerie with him. Is that all right with you?"

He held out the phone and invited her to take it, but she said in a loud, cheerful voice that of course it was all right. When would they arrive?

"When do you think you'll get here?" asked John.

"Suppertime," was the answer.

"He says suppertime, Grace. Is that all right?"

"Fine," said Grace. "Tell him we're delighted."

When they had finished dinner and the dishes were done, Grace took off her apron and went into John's study and said, "Well, what do you think about that?"

"About what?" said John, putting his finger on the line and word in the book he was reading.

"About Will and Val . . . whatever her name is."

"Fine," said John. "I was beginning to think there wasn't such a person. What do you think?"

"Fine," said Grace. All the animation had

gone out of her voice.

"Obviously you have very little enthusiasm for it."

She looked up and smiled without evidencing any joy and said, "I don't know. I just don't. He seemed so . . . well, so flat the last time he was here."

"Well, now," said John easily. "Everyone has his ups and downs. You worry too much."

"I know it," she said. "What do you think we ought to have for supper?"

"You'll think of something," said John cheerfully, returning to his book and apparently unaware that Grace stood there helplessly for a few moments, wondering if there was anything else to say. Finding that nothing came to mind, she went into the living room and took up her knitting.

Once Grace had made up her mind to accept the circumstances, she went all around the house dusting the tops of picture frames and doing other picky house-cleaning chores, as if she knew instinctively that Wilson was coming home with someone destined to join the family. In view of that, she wanted to pass inspection.

That weekend, Will ran up the steps and into the house, dragging Val and saying, "You see, I told you it wouldn't be so bad, didn't I?"

Val murmured something and looked embarrassed.

Ever since Sissy's wedding Eleanor had wondered about Val. She didn't see how anybody could be as beautiful as Sissy, but she was wrong. Valerie, a slim, graceful girl, was a Snow White to Sissy's Rose Red. The minute she saw her, Eleanor felt touched by her beauty and the look of innocence in her expression. Val seemed fragile and shy. She smiled and said, "You're Eleanor, aren't you?" And Eleanor said, "Yes I am. And you're Val?" The exchange, simple as it was, seemed somehow significant.

"We're so glad you could come," said Grace. "Will tells us you're from California. You must miss your family."

"Yes, I do," said Val, looking helplessly at Will as though to ask what he had told them. Didn't his parents know that they were planning to be married? She reached out and took his hand, and he said, "Val will be part of our family in another year, if she'll still have me."

There was a moment of silence in which Val might have said, "Of course I will, you nut," but she didn't. She stood there, holding his hand and waiting, and then Grace spoke up, as though she had known all along what

127

they wanted to do because she smiled agreeably, as though weddings in the family were announced daily. Clearly she was relieved that there would be time to do things the right way. That seemed quite important to her suddenly, and she smiled all round and said, "Well, time to think about supper."

They were having a cold supper because the weather was hot. Grace's rolls were rising under tea towels in the pantry and the refrigerator was full of strawberries, stuffed eggs, and sliced ham. She had been worried that perhaps it wouldn't be enough, but somehow, now that she'd seen Val, her anxiety vanished. As she turned away and headed for the kitchen, she heard Will say to Val, "How about a walk around the campus? The view from the chapel tower is great."

"Tower," said Val, her voice almost inaudible. "I don't like high places, Will. I thought you knew that." There was just a hint of disapproval in her tone, but Will said cheerfully, "That's right. I forgot. We'll follow the low road this time."

As they disappeared down the hill, Eleanor was somehow glad that there wouldn't be a wedding immediately.

Once again Grace sat at the kitchen table making a guest list. It seemed like a moment since she had been planning Sissy's wedding, but that had been over two years ago. Sissy already had a baby, a little boy named Matthew. "You see," she said to anyone who commented on either wedding, "how can we ever forget how things were at Sissy's wedding, but hasn't it all worked out happily?" Time goes so fast, she thought, returning to her list.

It was a hot day made hotter by the canner that steamed on the stove. In another fifteen minutes Grace would take out six quarts of strawberries to drain and cool. Then she would bathe and dress for supper. Meanwhile, she wrote the names of the guests who would be invited to Will's small wedding. There seemed to be more than she had thought there would be. She thought with some irritation that one didn't usually plan a son's wedding, but it wasn't Val's fault that her parents lived so far away. Such a beautiful girl, she thought, wondering why she didn't feel more enthusiasm for the wedding.

In the living room Jane was playing a Jose Iturbi–Deanna Durbin record. If things were different she might be planning Jane's wedding now, but Grace tried never to think about what might have been. She resumed her list and made a memo. *Punch.* And underneath that she wrote *pineapple juice, lemons, ginger ale.*

It was almost four and time to put on the teakettle. Grace never deviated from routine, which was the family's salvation. What would their life have become without its patterns? She wondered what would become of them if, one day, they failed to rise at seven, eat breakfast, struggle into the bathroom at eight to contend with the problems that atrophied limbs and shrinking organs imposed, and then proceed with a day identical to the one before.

There would always be something Jane could do, Grace consoled herself, for Jane was clever with her hands. Jane peeled vegetables, arranged flowers, and did the mending. She painted and wrote poetry and did needlework. It was Jane who wrote and addressed the wedding invitations, and Grace meant it when she said, "Jane is an enormous help to me."

In the evening she and Jane listened to the radio, laughed at Jack Benny, remembered which Sunday it was according to what had happened to Charlie McCarthy. Jane and her father shared long, silent games of chess, during which they sat and stared at the wall or the board or each other, and in those seemingly endless periods Grace breathed deeply and freely, as though she had put down a burden she had been ordered to carry day after day, for as long as she lived.

How could she worry about a wedding? It

was simply something to be fitted into the pattern of their lives, a normal event, considering Wilson's age. She was sure they would come to care greatly for Val once she was actually a member of the family.

What had begun as a small wedding for family and friends grew to become an event with houseguests. Polly, Val's sister and maid of honor, arrived by train on the day before the wedding, and, the same afternoon Will and Val and Charles Hammond, his best man, drove out from Cambridge.

When they arrived, they found Grace and Jane and Eleanor drinking tea and Will said, "Good Lord, Mother, it's sweltering. How can you sit here drinking hot tea?"

"It's very easy to sit here," said Jane. "If the British can drink tea year round in India, we can certainly do the same here."

"You can have something cold," said Grace, "once you're settled," and there followed a grand scurrying up and down stairs with bags as Grace showed them where to sleep.

Downstairs Charles was drinking tea with Jane and Eleanor, and Marmalade, their orange cat, was prowling around and rubbing Charles's ankles and purring loudly as Charles stroked her head.

"She likes you," said Jane.

Eleanor, who knew Charles had flown with Will in China, passed the cookies and said, "I'm surprised you like tea. Will came home from China with a vast dislike for tea and rice."

At that moment Will and Val came down the stairs. Val had told him privately that she didn't like the idea of sleeping with Polly, even though they were sisters, and Will had told her privately that there wasn't any other place to sleep and to make the best of it. God, he thought, if I ever needed a drink I need it now, but he knew better than to ask for it. He and Charles had brought along some private stock, but he wondered just when they'd be able to get to it.

Grace was in the kitchen working on supper. As soon as John came back from the station with Polly she would put in the casserole and call the chaplain and tell him they were ready to rehearse. What was there to rehearse? she wondered, feeling unaccountably glum, but, of course, even if the wedding was to be at home they needed some instruction. She would be glad when it was all over and they could get back to normal. Eleanor was due back at Smith in two weeks and Will and Val would be off almost immediately for Ann Arbor, where Will had taken a job.

The family was making its first move toward

separation. Ann Arbor was miles away, halfway to the West Coast, which would probably please Val. Once that far, might they not go the whole way? No wonder I feel glum, Grace thought.

Grace hadn't heard from Alice and was surprised when her black Buick turned into the drive the next morning. Her first reaction to this was irritation, but as she took off her apron and went out to meet her, Grace realized that Alice, who had been to so many of their family events, belonged here now. Giving her a hug, Grace said, "I didn't hear from you. I was afraid you weren't coming."

"Of course I've come!" cried Alice, moving briskly up the front steps and into the house, where Wilson and his father were struggling with a trellis that someone had insisted they borrow for the event. It seemed to want to belong in front of the fireplace, but when Alice saw it there she said immediately, "Try it in the arch, John, then you won't have the hearth to contend with."

She was right. The trellis fit perfectly in the double doorway between the living and dining rooms and, banked with jugs of goldenrod and ferns, it was lovely.

"There, you see," said Alice, and taking Grace's arm she started for the kitchen, saying,

"Now, Grace, you must put me to work. That's why I'm here. I can make sandwiches or wash dishes, anything you say. I suppose the cake has arrived."

Val's parents had sent a check for twenty-five dollars and written a note asking Grace to use it for the wedding cake. It was a nice note and made Grace feel somewhat better about Val's family. It was the thoughtful gesture that made them, distant and unknown as they were, seem ordinary and friendly.

Mrs. Ware's daughter, who worked in a bakery and knew how to use a pastry tube to make leaves and rosebuds, had made the cake. It was twenty-four inches high and had three tiers with a celluloid bride and groom on the top. It was a pretty cake, but not like Sissy's, which had been a dark fruit cake. Val's was a plain yellow cake with white frosting and pink roses.

When Alice saw it, she said, "Oh, what a sweet cake, Grace," and then she looked around for the little white boxes the guests would take home, but, of course, there weren't any. Not to be put off by anything, she said, "I know I'm early, but I thought I might help. Where's the bride?"

Val was in seclusion with her sister Polly. She had had a breakfast tray and a lunch tray, because it was bad luck to see the groom before the ceremony, she said, and her sister Polly had been trotting up and down stairs all morning.

"Well," said Alice, "just put me to work, Grace," and she went right out into the kitchen, where Mrs. Ware was making sandwiches. When Alice saw the trays of punch cups and coffee cups she said, "I should have brought my punch bowl. I didn't think."

"We'll manage, Alice," said Grace, who wanted to scream that it was their wedding and that they didn't need Dwire crystal, or Dwire china, or anything else for that matter, and she went quickly into the living room to find John.

"Can't you do something with Alice?" she asked in exasperation.

"What?"

"How should I know? Sit on the porch, go over to the chapel, walk around the athletic field. I don't care. Anything."

In a minute Alice and John were going down the steps and, as they strolled across the lawn, Alice said, "I feel so fortunate, John. I've simply put all my affairs in Ned's hands. You can't imagine the difference it's made. I never have to think about money anymore."

"I'm very glad to hear that," said John, "and how is Sissy?"

"Well," said Alice, pausing thoughtfully as

though she had, of course, given the matter real consideration. "I can't see any reason why she wouldn't be happy, but is anyone ever really happy, John?"

He patted her arm and they moved along toward the chapel.

Eleanor and Jane watched their father and Aunt Alice disappear through the hedge. They had seen the look on her face as she turned to say, "Is anyone ever really happy?" and, without thought, Eleanor's hand moved to Jane's shoulder. They watched silently as their father, tall and spare, moved away from them. Like figures in a dream he and Alice passed through the white hydrangeas, leaving them behind. Pretty soon the campus people would begin to arrive. Upstairs Polly was helping Val dress and telling her that being married was wonderful. In the kitchen, Mrs. Ware, lifting her arm to mop her sweaty face on her sleeve, was filling nut dishes and cutting sandwiches into thin strips. Wilson stood in front of the mirror, running his hand over his face. He was nervous, and everything seemed to remind him of Sissy's wedding. Upstairs Grace had just stepped out of the tub and was scrubbing herself dry with a heavy turkish towel. She reached for her bottle of Yardley April Violet toilet water.

"We'd better get dressed," Eleanor said abruptly. "They'll be coming soon."

"You'll be next," said Jane.

"I'll probably never get married."

"Oh yes you will."

"I doubt it," said Eleanor, and she grabbed the handles of Jane's chair and pushed it up the ramp.

Wilson's wedding was remarkable for a number of reasons. For Eleanor it was the beginning. Beginning of what? one might ask, for at that time in her life everything was a beginning. Later she would know that it was remarkable for being the first time she met Charles.

She would always remember Charles sitting with Jane, both of them surveying the scene with serenity: the trellis, the vases of black-eyed Susans and goldenrod, lunch spread out on the kitchen table to be eaten anywhere one could find a spot to sit down, Polly rushing upstairs with lunch for the bride on a tray. Jane and Charles seemed to find all of this interesting, but remote, as they talked and laughed. Charles bent down and stroked Marmalade, who had chosen to wind herself around his ankles.

Eleanor knew at that moment if Charles had been the Hunchback of Notre Dame that she would love him anyway, for he made Jane happy. He was not an extraordinary man, or so it seemed then. Just a nice man, dark-haired and solemn, solid and tall, a pleasant-looking man. The sort of man who seemed to have been created to manage troubling things with goodwill and ease. A man who would know what to do in a crisis, and, curiously enough, one arose that no one seemed to be aware of except Eleanor.

She and Polly stood together, wearing identical bridesmaid dresses made from a McCall's pattern. Polly stared at the back of Val's head and seemed to be holding her breath, while Eleanor, nearly overwhelmed by emotion, glanced away through the greenery of the arch and into the dining room where, to her horror, she saw the cat stepping silently among the plates on the dining table and sniffing at the wedding cake.

Her heart seemed to beat faster until it nearly choked her. Marmalade prowled delicately and Eleanor glanced at Polly, willing her to notice and do something. But Polly wasn't looking. Charles was, though, and the minute Eleanor saw that she thought, He'll do something.

But Charles didn't do anything. From his expression one would have thought he found it natural for cats to inspect wedding cakes.

Glancing up, he noticed Eleanor and smiled and winked, and suddenly, for the first time in her life, she realized that perhaps life wasn't quite as deadly serious as she had always felt it was.

Val and Wilson left in a shower of confetti and Aunt Alice drove away shortly thereafter in order to get home before dark. Charles, who had driven up from Cambridge, left soon afterward, taking Polly to the station in Greenfield, where she was to board a sleeper for Chicago.

Before he left he thanked Grace and John for their hospitality and then he bent down and took Jane's hands in his and told her goodbye. When he came to Eleanor he gave her a hug and said, "I'll be back." And while that seemed like an ending to her, it wasn't. It was really just the beginning.

6

In September 1950, Eleanor was to move to Cambridge to teach French at the Chambers School, and one hot day in July she and Grace drove to Boston to look for an apartment. They went in and out of old houses with narrow hallways and steep, dark stairs until they found two rooms with a bath and kitchenette that seemed passable. It was hardly how Eleanor had imagined her first apartment, which was with bright chintz and sunny windows, but Grace said it was in an acceptable neighborhood and that a little scrubbing and paint would help. It wouldn't be available until November, and until then Eleanor could stay with Aunt Alice.

"It's time for Alice to do her part," said Grace, and when they found a telephone and Grace had outlined the problem, Alice said, "Of course, Eleanor must come. There's plenty of room. You must be sure to let me know when to expect her so that I can be at home."

It was much too easy, thought Grace, but as she put down the phone she thought, It's no more than she should do, considering everything. Even so, she hadn't expected it to be so easy.

On the day John drove Eleanor to Cambridge, the leaves had not yet begun to turn, but there was the quick pulse of an advancing season in the air as summer flashed its last brilliance over the distant hills. Soon there would be frost, foliage would flame briefly, and a new school year would begin. As they drove along narrow, tarred roads through Athol and Gardner, John thought of the time thirty years ago when he had taken the bus from Harrison to Boston. A lot of changes, he thought sadly, thinking of Elliot and Harold and Jane.

Eleanor was thinking about Jane, too. Jane seemed content at home, but what other choice did she have? No adventures for Jane, thought Eleanor, although moving in with Aunt Alice could hardly qualify as an adventure.

"Write when you can," said her father, "it helps."

The bushes had been pruned around the house in Cambridge, and the stucco renewed. A black iron fence now separated the house from the street where, even then, the sluggish flow of traffic was quickening.

Aunt Alice threw open the door. "I'm so glad you're here," she said, "I have to rush, but here you are. . . . Come in."

She led them upstairs and down the hall, past windows John had washed and over floors he had waxed in those long-ago student days.

"Here we are," she said, stepping into a room at the back and raising the shade. "It's small, but it's private."

It was small and dark, the walls papered, the woodwork stained. It was a narrow room but it had its own bath. Eleanor opened the window. Already she was composing her first letter to Jane. Not exactly an attic room, she thought, and said, "This will be fine, Aunt Alice."

"Good," said Alice, "now let me show you my room, then we'll go downstairs. I was wondering, Eleanor, if you'd mind bringing me my coffee in the morning? Mrs. Briggs gets here at nine, which is much too late for me. I can't function until I've had my coffee."

"I'd be glad to," said Eleanor.

"Oh dear," said Alice, glancing at her watch. "I'm afraid I can't offer you anything, but John, would you mind stepping into the library with me? Something's wrong with the damper in the fireplace. I thought if you would just look at it."

John went briskly toward the library, and Eleanor mentally added a paragraph to her letter. *Aunt Alice put Daddy to work on the spot and I'm going to be her breakfast maid. You would die laughing, Jane. She never changes.*

Every morning at eight Eleanor carried a tray with coffee and toast up the back stairs and down the hall to Aunt Alice's room. By then Alice had brushed her hair and arranged herself among a collection of pillows. Propped up in bed and wearing a satin bed jacket, she was the fading beauty of an aristocratic era. In another ten years she would say, as she was surely already thinking, "Bones, my dear, it's all in the bones," and she would stroke the pale skin that covered her well-bred bones and tell Eleanor what her plans were for the day. As she accepted her coffee she looked up and said dramatically, "I live for others, Eleanor."

And she really thinks she does, wrote Eleanor to Jane.

"Now, Eleanor," she said one morning when Eleanor had been there for a week, "I want to know all about you. You don't need to tell me about Chambers because Sissy went there and things are probably just the same. I want to know about *you*."

"You know all about me, Aunt Alice."

"I don't know about your friends, dear. Have you any friends in Cambridge? How will you amuse yourself on the weekends, dear?"

"I suppose I'll be going home, mostly."

"You mustn't do that," said Alice, "except, of course, occasionally and for Thanksgiving, but there is so much to see and do right here."

"I do have a friend," said Eleanor. "You may remember Charles Hammond from Wilson's wedding."

"What Hammond would that be?"

"He's from California. He and Wilson flew together in the war."

"I see," said Alice. Clearly there was no significant Hammond connection to be made and she said, "Tell me about him, dear."

"There's not much to tell. He's a banker and he's nice."

"I'm sure he is," Alice said, dismissing him and wondering if Sissy might know someone suitable for Eleanor. Of course, even though Charles had no background that she knew of . . . but there again, things were changing. Background wasn't as important, perhaps, as it had been before the war. Many of her friend's children were marrying quite ordinary people.

Nevertheless, Aunt Alice put her book aside and looked sternly at Eleanor as she said, "I want to meet your Charles. Bring him to tea one day soon."

"I'd love to," said Eleanor.

"That's good," said Alice, "we'll make it soon." Then she paused, her gaze fixed on something across the room, and after a minute she said, "You'll forget, or I will. Make it this Friday. Write it down in my book, Eleanor, and don't you forget it."

Promptly at four o'clock on Friday Charles appeared at the front door of the house on Fresh Pond Park and rang the bell. Ordinarily he and Eleanor met on Fridays at the Fine Arts, but she had hurried home today so that Aunt Alice could give a tea party without Mrs. Briggs's help. When Eleanor heard the bell she ran to the door, bobbed a curtsey, and said, "You must be Mister Hammond. Come this way please, sir."

As they went through the dark hall Charles reached out and pulled her into his arms and kissed her.

"Lud, mister," gasped Eleanor, "what will the mistress say?"

"She won't know," he said, trying again, but Eleanor laughed and put him off. "This is the library," she said. "It is a hallowed spot.

145

This is the room that was the scene of my father's announcement to Aunt Alice's husband that he intended to marry my mother and live on saltines and water for the rest of his life."

He reached for her hand and pulled her gently toward him. "This is our hallowed spot, too. If you give me sixty seconds more I'll be down on my knees begging you."

"For what?"

Her tone was flippant, but the expression in his eyes was not.

"For anything you care to give me," he said.

As he kissed her she heard the sound of Aunt Alice descending the stairs and she pulled away. "Here she comes," she whispered. "Now stop being silly and behave yourself."

"My dears," said Alice, "here you are." And, stretching out both hands, she said, "And you are Mr. Hammond. How lovely of you to come on this gray afternoon to brighten the day for a fussy old woman."

Alice called herself an old woman for the pleasure of hearing others deny it, and did so until she was over seventy, when people accepted the phrase at face value. Charles rose to the bait, saying, "Madam, any day would be gray compared to the glow of your beauty, and you cannot say that you are old. Your eyes are as bright and your skin as fair as that of a woman half your age."

He clicked his heels and bent over Alice's hand and kissed it while she blushed and all but stammered, "Now, don't tease me. You are surely quoting someone of distinction and I am too ignorant to recognize the source. Sit down and we'll start over again. Eleanor tells me you're a banker."

"I am not a banker as such," said Charles, reaching for his cigarettes and pausing to ask if she minded.

"By all means smoke. Everyone does. Tell me, just what do you do?"

"I am an officer in the trust department of the bank."

"My husband was a broker," she said, "I didn't actually know what he did. At the time of his death he had done quite well for a young man, but of course the crash did its damage all the same. But I am getting off the track. One's own money is quite different from the money of others. Managing that must be a heavy responsibility."

"It is, indeed, but people in trust departments are supposed to have ironed out all the problems ahead of time."

"I must ask your advice someday," she said. "Ah, here comes Eleanor."

Scanning the tray, Aunt Alice said, "I see

Mrs. Briggs has made us some scones. Of course whatever she makes of that nature she uses Bisquick so there's no need to go into raptures.

"Tell me about your family, Charles?" she continued as she poured out and sent it around. "If you are a Californian what brought you to Boston?"

"Law school," he replied. "I did my undergraduate work at UCLA. For law my father wouldn't be satisfied by anything less than Harvard."

At that moment the fire collapsed with a shower of sparks and Charles was on his feet instantly. "No need to call the footman, miss," he said to Eleanor, "it's all put to rights."

"You are something of a wag, Mr. Hammond," said Alice, "but I like you all the same. Tell me where you two would have been right now if I hadn't ordered you to come to tea."

"Together," said Charles. "I am threatening Eleanor to fall on my knees and beg for her company eternally."

"Do so," said Alice. "Do so at once."

But he didn't. A joke would be taken lightly, and Charles already knew there was nothing about Eleanor that he wanted to take lightly.

Sissy and the baby came by occasionally to see Alice. Matthew was now going on five and was too old and too big to be called the baby.

He was a robust, handsome little boy who clung to Sissy as though he were three. This didn't seem to bother her. She would pat him and cuddle him and say, "Now be good, darling, Mummy wants to talk."

Generally she didn't stay long, but one Saturday morning in October she settled down and said, "I'm glad Mother's gone. There's no use trying to talk when she's here. Tell me what you hear from Will."

Matthew, who was sitting on her lap, began to squirm and she cooed, "There, there, darling, get down and see what you can find to play with," and she put him down almost as though she were dislodging a pet of some sort in the hope it would find some way to amuse itself.

"I've been talking to Ned about Will and Ned says there might be a place for a CPA in the New York office when he finishes at Harvard. When will that be?"

"He finished almost two years ago."

"What!" cried Sissy. "I can't believe it. Where is he now?"

"In Ann Arbor."

"Michigan! Are they living in squalor?" she asked hopefully.

"I don't know," said Eleanor. "They don't complain."

"I expect they are," Sissy said, "but we can

149

fix that. He couldn't go wrong with Ned," she continued briskly and, digging into her purse, she took out a piece of paper. "It's sort of a scribble. It tells him where to write for an application. Of course he won't have to go through most of that interviewing stuff, but there has to be a file. Send it to him. Please, Eleanor."

"I'm not sure I ought to."

"Don't be silly," said Sissy. "I'm over all that, if that's what you're worried about, so you can forget it."

She scooped up Matthew from the floor, hugged him, rubbed noses with him as though she hadn't seen him for a long time. "Well," she said, "how do you like being here? Does Mother drive you wild?"

"I hardly see her."

Sissy sighed and took out her cigarettes. "Life is such a bore," she said.

Inasmuch as she and Ned had an apartment in New York, a house in Palm Beach, the Wellesley place, and, of course, Chatham, Eleanor thought this was a stupid remark.

"Who is this man you're dating?" Sissy asked. "Mother says he is quite charming."

"He's a friend of Wilson's. He's nice and I like him and, as far as I know, he's not rich."

"Rich isn't everything," Sissy said, standing

up and attaching Matthew to her hip again. "You will get in touch with Will, won't you?"

"I'll try," said Eleanor.

7

One morning in January 1951, if she had been there, Eleanor might have seen Matthew, in his snowsuit and boots, playing in the garden of the Barringers' home in Wellesley with Miss Purse. It was a bright day and in the garden, which was surrounded by a high brick wall, it was almost warm. Icicles, hanging from the roof of the sun porch, dripped into the snow. Matthew headed for the fish pool, where he had skated around on his bottom all winter, but today Purcie stopped him. The ice looked thin and wet, she thought. She took his hand and said, "Come and sit on the bench, Matthew, and I'll tell you a story."

She had been with the Barringers since Matthew was six weeks old. She liked children, but it would be easier, she thought, when she could read him something besides Peter Rabbit and Ping. Reading struck her as being the heart and soul of her position, for Miss Purse thought of herself as a governess. Sissy thought of her as Matthew's nurse. Ned thought of her as a servant. Matthew thought of her as his other mother, and the house-keeper, Mrs. Barnes, who had been a war bride and come to the United States from England in 1920, thought of her as Nanny Purse.

They made a pretty picture sitting on the granite bench in the brilliant blaze of sun on snow, but no one saw them except Adam Jones, who was potting things in the green-house. They wouldn't be out long, he thought. Nice as it seemed now, it was raw and chilly. They could have a lot of winter yet, said Adam to himself.

As she pointed out the various things of interest in the garden, a cardinal in the bushes, two squirrels chasing each other along the top of the wall, Purcie thought of other things.

Mrs. Barringer and her mother were in the sun-room, drinking coffee and talking. As Purcie and Matthew, now shivering, came into the back entry, Purcie could hear every word they were saying because Mrs. Dwire was hard of hearing and Sissy spoke to her in exaggerated tones, as though she were a child.

"I would say Eleanor is smitten," said Sissy. "Some people do marry for love, Mother."

"I should hope so," replied Alice.

Miss Purse would have liked to hear more. There was a sharpness in the exchange, short as it was, that piqued her interest. Miss Purse had lived long enough to think she knew when people were in love and when they weren't, and even though her own small experience in that area had not worked out happily, she clung to the romantic notion that marriage without love among the rich could have other satisfactions. Therefore, it surprised her somewhat to note the bitter tone in Mrs. Barringer's voice as she spoke. I wouldn't be surprised, thought Nanny Purse, to find out she had a boyfriend somewhere. All those trips to New York and Philadelphia to see one friend or another. She could be wrong, but she doubted it.

"By the way," said Alice, "What is this about Will? I've just had a letter from Grace and apparently Will and his wife are moving to New York. Did you know that?"

"Really?" asked Sissy in surprise. "Ned did say something about it. There seems to be an opening for a CPA in one of Ned's companies, but I didn't know about Will. Ah, me," she said, "whoever would have thought it?"

Alice knew better than to believe Sissy was as ignorant of the move as she said she was. But what can I do? thought Alice. Trying to control Sissy was something she had given up years ago. She wished Sissy were more like

Eleanor, who came and went with hardly a sound. She dreaded the time, which would surely come soon, when the apartment would be ready and Eleanor would leave to live on her own.

Eleanor was dreading it, too. The house on Fresh Pond Park was not only near Chambers, it was also more convenient for Charles, and one morning when she took Aunt Alice her coffee Eleanor asked if she could stay on.

Alice was reading the paper and muttering to herself that papers ought to be smaller. She welcomed the interruption and said, "Leaving? You mustn't leave. Who will bring me my coffee? I would miss you greatly."

"I don't pay any rent and I don't pay for the food I eat. It really isn't right."

"Nonsense," said Alice. "I don't want you to leave and you don't eat a thing. I want you to stay. Mrs. Briggs is always late with my coffee. She will be glad to have you stay and so will I."

"Are you sure?" asked Eleanor.

"Of course I'm sure," said Alice in her that's-settled tone of voice. And then she poured her coffee. It was just the way she liked it, boiling hot. She would hate to lose Eleanor, she thought, and called out one last time, "Have a happy day, dear," and then she picked up the phone and called Sissy.

★ ★ ★

"What's wrong?" asked Sissy. "It's early, Mother. Why are you calling so early?"

"I just thought you'd like to know that Eleanor will be staying on. It will be so nice for me."

"I'm sure it will," said Sissy, "and for Eleanor, too."

Sissy found early morning calls irritating, but, once bothered, she tried to make the best of it. Personally, if she had lived with her mother she couldn't have escaped fast enough, but Eleanor was different. She always had been. "How is Eleanor?" she inquired, trying, despite the hour, to be civil.

"She seems to be fine," said Alice. "She is seeing a great deal of Charles."

"Who is Charles?" Sissy yawned, stalling for time and trying to wake up. "Have you met him?"

"Of course I've met him. They see a great deal of each other. He had something to do with Wilson in the war."

"Oh, yes," said Sissy, "Will has mentioned him."

Alice opened her mouth to say something and then paused. "When have you seen Will?" she asked.

"I can't remember," said Sissy, who had been with Will a short week ago. "Sometime.

I shall try to make a note of it the next time I happen to see him."

A feeling of frustration and fury fluttered within and Alice said, "I suppose now that they are living in New York you see Will and his wife fairly often."

"Not really," said Sissy.

But Alice knew better. There had been a change in Sissy lately. She had seemed happier than she had seemed at any other time since her marriage. She seemed sometimes almost to dance when she was actually walking. She hummed little snatches of songs that had been popular years ago. She talked about divorce in a careless way, as though nothing mattered except her own happiness. It made Alice shudder just to imagine what might happen if Sissy did anything foolish and Ned found out about it.

"Is that all, Mother?" asked Sissy. "Do you like this Charles?"

"I had hoped for something better for Eleanor, but he seems nice enough. He is an attorney as well as a banker," Alice said, as though this explained everything and made the unthinkable acceptable.

"Well," said Sissy, "I'm running late. Give Eleanor my love and tell her Merry Christmas for me."

"Merry Christmas! Good heavens," said

Alice, "it will soon be upon us."

Charles and Eleanor drove to Harrison two days before Christmas. It was a cold, clear day. Snow sparkled on the fields and great drifts of it were piled high on either side of the road. In the larger towns Christmas decorations adorned the lampposts, and ropes of evergreen were stretched across the streets of many villages they went through. Saturday afternoon traffic choked the main streets and traffic moved so slowly one could almost hear the ringing of the Salvation Army bells as red-faced bell ringers, wearing caps and mittens, stood at their posts, jingling and stamping their feet and calling out, "Merry Christmas!"

"Why so quiet?" asked Charles, reaching over to pat Eleanor's knee.

"I was just wondering what you would think of our Christmas."

"And what is so unique about your Christmas?"

"Well, for one thing, we're all grown up, but we still hang up our stockings."

"What else?" he asked.

"We always have the same things for breakfast and dinner. Breakfast is grapefruit with confectioners' sugar and topped with a cherry, then sausage and toast and mince pie."

"Is that all?"

She laughed and said, "We dress before breakfast and after that comes presents, which takes forever because it's just one gift at a time and we all watch and say, 'ooo, and ahhhh.' It takes forever."

"Gifts," he said, looking shocked. "I forgot about gifts."

But of course he had not forgotten. He already had her present. It was in his pocket, and that evening when the others had gone to bed and they had lingered by the fire, he reached into his jacket pocket and took out the small box that held the symbol of all they hoped for.

"It's for you," he said, holding it out to her. "You can't turn it down. It's nonnegotiable."

"Oh," she breathed when she saw it. "Oh, Charles, it's beautiful," and she handed it back to him and said, "You put it on," and her hand trembled as he took it in his.

"With this ring," and he slipped it on her fourth finger left hand, "I will thee wed."

"It fits," she murmured. "See, it fits perfectly."

"And when will we be married?"

"In June?"

"Sooner," he replied.

"In June," said Eleanor.

Two months later Charles was called back by the air force. His orders were specific: he was to report to March Field in California for six weeks of refresher courses before his embarkation to Korea. His orders hit without warning, although flying personnel had high priority and he knew it.

Eleanor was totally unprepared. The war was over. Of course she knew what was happening over there, but it was a different war and men who had been discharged didn't have to go.

"But you've been discharged," she said desperately. "They can't take you."

"Darling, they can," he said. "Commissioned officers were commissioned for the duration plus six months. I was separated from the service, not discharged."

"It's the same thing," she said. "Furthermore," she said, "that war is over. The duration, or whatever you said, is over and done with."

He took her hands in his and said quietly, "It will be over when Congress declares it is over and God only knows when that will be."

"It isn't fair," she said. "You had your war. What about Will? It's not fair."

"The army is never fair," he said. "Fair is nothing but a weather word in the army.

Will won't be called because of his leg. He broke it that first year back at Dartmouth."

"Somebody can go in your place. Someone who hasn't been to war yet."

"There aren't enough trained men."

"Then break something," she said.

They had been on their way to the Union Oyster House for lunch. It was something they frequently did and Charles, with his orders burning in his pocket, saw no reason not to. I wish I had not had to tell her, he thought, as they raced arm in arm, through rain turning to sleet and rising wind. But he hadn't been able to keep it to himself, and suddenly the rain and the wind were nothing as the bad news began to register.

She stopped abruptly and turned to face him. "It's not fair," she said. "There must be something we can do. You can't go. We're going to be married in June."

"We're going to be married *now*," he said. "We're going to call your parents and tell them we want to be married tomorrow."

"The next day," said Eleanor.

"The next day," he repeated, and he grabbed her hand and they began to run, squelching through puddles, laughing and panting as they burst into the warmth of the Oyster House. There they sat facing each other, hands locked, staring at each other through a haze of steam that drifted from bins of clams buried in seaweed like the harbor mist that had swirled around star-crossed lovers of all times, as they prepared to part.

Before Eleanor left Cambridge the next day, Aunt Alice called her into her room to offer some words of wisdom, of which she had a vast supply. "Are you really sure that you want to rush into things, Eleanor? Are you sure your parents won't object? There's still time to think about —"

"I am positive," said Eleanor. "The only thing that matters is what we want to do and when we get home this afternoon if they try to stop us we'll leave for California and get married on the way. In Reno."

"Oh, dear," said Alice, who considered Reno tawdry beyond expression. She scrabbled about among her letters and reading matter and, finally finding what she wanted, she handed Eleanor a check.

"This is for you, dear," she said. "I thought it might be more useful than a gift."

She had written it for one hundred dollars, which seemed like a great deal of money to Eleanor, and she said, as though she had suddenly become the recipient of a lifetime endowment, "Thank you, Aunt Alice," and then, as an afterthought, "I am sorry about your coffee."

"Oh, my dear. Don't be foolish," and then she continued, "I wish I could come for the wedding. If only I had known," she said, inferring that someone, the army in this case, had been at fault not to warn her in advance. "I was there for Wilson; I should be there for you."

"It's all right," said Eleanor, "no one's coming."

"But you must have a real wedding!" cried Aunt Alice, looking genuinely stricken. "If I had known . . . I could have ordered a cake, or flowers, and what will you wear? Isn't there something of Sissy's you'd like?"

"I have a new dress."

"Oh," she said, "a dress . . ." And then she murmured, "You children have all married so fast. I'm sure Charles is a fine man, but I wish you were having a real wedding."

When Eleanor and Charles walked into Drury House that raw and forbidding day, there was a fire burning and Grace and John and Jane were sitting around it drinking tea. There were two empty cups on the tray, and Grace looked up with a smile and said, "You're just in time for tea. We hoped you would be," and she began to pour out as

163

though it was an ordinary day and that now that they had arrived things were all right again.

Will and Val were expected by suppertime. It could have been an ordinary weekend. Her father asked logical questions about the war. Her mother said she was glad Charles's family lived relatively close to March Field. She would be glad, she said, to think of Eleanor as being close to family instead of being in base housing, which might not be available. Jane and Charles started a game of chess, which was finished eventually by Jane and her father. None of them commented on the real war. No one said it wasn't fair. No one prayed audibly or cried openly. Community joy and sorrow, anxiety and faith, hope and fear flowed with equal force through them all.

Before Eleanor and Charles walked over to the chapel to be married by the chaplain, Val came into Eleanor's room to see if there was something she could do to help. She sat down on the edge of the bed, clasping and unclasping her hands nervously as she said, "I want you to be happy, Eleanor. Isn't there anything I can do to help?"

"Zip me up," said Eleanor.

Val hadn't meant that sort of help, but she pulled up the zipper of Eleanor's dress and fastened the hook. Eleanor reminded Val of her sister, Polly, and she said, "You are just like Polly. She never gets ruffled."

I wish I were, thought Eleanor, but she didn't say so. She said, "How do you and Will like New York?"

"All right," said Val. "I don't know. It's so big. I wonder if I'll ever know anyone. Will's gone so much. When we lived in Ann Arbor they sent him to Philadelphia, and now that we're in New York they send him to Chicago. I didn't know he'd be gone so much."

"It won't be that way forever," said Eleanor.

Val gave a little shrug, dismissing the subject, which obviously bothered her, and saying, "Well anyway, you look lovely and I came to give you a present, not to talk your ears off."

She pulled a little box out of her pocket and handed it over, watching with shining eyes while Eleanor untied the ribbon and opened it.

"It's a cross," said Val unnecessarily. Anyone could see that it was a gold cross on a gold chain. "It's for something new," Val said. "From me to you because you'll be traveling and because of Charles and the war. I just thought it might help. Here, let me fasten it for you."

"Thank you, Val," said Eleanor, "it's lovely. I'll wear it all the time."

"Why do you wear that thing?" asked Charles later.

"I made a vow."

"What sort of vow?"

"I vowed not to take it off until you come home."

He laughed. "What happens if you break it — the chain, I mean, not the vow."

"Nothing," said Eleanor. "I get time off until it's fixed."

"You're sweet," he said and, making a point of being careful when he touched her, he kissed Eleanor's neck tenderly and wished things were as simple as hanging a cross around your neck and coming home free.

Charles's parents lived in a white brick house on a quiet street in Beverly Hills. The property was surrounded by a wrought-iron fence with a double gate that was always left open — for convenience' sake, said Charles. As the cab turned in at the drive, Eleanor had a glimpse of a flower garden at one end of the house and a cluster of cedars at the other. Out of sight, but beyond the cedars, was a swimming pool and beyond that a tennis court.

"You see," said Charles. "Very simple.

Nothing to be scared of."

On the train coming out she had talked endlessly about his parents and their home in Los Angeles. "Who will be there?" she'd wanted to know. "Suppose they don't like me. I haven't the right sort of clothes."

At all of this Charles shrugged. What did it matter? "I love you," he had said. Or he'd teased, "It's just a white house with some trees and a nice lawn. It isn't a palace. My parents will be there because they know we're coming. My sister lives in Boise, Idaho, and is having a baby next month. They won't be there."

At this time next year would she be having a baby? Eleanor wondered, but she tried not to think about next year. Day by day was enough. What she held in the palm of her hand right now was what counted.

She was tired and dirty. If she was dirty despite the shallow stainless-steel washbasin in their compartment, how would she feel if they had come coach? "A bath, a bath," she said, "my kingdom for a bath."

"Bear up for five more minutes and the tub is all yours."

He pushed the doorbell again and they heard it echo, faint and far away, somewhere in the nether regions of a house that suddenly seemed enormous to Eleanor.

And then the door swung open and there

was Mrs. Shimuboku in her black uniform, bowing and smiling, and down the spiral staircase raced his mother, her head wrapped in an apricot satin turban that matched the lounging pajamas, sleek and wide legged, that rippled as she ran down the steps with her arms outstretched as she called out in little squeals of excitement, "Dahlings, dahlings, you're here, you're here." And she threw her arms around Charles and said, "You old sweet thing, you, and this is Eleanor, aren't you a pretty thing," and she hugged Eleanor too and, turning to Mrs. Shimuboku said, "Quick, quick, remember what I told you? The champagne on the tray. Take it to the library."

Turning back to them, she said, "It's been on ice all day. We are just so thrilled you're here and married, too. It calls for a toast. Now! Right now."

"I'm so grubby," said Eleanor. "May I just go up and take a quick bath?"

"Of course you can. In a minute, honey. This won't take two seconds. I've been counting on this for months. Terrible that it takes a war to get you home, dahling."

When she saw the bottle she said, "Mrs. S doesn't like to open champagne. She says the pop upsets her, poor dahling. You do it, Charles. There, you see, perfect," and she lifted her glass and said, "Here's to the most beautiful couple ever. Happy days, happy years!"

As they sat and sipped, Mrs. Hammond continued to babble. There was something familiar about Charles's mother, thought Eleanor, but, of course, in any group of women there was usually one like her. And then, curiously, Eleanor thought suddenly of Aunt Alice. It was as if Charles's mother were an imitation Aunt Alice. Like but unalike, a dreadful, playacting Aunt Alice, unique and foreign.

When it was decently possible, Eleanor asked to be excused and, as she reached the stairs, she heard Mrs. Hammond say, "I've asked Babs, Charles. She is so excited. She says she hasn't seen you in years and she's dying to meet your sweet little wife."

Charles glanced up and saw that Eleanor had now disappeared and was out of earshot. He took a deep breath. "I wish you hadn't done that, Mother. There's nobody left here that I want to see, except you and Dad. Call her up and cancel. You can have her after we've gone."

"That's one of the things I'm thinking about, Charles. I want Eleanor to have some friends to fall back on. Don't you want her to stay with us? I thought you would, and most of the crowd are married or gone. I thought of Babs because . . . well, you know. There was a time when we thought you and Babs —"

"You thought wrong," Charles retorted, "and I doubt Eleanor will want to stay. She has a job to go back to and a family. I'd really rather you'd call up and put Babs off."

"I can't do that, dahling. What would she think? But I won't ask her again. I just thought it would be nice for Eleanor to get to know at least one of your old pals."

Eleanor lay back in the tub under a blanket of bubbles. There was a painting on the bathroom ceiling that seemed to be a harem scene showing half-naked girls bathing. She raised her foot and patted the gold swan's-head faucet with her big toe. Nearby was a footbath large enough for a child to play in. What luxury, she thought. What splendor.

When she had drawn the bedroom shades before she undressed, she had seen the pool and tennis court and a little house between them that must have been a cabana or a guesthouse. Looking farther, she had seen a man, wearing a straw hat like a lampshade, among the roses. That must have been Mr. Shimuboku and she wondered if he and his wife had been interned during the war or if people like the Hammonds were allowed to intern their own servants behind the gate and the fence, where the servants had spent the war years cultivating the roses, cleaning the swimming pool, and maintaining the comfort of their masters inside the big house.

When she heard Charles in the bedroom, she stepped out of the tub and, wrapping herself like a warrior chief in a towel that was as big as an Indian blanket, she opened the door and said, "Tub or shower or both, not to mention the footbath."

"I could do with a couple of those," he said.

"Your mother is very nice," said Eleanor. "However, she makes me feel somewhat dowdy. As dowdy as a New England missionary put down in Hawaii before the first tourists arrived."

He crossed the room and grabbed her, and, giving her a little shake, he said, "You are not dowdy. You are beautiful. You are dear to my heart. You are what I want. Always. My mother is rather a silly person, but she tries in her own way."

"I was only teasing," said Eleanor. "She's different, but nice."

"She's done something stupid, darling," said Charles. "She's asked an old friend of mine to dinner. She's a nice enough girl, I suppose, but I haven't seen her in years. I can't imagine what we'll have to talk about

171

and it will be dull for you."

"What's her name?"

"Babs."

"Ah-ha," said Eleanor, "and what sort of friends were you?"

"She was my girl in high school."

"I'll be obliged to hate her then," said Eleanor. "Do you mind?"

"Hate away," he said. "I expect you'll be too bored to bother."

When Charles had shaved, showered, and dressed he said, "I think I feel too rotten to go down for dinner. Ring up and ask Mrs. Shim to bring us a couple of trays."

"We can't do that," said Eleanor.

"I don't see why not," he said, "and besides, you look a bit peaked. I'm afraid you're not up to it. I think I should get you to bed right now."

"Patience," she said, although she would have greatly preferred it.

Babs, who had arrived on time, was talking earnestly to Mr. Hammond, and when she saw Charles she rushed across the room with her arms out. "Give me a hug, you wonderful man. Where have you been and where is your little wife?"

She knew perfectly well where Eleanor was. "There you are," said Babs. "Everybody's been dying to meet you."

Mrs. Hammond began to flutter around them. "Booze or bubbly?" she inquired. "It's all right here. For heaven's sake, Walter, make us something to drink. We can't be helpless with guests here and Mr. Shimuboku is busy in the kitchen with Mrs. S. I want a martini. With an onion. Just some ice and gin and a drop of vermouth. Babs, dahling, I can't remember what you drink?"

"Probably Coca-Cola the last time you saw me," said Babs. "I'll take a Manhattan, Mr. Hammond, if you have the makings."

"Will do. And Eleanor . . ."

"I'll take care of hers and mine," said Charles.

For a while they talked about the old days. Both Babs and Mrs. Hammond (who kept insisting that all of them, even Charles, must call her Aileen) kept interrupting each other to add some detail that seemed remarkably insignificant to Eleanor. Once it was settled as to where the event in question had taken place (before or after the war), and who was involved, Babs would say, "Oh, but this isn't fair. Eleanor doesn't know any of these people. We had better stick to things that are happening now, or try to fill her in. Which would you prefer, honey?"

During the first drink, Eleanor replied, "I

love listening. I've wanted to know more about Charles. Don't let me slow you down."

"You're a sweetie," said Babs. "If I were you I'd hate it." Then she turned and said, "Who knows whatever happened to Elsie Jackson?"

"I don't remember an Elsie Jackson," said Charles.

"Yes, you do," said Babs. "We used to double-date with Elsie and Paul somebody. What was his name? He had a car before any of the rest of us did. Surely you remember."

Charles said he didn't remember and that he had more important things to think about.

During the second drink Babs forgot about turning to Eleanor and saying nice things to her, and after the third drink they were all talking and nobody was listening.

Walter (Charles's father) was trying to explain to his wife why it was necessary for him to tee off at exactly nine A.M. the next day. Aileen (Charles's mother) was saying he was married to his golf buddies, not to her, and one of these days he would be sorry. Babs was trying to convince Charles that they had met at Teenie Peacock's Christmas party and that he had said to her, "I don't suppose you'd want to go to the show with me on Friday."

Charles said he wouldn't have handled it that way and, turning to Eleanor, he said,

174

"What do you think, honey?"

"I think," said Eleanor, "that I do not like to be called honey, and, furthermore, I'm hungry."

Charles stood up immediately. "We are hungry, Mother," he said.

Midway through the meal when Mr. Shimuboku served the salad, Aileen hastened to say that salad after the main course was the French way. Not served on the side and not served after the appetizer because the French believed . . .

Mr. Hammond didn't care when the salad appeared. He was trying to talk seriously with his son about Korea and when they might hope it would be over.

"I don't speculate," Charles said. "It's pointless." Five minutes after going into combat good men died. Five days after a cease-fire was announced, men died of wounds. "I don't think about it," he said to his father.

Babs, who was busily trying to trip up Eleanor in the hope of getting her to say or do something foolish, gave up and said loudly to all of them, "Things will never be the same. It was a terrible thing. There isn't a single person who hasn't been hurt in some way or another. Or won't be this time. Don't you agree, Eleanor?"

"No," said Eleanor.

"Why don't you shut up, Babs," said Charles.

"I'm sorry, honey, I didn't mean to say that. Of course lots of people get through any crisis unscathed. I was trying to be helpful," Babs said.

Charles reached for Eleanor's hand and held it tightly. Mr. Shimuboku began to clear the plates, and Charles said pleasantly, "No need to worry about me. I am indestructible."

"Isn't he wonderful?" said Babs. "If you were a racehorse, I'd put all I had on you."

Charles's mother said, "How can you two joke about it? I can't even bear to think about it. What can the government be thinking of? Wasn't one war enough?"

"The thing is, Mother," said Charles, "the government doesn't think about anything. Things are so much simpler that way."

Mr. Shimuboku was now presenting the finger bowls, and everyone stopped talking until he retired. Then Babs said in an undertone, "None of us feel the way we used to about the Japanese, but there it is. Life goes on. Do you remember Dicky Pearce, Charles? He came home from Malaysia where he had been interned for three years and the first thing he discovered when he walked into his house was his old friend Howard Roberts in bed with Susan."

"Tut, tut," said Charles, "and what did he do about that?"

"He went down to his study and got a gun and blew the top of his head off."

This was too much for Mrs. Hammond, who glared at Babs and said, "Dick Pearce was a fine fellow. He deserved better than that."

"Of course he did," said Babs. "I'm sorry. I shouldn't have mentioned that. Eleanor doesn't know who any of these people are. I must be boring you to death," she said to Eleanor.

Eleanor didn't bother to answer, but Charles stood up and said to his mother, "You must excuse us, Mother. We had a tiring trip and need to turn in. It was nice to see you, Babs. Good evening, Father."

They went hand in hand up the curving staircase, leaving behind them the idle chatter, the loud voices, and when the lights were out and they were lying together and alone, she said, "It won't be easy, will it?"

"No," said Charles.

"But they are nice," said Eleanor. "Your mother had champagne and she probably thought you'd like to see one of your old friends."

Charles didn't answer. He kissed her tenderly. He put his face against hers and held her tightly and said gently, "No, darling. She wasn't trying to help. She wasn't thinking at all. She was doing what she's been trained to do. She and my father are alike. They use people. They collect interesting people and make 'contacts,' not friends."

"How sad," said Eleanor.

The next day they moved into the guesthouse and for the six weeks thereafter they had an unforgettably good time.

8

When Charles shipped out Eleanor went home to Jane and her parents, to her own room, her bookcase where Nancy Drew and Madame Bovary kept company, to tea at four and supper at six, to chapel and vespers on Sunday. Sitting in the gallery, where she could see the backs of five hundred heads, ranked from Adams to Zyvanah, she tried to persuade herself that basics didn't change. Miserable as she was, she thought bitter thoughts as she sensed the anticipation of life pulsing below her. What do they know? she thought. They're only boys.

At home her mother took a ham out of the oven and asked cheerfully, "How was chapel?" and her father, pushing Jane's wheelchair up the ramp and into the house, answered, "A good sermon, Mother."

When she left Chambers to be married Eleanor had resigned her position. Now she had no enthusiasm for trying to take it up again.

"Well," said Grace, "if you don't want to go back to Chambers, why don't you apply for something here, Eleanor? They always need help in the library and the alumni office. Or, if you don't feel like doing that you could go to New York to see Wilson and Val. I'm sure they'd love to have a visit."

Grace sounded positive enough, but she wasn't at all sure Will and Val would want a visit from anyone. She couldn't base these feelings on anything except intuition. They came home occasionally, but stayed only one night and had very little to say. Grace tried to talk about it to John, who answered in platitudes, and she would welcome a firsthand report from Eleanor.

"Yes," echoed Jane, "go for a visit. They would probably be delighted."

"What's all this?" asked her father. "Somebody going somewhere?"

It seemed to Eleanor as they regarded her, forcing her attention to the various expressions of concern on their kindly faces, that they had become strangers. For the first time she noticed that her father was losing his hair and that somewhere along the way her mother had begun to stoop. Jane's smile rendered her face a luminous oval above the pitiful contortion of her body, and her words "they would probably be delighted" seemed to have been uttered by someone Eleanor didn't know, someone whose definition of suffering extended to realms Eleanor could only guess at. Only her mother, nodding approval and speaking casually about Will and Val and their apartment, appeared familiar, but then, of course, Eleanor reminded herself, she could remember when her mother had been different and able to say what she really thought. Back before polio and all that came with it. The naturalness (unwavering good-naturedness) that she had acquired to accommodate her problems cost more than anyone knew.

And so one cold drizzly day late in March, Eleanor packed her bag and bought a round-trip ticket to New York. The train steamed and rattled, whistling its way through cross-roads, streaking down the valley, where the sodden fields were patched with dirty snow. She had brought a book but didn't read.

Val met her in Grand Central, pushing through the crowds and grabbing her arm. "Come on," she said. "If we hurry we can meet Will for lunch," and, taking Eleanor's bag, she scurried along toward the street.

"There's always a cab," Val panted, "just watch me," and she stepped fearlessly into traffic, waving her gloved hand and shouting, "Taxi!"

"There," she gasped when they were settled. "All you have to do is assert yourself, Eleanor. Remember that," and her eyes darted around as though she assumed the driver would miss their restaurant and that things would go wrong unless she, personally, remained alert. She barely turned her head to answer when Eleanor asked about Wilson.

"He's fine, I suppose," Val said, stiffening suddenly and leaning forward to call out, "It's on the right. Up there." And she began a frantic rummaging in her purse.

Inside the restaurant it was crowded and noisy, but Val marched through the main room, peering here and there as though she were looking for a child playing hide-and-seek. "He's not here," she said angrily. "I told him we might be late and we're not that late."

"He might have misunderstood."

"He doesn't listen," said Val. "He never hears anything I say," and she drew herself up indignantly. "We'd better go home and get settled. We're going out tonight."

"Oh, please," said Eleanor. "I don't want to be entertained."

"It's only the Barringers. There's always a party at the Barringers'. Will goes alone mostly, but *she's* supposed to be down this weekend and found out some way that you were coming."

Then she turned abruptly, as though it had

suddenly occurred to her that even without Will they might eat here. "Do you want to have lunch here," she asked, "or shall we go home and open a can of soup?"

"Go home," said Eleanor.

Val opened a can of tomato soup and a box of crackers, and when they had eaten she looked around helplessly as if the crumbs on the table and the saucepan on the stove were too much. "I hate to desert you," she said, "but I simply have to lie down. Why don't you go out and shop or something?"

Eleanor picked up the dishes and Val said testily, "Oh, don't do that. Dishes wait. Go on and do something you'd like to do. It must be deadly living at home and waiting for letters. I know all about it. Go to a movie or something. Have a good time. I'm not much fun these days. I don't like the city. Come to think of it, I might like being holed up in a place like Harrison, but what would happen to Will," she said vaguely.

Eleanor took a bus up Madison, getting off at Forty-sixth and walking over to Fifth Avenue. The wind was high, whipping dust and grit along the street, and she pulled her scarf over her head and tied it under her chin. Here and there she saw men in uniform — not many, though, not the way it had been in 1945, only token soldiers now to remind people there was a war somewhere. She wondered if there might be a letter from Charles waiting for her at home. She would write him a letter when she got back to the apartment, and bring him up to date.

Dear Charles, she would write, *I am visiting Val and Wilson. It's cold, but I actually saw some crocuses beside the steps of a church that is now a city mission. I've seen so many desperate-looking people on the street. . . .*

Glancing up, she saw that she was at Forty-ninth Street, and she paused.

I decided to go into Saks, not my usual objective, but there's going to be a party at the Barringers' tonight. Sissy's here. . . .

It was warm inside the store. Heat rushed forward to greet her, drawing her along past counters of gloves and perfume to the elevators and up to the third floor and into a forest of dresses. It occurred to her that she had never had a dress from a store like Saks and that it would be something different to write to Charles. She could imagine him sitting on his bunk reading her letter about a dress from Saks. How incongruous and obscene it would be, and yet it might give him a moment's escape and pleasure.

She drifted along past the racks, letting her

hand trail from one garment to another, rejecting them all until she came to one that appealed to her. Turning the tag, she saw that it was marked $200. It was more than half the allotment she got from the government each month as compensation for Charles's labors. It would be absurd even to consider such a dress — what sort of person would? — and as she turned away she caught a glimpse of herself in a mirror and wondered, Is that really me, that woman with the shocked eyes and limp brown hair and a plaid scarf hanging around her neck?

Look at you, she said sternly to herself, you are drab and you are dowdy. Perhaps Charles would like to be married to somebody who wore dresses from Saks, but then it occurred to her that if he had wanted such a wife he could have married Babs, or someone like her. She smiled at herself in the mirror and straightened her shoulders. Maybe, she thought, my poor old polo coat will be good enough for another winter after all.

The wind snatched at her coat and tore at her hair as she raced up the steps of St. Patrick's and into the warm vestibule. People passed purposefully around her, their heels making hard clicking sounds on the stone floor as they moved rapidly into the body of the cathedral.

Candles flamed and sputtered in shining banks before which people knelt, praying with hands gripped together and eyes glistening. Oh, she thought desperately, if I could I would light a hundred candles, a thousand, and fall down on my knees and beg God to send Charles home. But kneeling didn't come naturally to Eleanor, and the shining eyes and working mouths and clasped hands were evidence of a faith she didn't feel, so she turned rapidly and started home.

"Ned gives nice parties," said Wilson. "I know you aren't much for parties these days, but maybe it won't be so bad."

"Yes, have a good time," said Val, pulling on her gloves and slipping into a black coat. "This is my new coat," she said, "Will says I have to try to look smart."

"I said you needed a new coat," he replied. "You always look beautiful, Val."

"Oh, I know," she said, "but beautiful isn't smart, is it, Eleanor?"

"Come on, Val," he said, "try to have a good time for once. Sissy said particularly that she was looking forward to seeing you again."

"Really," said Val, "and when were you talking with Sissy?"

"She called this afternoon. She wanted to be sure you'd come, Eleanor."

At this Eleanor began to regret passing up the dress in Saks. It was, after all, smart looking, she thought as Val took her arm.

"Just don't drink too much," Val said. "Watch out for the punchy things. You know, with slices of orange and cherries. Sissy likes to get people drunk but then, of course," she said, "people who drink too much do."

"Come off it, Val," said Wilson.

"Well, she does. She doesn't get disgusting or anything," added Val, squeezing Eleanor's arm. "I'm sorry, Eleanor. I know she's your friend, but she does drink too much. You can deny it all you want to, Will, but she does."

"I deny it."

"Will is so gallant," said Val. "He's going to be a great success in New York. I can tell it already. Besides, Sissy told me so. She came up to me, I forget when it was, I've only seen her a few times, but she came up to me and said that she hoped I appreciated my wonderful husband because she had known him for years and always knew he was going to be a success."

"I wouldn't pay any attention to Sissy," said Eleanor. "She exaggerates."

"Oh, I don't pay any attention to her," said Val. "That's Wilson's job. He pays attention to her."

★ ★ ★

It seemed to Eleanor that through the long evening Sissy drifted from group to group, as though she were looking for a place to put herself, or wondering perhaps if she was at the right party, until it began to seem that she was not a person at all, but just one of the lovely things in the apartment. It was a spacious and elegant place, filled with beautiful things, a sort of wonderland of luxury suspended over the dark, squalid streets below where, surrounded by soft lights and music and the pleasant murmur of voices, all of them were separated from the painful urgencies of the world.

If Sissy drank too much it wasn't evident to Eleanor, and she found herself pleasantly distracted, almost as though this was reality and the war and all the lesser sorrows that touched her life were remote and unreal.

Later, in the bedroom, she found Will and Sissy together. Sissy was rummaging through the wraps on the bed, saying distractedly, "I know it's here, Will, I saw where she put it," and he was leaning over her saying harshly, "For God's sake, Sissy, stop digging around. It's right there."

She looked up, pain flashed from her eyes, and she said, "When are you going to call me? I can't bear it, Will. Please, please call me."

"I can't," he said. His face was white and he looked at her as though he were dying.

"Well," said Eleanor, "private party?"

Sissy whipped around. "Hunting for coats," she said. "Wilson bought his wife a spiffy new coat that looks like everybody else's spiffy new coat."

"No problem with mine," said Eleanor. "It's that old polo over there."

"Good grief," said Sissy. "I think we ought to buy you a new coat, Eleanor. I think you and I ought to have lunch tomorrow and go down to Saks and buy you a decent coat. You don't want Charles to be ashamed of you, do you?"

"Fine," said Eleanor, "but not Saks. I don't shop there, not even for Charles."

During lunch they talked about Matthew. At least Sissy did, and Eleanor listened.

"I thought it was silly, having a nurse," she said. "If there's anything I love it's taking care of Matthew, you know that, Eleanor, but we're always going somewhere."

"That's what you get for being rich."

"I suppose so," she said. "It's made a new woman out of mother."

She paused and looked around, and almost instantly there was a waiter at the table. One would have thought he had been assigned a spot in the palms just to watch her. How had he known she wasn't simply looking aimlessly around the way people do? But she wanted another drink.

"Aren't you ready?" she asked. "What are you doing, diddling along that way?"

"I'm fine. I don't drink much. You know how it is."

"Oh, dear," Sissy said, shrugging, "campus life and all that. What are all these letters Mother keeps getting about giving money?"

"Would it be the Dwire scholarship fund?"

"I don't mean that. We contribute to that, of course, but this is something called development. They have all those beautiful buildings. What do they need to develop? Ask your father, Eleanor. Not that it matters," she said. "I leave all that to Ned, and Mother's awfully cagey with her money."

Sissy picked up her drink and her eyes brightened. "Oh Eleanor, don't you wish we could go back? Wouldn't it be wonderful to have it summer again, before Jane was sick or Harold was killed? I think of those visits and I wonder how your poor mother stood it. I can remember when I wouldn't eat anything but peanut-butter-and-banana sandwiches."

She sighed happily. "Do you remember when Harold wanted to help Jane walk again?

I think he really thought she could, if she tried hard enough, and your mother came screaming down the back steps waving a dish towel." She paused. "Harold thought that if you wanted something badly enough all you had to do was make up your mind and go after it," she continued. "Do you believe that, Eleanor?" she asked.

"Believe what?"

"That if you want something badly enough all you have to do is take it?"

"No," said Eleanor.

"I'm sorry," said Sissy, reaching out and touching Eleanor's hand. "I am such a dumbbell. What a stupid, stupid thing to say."

Lunch arrived and Sissy ordered another drink. "I know just the place for your coat," she said. "There's a place on Madison where they have lovely things, good things, but not so ridiculously expensive. I think we'd better buy you a blue coat."

Sissy ate hungrily and continued to talk, as though she had bottled it all up and saved it for this particular moment.

"I suppose I shouldn't talk to you about Ned, should I?" she mused. "It wouldn't be very loyal, would it?"

Eleanor thought that perhaps it wouldn't be, but this didn't stop Sissy.

"You know, he's a wonderful man," said

Sissy, whose speech was beginning to slur, and it occurred to Eleanor that the coat might be forgotten. She wanted it to be forgotten.

"He's a wonderful father to Matthew," said Sissy.

"Good."

"And," Sissy said archly, "he doesn't ask very much of me."

"I'd like some coffee," said Eleanor, turning hopefully, but evidently none of the waiters had been engaged to keep an eye on her.

"Some men aren't like that," continued Sissy. "I don't know what I'd do if he was demanding, if you know what I mean, because, to be perfectly and utterly frank, Eleanor," she said, sounding suddenly very sober, "because, if the truth were known, I'd cut off his balls if I could."

The coffee came and eventually they were in a cab heading for Sissy's shop on Madison. While Eleanor went through the racks at the front, Sissy walked to the back. "You won't find anything there," she said as she went, "but you can look if you want to. I'm going to prowl around in the back. That's where all the good buys are."

Pretty soon she came out with three coats. They were all blue and the prices were right. Eleanor knew, of course, that Sissy had had them marked down and the difference billed to her, but she took one anyway. It seemed, at the time, the kindest thing she could do for her friend.

There was a note from Val in the apartment. She had gone to a church meeting and expected to be home before five. *We're going out for dinner*, wrote Val, *no cooking, no dishes! Hurrah.* On paper Val sounded like anyone else, and it occurred to Eleanor to wonder if Val might be pregnant. That would account for the shrillness and erratic behavior, but, of course, if Val were pregnant, wouldn't she seem happy?

Alone in the apartment, it struck Eleanor that the rooms were narrow and dingy. She had smelled cabbage in the hall and from the living room window she saw only the blackened brick of the building across the alley. Radiator heat streaked the walls and filled the place with its hot, suffocating presence. She went into her room and pulled off her dress and lay down with a book.

It was dark when she woke and she could hear water running. As she lay there, half awake, she knew that she would rather have scrambled eggs for supper than go out again. She heard a door close, and the toilet flush, then Val's angry voice.

"Where have you been?" said Val. "You're late again."

"It's only six-thirty."

"You know your sister's here. You might have tried to make it earlier."

"I'm sorry."

"I'm not going to take much more, Will."

"I don't know what you're talking about."

"Liar," she hissed. "Do you think I didn't see you last night? Do you know how many times you looked at her during the evening? Have you any idea what it's like to watch your husband mooning over another woman?"

"Come on, Val. You know better than that."

"I know what I need to know."

"I've told you before and I'll tell you again," he said patiently. "I've known Sissy all my life. If I'd wanted to marry her I would have. We can't refuse their invitations. I wish to God I'd turned the job down, but I didn't, and it's better than the one I had."

"Ha!" she said.

"Where's Eleanor?"

"Asleep. She was asleep when I came in."

"You better go wash your face and calm down," he said.

"Why should I wash my face, I just took a shower. Do I look dirty, Will? Look," she said.

Everything was silent for a minute and then

he said in a strained voice, "Quit it, Val. Tie up your robe."

"Why should I?" she said. "Don't you like to look at me, Will? Don't I look as good as she does, or haven't you ever seen her this way?"

"For God's sake, Val, shut up," he said. "When are you going to stop imagining things and act normal."

Eleanor pulled the pillow over her head, but even so she could hear sounds in the kitchen — ice dropping into a bucket — and the sound of Val crying in the next room. I should have known, she thought, because of course this could only mean that Val knew about Will and Sissy, and had known for some time. She wasn't surprised and she had never warmed up to Val, but Will and Sissy ought to have been strangled.

Eventually the television came on and Eleanor stumbled up and into the shower. By the time she was dressed, Val was sitting on the sofa reading a magazine and Will was watching the news with a drink in his hand.

When she had had a drink, she put on her new coat and showed it to them, swinging around the room with her hands in her pockets and giving them something to look at so they wouldn't have to look at each other. She didn't say that Sissy had been with her when she bought it. Instead she said, "Tonight's my treat, and tomorrow I've got to go home."

9

In August, that sultry month when in the past they might have expected Aunt Alice to descend with the children, unannounced but expected, the telegram was delivered that changed everything. What there was of innocence and trust in Eleanor was shattered as she struggled to get the message out of the envelope. Her hands shook so terribly that Grace took it and ripped it open. She spread it out on the kitchen table and they read it together.

Charles had been killed when his plane crashed on takeoff. Mr. Giles, who had delivered the telegram, stood in silence and waited. The government required him to wait until the message had been read and understood, and so he stood there, witnessing their agony, while sweat ran down his face and his own anguish nearly choked him. He had known the Richards for years. Known them when Eleanor was a toddler. Known them when Jane was so sick. He was relieved when Grace said, "Thank you, Mr. Giles. You needn't wait. We'll be all right."

Jane, who was working a jigsaw puzzle in the living room, didn't know what had happened until suddenly she realized that she had heard a strange voice in the kitchen and now, suddenly, there was only silence. She pushed away from the table and turned her chair toward the doorway, and when she reached the kitchen door she called out, "What's wrong? What's the matter?"

Eleanor, clutching the yellow paper in one hand, had begun to shudder, her teeth chattered, and, although it was suffocating in the kitchen, she was shivering uncontrollably. When she saw Jane she held up the telegram and Jane didn't need to be told anything more. The news about Harold had come in a letter, but this was no different.

Grace looked up and said, "It's all right," and she took the telegram from Eleanor and passed it over to Jane. "Call Daddy, Jane, and tell him to bring the doctor."

Then Grace put her arms around Eleanor and said, "It's all right. It's all right, Eleanor."

But, of course, it wasn't all right and the three of them knew it.

Grace led Eleanor toward the stairs, murmuring to her as though she were blind, telling her to watch the stairs, to hold on to the rail, telling her that everything was going to be all right. It was hot in the upper hall and stifling in the bedroom, although the shades were pulled to keep out the sun. Still Eleanor shook and, as her mother eased her onto the bed, she pulled up the spread and wrapped it around her. Then, sitting on the edge of the bed, Grace began to smooth Eleanor's hair away from her forehead. Grace had stopped saying that everything would be all right.

"Try to breathe slowly," she said, taking Eleanor's shaking hands in her own and rubbing her wrists. "Oh, my dear," she said, "I am so sorry."

Downstairs Jane had rolled herself into the hall and reached for the phone. "I think you'd better bring the doctor when you come, Daddy," she said.

The doctor gave Eleanor a sedative and for the rest of the day the house was silent. Through the afternoon people came and went, whispering their sympathy and passing silently in and out with their offerings of food and flowers. There were some, Grace's closest friends, who sat in the living room all afternoon to keep Jane company, and Jane, with her hands clasped tightly together, struggled to respond. She would have preferred to be alone.

Upstairs, Grace sat by the window, waiting for Eleanor to wake up.

At six John came upstairs. "You'd better come down and have some supper," he said. "She'll be awake all night. You'll be worn out, Grace."

"I'll come after a while."

"Jane has got it on the table, Grace."

"Tell Jane I'll be down soon."

When Eleanor woke up, Grace had raised the shades and the pale pink of evening shone at the windows. Outside the birds were settling in the trees and from the fields at the back of the house came a faint whine of insects. Grace sat where she could watch the illuminated face of the chapel clock. The hands pointed to eight o'clock. Across the lawn fireflies flashed and winked in the gathering shadows.

When Eleanor moaned, Grace rose quickly and crossed to the bed.

Leaning down, she said, "It's Mother, Eleanor. I'm right here, dear."

"What time is it?" asked Eleanor.

"Eight."

"Is it still Monday?"

"Yes."

"Have you had supper yet?"

"Would you like some supper, dear?"

Eleanor shook her head.

"You're a brave girl," said Grace.

Eleanor turned her face to the wall and closed her eyes.

After a while her father came down the hall and into the room. It was dark now, and when he turned on the hall lamp it made a vivid flash of light. Grace looked up quickly and shook her head, but he paid no attention. Taking her by the hand, he pulled her to her feet. "Go downstairs, Grace, and have some supper and keep Jane company," he said. "I'm going to sit here with Eleanor."

"I'm all right," said Eleanor.

"I know you are," he said, sitting down.

It was silent in the room again. From downstairs came a murmur of voices and then the sound of water running and dishes being washed. Once or twice the telephone rang.

"I've talked with Charles's parents," said her father. "They sent their love."

Eleanor tried to visualize the Beverly Hills house, which now seemed remote and strange, even though they had been there less than a year ago. She could see his mother on the stairs, her face vivid with makeup, her dress a sheer confection of white and navy, her voice chirping "dahlings, dahlings." Would she ever see them again? What would become of them all? How many years of martinis would it take to blot out the sadness they must be feeling?

Suddenly she heard her father say, "Time will help," and she realized he must have been talking for some time. How would time help? she wondered. Charles was not coming back. Was it just this morning that they were canning tomatoes? Why was it so dark, and who had turned on the light in the hall? She turned toward the wall and closed her eyes.

One day Eleanor was aware of someone speaking loudly somewhere nearby. She could hear her father saying, "Now, Grace, I want you to stop this. No more trays. No more sitting with the shades down."

"It's only been three days, John. That's not much time. She did eat some of her supper last night."

"I mean it, Grace. She has to face it."

"Face it!" cried her mother. "Do you think she won't face it? She'll face it for the rest of her life. She's only twenty-four. What did we have to face when we were that age?"

"I know, I know," he said. "I'm thinking of her."

"So am I," said her mother.

After a minute there was a rap on the door and then her mother entered carrying a tray. There was a white napkin spread on the tray and a juice glass with some flowers in it. Eleanor watched as her mother set it down and then she allowed Grace to fluff up her pillows and prop them up behind her.

"Now then," said Grace cheerfully, "have some breakfast. Mrs. Ware brought us some peaches. I thought you might like them on your cereal."

There was a dish of sliced peaches, another dish of Rice Krispies, a small sugar and creamer, a cup and saucer. Her mother poured coffee from a tiny flowered pot and spooned peaches on the cereal.

"Sugar?" asked Grace, as though she didn't know.

Eleanor nodded.

"I think it's a little cooler," said Grace, "maybe that will help."

Eleanor submitted to the cereal, taking two or three spoonfuls, as though she were an invalid or a child, and listening as Grace rambled on about Jane's painting.

"She's painting one of those Gypsies," said Grace vaguely, as though she had almost forgotten that there had ever been Gypsies camped nearby. "A girl on a stone wall. You remember, when they were down there in Purple Meadow. That terrible summer," she said, as though it had just occurred to her to couple the Gypsies with the disaster they had left behind them.

"Well, now," she said briskly, dismissing it, "you might get dressed, dear, and come downstairs after a while. Jane is miserable. She wants to be up here with you . . . and then, of course, she can't help but think of Harold, too."

Eleanor cried out as though something had suddenly pierced her. Through the gray mist of pain and disbelief surrounding her came this terrible thing. Harold. Harold in his uniform, holding her in his arms, saying that he loved her and he loved Jane and he loved them all. Charles, gripping her shoulders on that gray, sleety day in Boston, telling her she was going to marry him. And suddenly she covered her face with her hands, her shoulders shook, and she began to cry. As she sobbed, Grace took away the tray, and then she took Eleanor in her arms. Tears ran down her own face as she rocked Eleanor.

That evening John came in late. Eleanor heard the screen door and his voice in the kitchen. Next came the sound of his feet on the stairs, a sharp rap on the door, and then he crossed the room and pulled up the shades, snapping them to the top of the rollers, where they spun and flapped.

"I'm told supper will be on the table in ten minutes," he said.

"I'm not hungry."

"It looks good," he said.

"I can't help it, Daddy. I'm not hungry."

"Get up, Eleanor," he said sternly. "I want you to get dressed and come down to supper."

"I can't," she said. "I can't. I don't want to. I don't feel well. I can't."

He reached for her hand. "I know," he said, "you don't feel well, and you don't want to get up, but you can. Now get up and get dressed."

"But I'm not hungry. I want to stay here."

"No," he said, "You're coming down. Your mother's worn out and your sister is half-sick with worry. Get out of that bed, Eleanor. Right now."

I won't, she thought childishly, he can't make me. But she rummaged around in her drawers until she found her Smith gym suit, which was soft from dozens of washings and cool, and she pulled it on. Then she went into the bathroom and washed her face and brushed her hair. She scarcely glanced in the mirror. She didn't want to see the face of grief, the limp hair and sunken eyes and trembling mouth of sorrow.

It had grown ominously quiet downstairs, but no one stood at the foot of the stairs looking up hopefully. They were already in the dining room, she supposed, already blessed, already eating.

Not so. When she entered the room they bowed their heads and folded their hands, and when she was seated her father began.

"Heavenly Father," he said, "we give Thee thanks for all Thy goodness and loving kindness to us. May we ever be deserving. Bless us and strengthen us as a family, both those here with us now and those absent. Give us, we pray, the strength to bear all sorrow that we may live according to Thy plan, both now and forever. We ask this in Christ's name. Amen."

What goodness and loving kindness, thought Eleanor, and yet, as she pulled the napkin out of its ring, she felt a rightness in what her father had demanded of her. Together there was strength. In the "outward and visible sign of the inward and spiritual grace" there was peace of a sort. At least something to hold on to.

10

For a while after Charles's death, there were always people in the house and eventually Eleanor managed to meet them again. Like Jane and her mother, she submitted to routine. She never considered going back to Cambridge and she declined invitations to Wellesley.

When September came and the leaves began to turn and there was frost in the morning, the boys returned and something stirred within her. The voice of school called out in its familiar way. She almost expected Grace to make her a new dress and buy her the annual new shoes for school, but Grace didn't think in those terms anymore. She said daily, "Why don't you go and talk to someone about a job? How about the library, or the alumni office? They may have an opening in the French Department. You'll never know if you don't try."

At the dinner table Grace said, "Don't you think, John, that Dave Edwards might be the one she should see about a job. If not him, then who?"

Eleanor looked at Jane in despair, but Jane only smiled and nodded. Their mother would always want to help, to be involved, to shape their lives as she shaped a loaf of bread. One might as well accept it, Jane seemed to say.

Eleanor didn't point out that she had no immediate need of money. Charles had left her his car and his insurance. Why must she rush out and find a job, she thought, knowing perfectly well that day after day of idleness would soon become unbearable.

Dave Edwards had been at Harrison almost five years. He had come as a math teacher and was now dean of students. The opening of school was a particularly rushed time, and, while he knew Eleanor and knew what her situation was, they were virtual strangers. The fact that his wife had left him during the summer put him at a disadvantage. It shouldn't have. Eleanor knew about the separation as he knew that she was a widow. These two facts might have worked to make them feel they had a common bond, but it didn't seem to.

On the morning she finally gave in to Grace, she called and made an appointment and walked across campus to see what he would say when she asked about openings. She found him at his desk, which was a hopeless confusion of open files.

"Hello," he said. "Terrible mess, I'm afraid. Sit down. What can I do for you?"

"You can give me a job. My mother recommends a spot in the library or the alumni office."

"What about French? Isn't that your forte?"

"Not now," she said. The thought of meeting a class regularly, responding to their questions and needs, was unbearable.

"Well, how are you? How are things going?"

"Well enough. And you — aside from all this?"

"I'd like to put you to work right here. However, the library might be better. How would you feel about taking orders from Doug Parsons? He's not the easiest man in the world to work for and he's due for retirement in two years. That can make people testy. What do you think about part-time there?"

"I'd like it," she said.

He grinned and said, "Will your mother like it?"

"It will suit her right down to the ground."

"I'll give him a ring. If he's free you could go along to the library now," and he picked up the phone, which rang seven times before he heard Doug Parsons's familiar bark.

"Library. Doug Parsons here."

"Good morning," said Dave. "This is Dave Edwards. I hope I haven't caught you at a bad time."

"You have," said Doug.

"Very good," Dave replied. "I have Eleanor Richards, that is Eleanor Hammond, here in my office and I want to send her along to see if you think you could keep her busy for a while. Part time for the moment. Full time if things work out."

"Blessed *Sauveur*," moaned Mr. Parsons. "In my golden years must I be plagued with 'helpers'? I need someone who knows about libraries."

"Good," said Dave. "I'm glad you feel that way. I'll send her along."

"Hold on, there," said Doug. "You know how I feel about student help, but, to be truthful, I'd rather have an intelligent student than a faculty child. Worst of all a faculty wife."

"Very good," said Dave, "I'm inclined to feel that way myself."

He smiled and nodded at Eleanor as Doug continued.

"Why do you do this to me, Dave?"

"That's fine, Doug," he said. "She'll be there in five minutes."

He put the phone down and stood up. "He

210

seems to be swamped at the moment, but that's to be expected at this time of year. He's inclined to be gruff, but, of course, you know him."

"Actually I don't."

"You will," said Dave. "Good luck," he said at the door. "If this doesn't work out we'll try the alumni office."

When the door closed behind her he went back to the phone. Doug picked it up on the second ring.

"This is Dave again. She's on the way. She's had a bad time and —"

"Another of those. Why do people think that anyone who can read can work intelligently in a library? I'm not going to take her unless she looks good on a ladder."

"For God's sake don't say that to her. Have a little compassion. She's lost her husband and John Richards hasn't had an easy time of it. He and Grace . . ."

"Yes, yes, I know."

"If it doesn't work out I'll try to find a spot for her in the alumni off—"

"That catchall," said Doug. "Ah, well, I'll do my best."

Eleanor found Mr. Parsons in his office, surrounded by open cartons of new books and a desk top littered with book catalogs and correspondence. Mr. Parsons, who was old and stooped, looked for a moment as though he was trying to decide whether to stand up or shake hands. Oh, bother, he thought, waving at a chair and saying, "Sit down."

"Thank you," she said.

He studied her over the top of his glasses and said, "Now then, tell me what you know about libraries."

"Libraries are for books and books are for people who like to read or are required to do research of one kind or another."

"Is that so," he replied.

"I have always thought so."

"And what would you do with this mess if I turned you loose on it?"

"I don't know," she said. "Make some surface effort to straighten it out, I suppose."

"Ah," he said thoughtfully, peering at her with eyes that never seemed to blink. Then without warning he said, " 'You are old, Father William, the young man said, and your hair has become very white.' "

He paused and regarded her thoughtfully. He must be mad, she thought. He is certainly rude. I suppose this is his way of testing people. And she replied, " 'And yet you incessantly stand on your head. Do you think, at your age, it is right?' "

His eyes began to sparkle and he retorted,

" 'We are so very 'umble.' "

"Uriah Heep," she replied, "David Copperfield. Charles Dickens."

"Good," he said. " 'May flights of angels sing thee to thy rest.' "

"Hamlet."

"Source."

"Everyone knows the source."

He laughed. "Let's try another. 'In the beginning was the word and the word was with God and the word was God.' "

"The Bible. Book of John. First chapter, first lines."

He leaned back and folded his hands across the plaid vest that covered his spreading paunch and said, "This proves nothing, of course, except that you, and probably all of your family, read and no doubt went to Sunday school. Would you like a cup of coffee?"

"That would be nice," she said.

He shuffled over to a table where there was a hot plate and a teakettle.

"The water is through that door in the lavatory and the cups are in that bank of files, under T for tea."

The door rattled as he pulled it open and, glancing inside, she saw that there was a shoe box there, stacked with tea bags, instant coffee, and sugar. "You will note," he said, "that we have no cream, as we have no refrigeration."

"I take it black."

"And please note, as well, that I do not expect you to fix mine."

"Is it against the rules to bring cookies?" she asked.

"Certainly not," he replied.

By the time she had been working there a month she knew that in the quiet of the library she had found just the refuge that suited her. Working in the maze of the stacks, she had the security of being almost invisible, and by the time she had been there for four months she enjoyed sitting in Mr. Parsons's study with coffee at ten and tea at three-thirty. At those times she surprised herself by feeling almost happy. If Mr. Parsons were twenty years younger, she might have married him. He was the sort of man one could feel safe with. He was so fond of his characters in books, the most he would ask of a partner was that she be fond of them too. He could never be handsome, but he was comfortingly Dickensian with his florid face, his large reddish nose, and monk's fringe of fine, white hair.

Now and then he pulled books from the shelves and presented them to her. "If you haven't read this, you should have," he would say. And sometimes when he was rattled or irritated by students, he would simply turn away and escape to the rare book room, which was out of bounds to students unless they were accompanied by a library aide.

"It will be terrible here when you retire," she often said.

"You are right, my dear," he agreed. "Retirement is barbaric. After years of struggle, when we are finally fit for the job, we are no longer allowed to go on. Hence, retirement."

She had scarcely been there a month before she realized how much she would miss him when he was gone.

It was strange, perhaps, that she found him stimulating, but here in the domain of this fragile old man she seemed to have found life again. She woke in the morning feeling rested and ready for the day. Things happened at the library and, in telling about them, she stirred up little flurries of conversation at the dinner table. For six hours a day she had somewhere to go and something to do. To be a willing prisoner in the library, in some curious way, seemed to liberate her, and she realized that this was probably as much happiness as she would ever know.

11

Two days before Thanksgiving, Val had her first baby and named her Allison.

"What a lovely name," said Jane in surprise, for they were a family with names like Jane and Grace and Eleanor, a family of Marys, Margarets, and Catherines. Now here was Allison, six pounds two ounces, reported Will, with black hair and blue eyes.

"All babies are born with blue eyes," said Grace. "When can we go to see her?"

"Better still," said John, "when can they come here?"

"For Christmas," said Jane.

"How wonderful to have a baby for Christmas," said Grace, almost as though she had decided that a baby, like a tree or a toy, was something they all needed to make Christmas complete.

They didn't hear very much from Will, but Val wrote one or two sketchy little letters. Yes, they would come for Christmas, but they mustn't count on much because she was so tired, and the baby cried too much, but they would come.

A year ago, thought Eleanor, she and Charles had been the ones coming, and as she helped with the tree and the baking and all the usual Christmas things, she felt desperately lonely. I have been a widow for five months, she thought, only five months and it has seemed an eternity.

Val wrote again. This time the baby had gained five ounces. Mrs. Dwire had sent a sterling cup with Allison's name engraved on it, and Mrs. Barringer had sent a complete layette from Lord and Taylors — *as if we were a charity case,* wrote Val.

"Why would Val think that?" wondered Jane. "It sounds like a lovely and generous gift."

"Who knows," said Eleanor lightly as she went on rolling and cutting cookies that looked like Christmas wreaths. But she knew why Val had written that. It was because of Sissy. Val hated Sissy, for all the things she knew about Will and Sissy and all the things she only suspected.

"Oh well," said Jane, who was addressing Christmas cards for all of them, "I expect she'll appreciate it eventually."

Jane worked slowly and carefully, calling

out things like, "Didn't the Moores move last summer?" and now, more often, "I thought Mr. Kendall died last year, but the book still says Mr. and Mrs.?" Someone among her parents' friends was undoubtedly dying at that very moment. Grace was aware of that, but Jane, whose health grew increasingly more tenuous, seemed surprised. It was as though she recognized her own physical decline but wondered why anyone who had lived life fully would ever die at all.

For years a subdued vitality beat stubbornly in Jane's twisted body, but now in the winter of 1952, as the world froze and cracked around them and the shadows of bare branches spread gray, grasping fingers over white yards, Jane, with a new serenity, seemed content to watch the birds at the feeder, happy to listen when Grace read the mail, indifferent to meals and the endless cups of hot cocoa her mother brought her. Day by day she grew more transparent. Sometimes when Eleanor came into the room and found Jane asleep, leaning back in her chair with her eyes closed, a red and blue afghan over her knees, she felt acutely the distance that separated them. Her own robust good health then repelled her and she thought she would have changed places with Jane gladly, if only it were possible. What was her life without Charles, anyway? she thought

. . . but she could no longer hear his voice, for he too was slipping away, becoming blurred and remote, and there were even times when it seemed to Eleanor that both Charles and Jane were in deliberate retreat, deprived of escape only by the force of her own heartache.

And yet Christmas seemed almost to bring its own joy into the house, and to know that Val and Will were coming with the baby added to it. By the middle of December John had brought the crib down from the attic and Grace was re-covering the mattress and making new crib sheets. Her foot on the treadle of the sewing machine went up and down — *rickety rackety* — sounding like old times when she had made the girls' clothes, and she said, as though it had just occurred to her, "You see, John, how nice it is to have a sewing room."

When Wilson and Val finally arrived late in the afternoon on the day before Christmas, Grace rushed forward with her arms out and took the baby with a little gasp. "Oh, you darling, you," she crooned, untying Allison's bonnet and kissing the top of her head. "Just look, John, she's the image of Jane when she was a baby," and, crossing to Jane's chair, she held the baby out to her.

Jane's hands fluttered toward the baby as

Grace leaned down to put Allison in her lap, but Val shot forward.

"She's too heavy for Jane," said Val, snatching Allison away and clutching her tightly as she looked around in desperation. One would have thought Allison too fragile to be touched. Suddenly, it seemed, disaster lurked on the stair landing and this visit to the family took on aspects as dangerous as crossing a bottomless body of water on thin ice.

"It's all right, Val," said Wilson, taking the baby and offering her to Jane, but Jane shrank away. "Just let me look, Will," she said.

"Well," said Grace loudly, "it's time to put the kettle on," and she and Eleanor went into the kitchen, leaving the rest of them to admire the baby. This was not at all what Grace had expected. Grandchildren running in and out of the house all summer and dragging their sleds over to Chapel Hill in the winter was what she had envisioned. But of course, Allison was only a baby and Valerie had always been nervous.

Eleanor stood at the sink washing teacups while her mother shredded cabbage. Baked beans and brown bread and cabbage salad, their usual Christmas Eve supper, followed by steamed pudding and hard sauce. Perhaps after supper people would relax. The Campus Carolers would come and then it would begin to feel like Christmas.

As Eleanor went back and forth to and from the dining room, she glanced into the living room, where Val and Will sat on the sofa with Allison lying between them. Wilson, mesmerized by the fire, might have been anywhere, remembering Christmases past, wondering about Christmas future, but Val looked tired and unhappy. Now and then she touched the baby, as if to make sure Allison was still there and asleep, but for the most part she sat with her eyes closed. It was not the lively Christmas Eve they usually had, and John poked the fire, patted Jane on the head, and said, "How's it going, Janie?" He paused to ask Will if he wanted anything, but Will didn't hear him and so he went into the kitchen and said to Grace, "What's the matter with her?"

Grace glanced up and smiled her smile of resignation, an expression that revealed distress and surrender simultaneously. "She's young," said Grace. "Allison's only a month old. Val is tired; she has a right to be tired."

"I don't like it. It doesn't seem like Christmas," he said.

"You don't have to like it. It's only for two days," and then she glanced around as Eleanor went into the dining room. Grace murmured, "Please, dear, please try to be cheerful for Jane's sake. And Eleanor too. Charles was here

221

last year. She must be remembering that."

"I'll do my best," he muttered as he moved restlessly about the kitchen. There had always been the faint suspicion in his mind that his daughter-in-law was one of those beautiful but cold people, who aroused passion in others without participating in it themselves. Poor old Will he thought, picking up a piece of the cabbage heart and beginning to eat it.

Christmas day was dazzling, and the rather pathetic procession down to the living room with stockings to open started them off in the usual way. Then came the grapefruit with powdered sugar and cherry, the sausage and mince pie, and then conversation came more easily. There was all the rustling of tissue and one of the girls (it didn't matter which one) said, "Mother, you're not going to save the paper and ribbon this year?" And Grace replied, "Leave me alone. I'll do it my way. I *like* doing it my way."

While the others went to chapel, Grace put in the turkey and started peeling vegetables. Then she thought about Val, who was up with the baby, and Grace took her courage and her heavy heart up the back stairs to Wilson's room. Val was leaning over the bed changing the baby. As she wiped and powdered and pinned with tense little motions, she cooed,

"Now you feel better, don't you darling? Are you hungry? Do you want Mommie to get you a nice warm bottle of milk?" And she lifted the baby, holding her tightly and possessively. She began to hum then and when Grace spoke, she started up as though terrified.

She is so thin, thought Grace, and she doesn't know how to relax. Poor child. But, remembering the first months just after her babies were born, Grace said gently, "Don't you want me to give her her bottle?"

Val held the baby closer and said, "No. No thank you. She isn't used to strangers." Then Val took the bottle from the warmer, sat down in the rocker by the window, shook a few drops of milk onto her wrist, and offered the bottle to Allison. When she could see that the baby was taking it, Val looked up and said, "I didn't mean to sound ungrateful, but she is fussy about other people. Even Will sometimes."

"Babies are like that," said Grace. "I just thought you might like a rest. I know how tired mothers can be during the first few weeks."

"I'm not tired," said Val.

Forcing cheerfulness, Grace said, "I hope Wilson does his part."

She had not expected to feel shut out, but

she did. Here in her own house with her own grandchild. It was not what she had expected, and as she went back downstairs the murmuring started again, soft and indistinct, as Val began to rock.

I wish they'd wait and go home tomorrow, Grace thought. They wouldn't get off until three o'clock the way things were going now and when she reached the kitchen she checked the oven, stuck a fork in the potatoes, and did what she could to hurry the meal. Getting them on the road as soon as possible seemed to be the only thing she could do. She hated to have anyone drive after dark in uncertain weather. Will said he didn't mind, and she said she supposed he didn't. "But I do," she said.

Their dazzling day had become overcast. The sky threatened snow. Will would have liked to stay for another day, but Val was ready to get home. He had hoped his mother would be able to do something about Val and the baby. He wasn't sure what, but he had a foolishly romantic notion that grandmothers were somehow capable fairy godmothers whose powers to soothe fussy babies were almost magical. It hadn't seemed to work that way, however, and there wasn't going to be time to have anything like a private conversation.

If he could have, he would have told Grace that nothing was going the way he thought it would. Val was tired all the time. The baby cried and spit up and always had messy diapers. Why did people have children? he wondered.

When the car was loaded he kissed Grace and said, "Well, Mother, we're on our way." Then he went around the room looking vague, as though he might have missed something, but apparently he hadn't. He shook his father's hand, kissed Jane and Eleanor, and then shouted up the stairs, "Come on, Val. The car's packed. We're ready to go."

Val came down the stairs with the baby in her arms. She looked around and smiled and said, "Thank you very much for everything. It's been a nice Christmas."

Only Grace stepped up and kissed her and peeked one last time at the baby, but all of them, even Jane, went out onto the front porch and waved as the car went down the drive and disappeared down the hill.

For at least forty miles they drove in silence. Allison slept. As they went through Holyoke, Val said, "I wish we could live in a house. I think about it all the time."

"Since when," he said. "This is the first I've heard of it."

"You never listen," she said.

He didn't deny it. Listening and talking seemed to invite argument, and they had too many arguments as it was. "Where do you want a house?" he asked.

"Anywhere. Just as long as it's out of the city. I hate the city."

"We'll take a look at Darien. I know quite a few people who live there."

The next time Will saw Sissy, he told her that he and Val were going to look for a house in the spring. The more he thought about a daily commute, the less enthusiastic he was about Darien. He tried to explain how he felt to Sissy, but she was talking about Matthew. She always did and he was glad to know how Matthew was doing, but Sissy's long rambles about his intelligence and athletic ability and especially his good looks began to bore him after a while. She had never said anything pointed about why she thought he should be aware of these things, and, until she did so, Will simply closed his mind to the possibility that there might be reason for his concern.

"Have you heard anything I've been saying?" he asked.

"Yes," said Sissy. "I heard every word. You and Val are going to look for a house in Darien and you don't like the idea of commuting."

"Well," he said, "what do you think?"

"I'm not sure," said Sissy. "No one likes to commute, but if she was way out there in Darien, she would be just that much farther away from us, and the farther the better."

"I don't know," he said.

"Well, put your mind to something else. Isn't there something we could do for Eleanor? Between the two of us we ought to know somebody nice, or at least suitably rich. Think!"

"About what?"

"You're not listening," she replied. "You're as bad as Mother. She can't hear and you don't listen. She won't get a hearing aid because she says it won't help. It's simply a matter of vanity."

Wilson wasn't interested in hearing aids or anything else that Sissy had been talking about. "I think I ought to get a divorce," he said abruptly, "and I think you should get a divorce."

"Oh, darling," said Sissy. "Wouldn't it be wonderful if we could, but think what a mess it would be. Ned is too stupid to even imagine I might, and he is generous. But if we divorced . . ." She let her words float off into oblivion, where she hoped they would remain, and then she said, "Oh yes, news. Did I tell you we're going to Paris soon? He's taken a floor in a hotel. For the whole family. It seems absurd to me, a whole floor, but he says it's a small hotel on one of the islands. I think it will be ghastly, all of us, even his half-grown-up children. Matthew doesn't even know them."

Wilson had always wanted to take her to Paris and all the romantic places like Paris that people wrote songs about, places where pictures were painted and books were written.

"It must be nice to be rich," said Will bitterly.

"Don't be like that, darling. Money isn't everything. Ned used to be such a stick in the mud and now he seems to want to travel, but Will, darling, I wish it were us."

"It will be someday," he said.

"Of course it will, darling," and she patted his hand and smiled at him as though they hadn't a care in the world. Why couldn't he see it as she did? They had a wonderful, beautiful love that was going to last for as long as they lived. What would be the use in divorce? Years ago when she was first married she might have felt that way, but now? Horrors! Ned hardly ever bothered her anymore. She had the best of two worlds and she wanted to keep it that way.

12

Sissy had what she thought was a brilliant idea early in January 1953, and she sat right down at her desk and wrote Eleanor a letter. Some days later, Eleanor pulled it out of the box and, after stamping up the back steps and knocking the snow off her boots, she came into the house rosy and panting. A letter from Sissy was rare and usually focused on some impracticality or another. What would it be this time?

Shedding her coat and waving the letter in her hand, she joined Jane and her mother in front of the fire, where tea was waiting. "Look at this," she said. "A letter from Sissy. It's so fat it feels like parchment. I won't be surprised someday to have her close it with sealing wax and smush it with a Barringer crest, if there is one."

"If there isn't," said Jane, "she'll invent one."

"Let's guess what she says. My guess is that

she wants to go away somewhere and wonders if she can bring Matthew here because she certainly can't take him with her and Miss Purse is indisposed and the other servants are horrid to her precious Matthew."

"Shame on you, Eleanor," said Grace.

"Let me see," said Jane. "My guess is that Ned has lost all his money and Sissy is going to move back to Aunt Alice's house and wants you to tell her how she can survive under the circumstances."

Grace, who was slow to warm up to such flights of the imagination, said, "I expect it's just an ordinary letter. I hope no one is sick."

Eleanor took a sip of tea and tore open Sissy's letter. As she read she began to smile, and when she finished it she handed it over to Jane and said, "We're all wrong. She wants me to go to England with Aunt Alice."

"Go to England with Alice," said Grace in amazement. "What on earth for?"

"To be her companion, I suppose."

"It's meant as an invitation," said Jane, and she read aloud Sissy's so-called invitation.

" 'I've had the most wonderful idea,' " read Jane, " 'I think it's time you had a change of scene and a little fun. Ned and I are taking the family to Paris, but it's not the sort of trip for Mother. Of course she wants to go and it occurred to me that England would be just the right place for her and if you would go with her, Eleanor, I wouldn't have to worry about her, and, of course, darling, it would be all expenses paid for you.' "

"Really," said Grace in exasperation, "Alice does a very good job of looking out for Alice. Sissy is the limit. She wants you to have all the responsibilities, and —"

But Jane interrupted her and said, "Go. Think about it. Really think. Two flights. You'll hardly get on the plane before you're there. Then two weeks at the Savoy. Then another flight and zip, back to Boston. I'd go in a minute."

Eleanor had thought of all that, and then she remembered that Doug was beginning to brood about retirement. Half the time he muttered that there was so much to do he would never finish by commencement next year and at other times he marched through the halls wringing his hands and saying, "Look at this. I will be glad to be rid of it all. It means nothing to me now. Nothing."

"It's not a particularly good time for me," said Eleanor. "Mr. Parsons is frantic about retirement."

"How foolish," said Grace. "Retirement is a fact of life. I certainly hope your father won't carry on when he retires."

Grace didn't seem to realize that John would

be retiring at the same time: June 1954. As well as she knew him, she realized it wouldn't be safe to predict anything at this point.

When Eleanor asked for time off, Doug's eyes flashed and he beat on the top of his desk with open hands and said, "Oh, to be in England, now that April's here."

"I'm afraid it will be March."

"March, April, anytime, my dear, and the Savoy! London at the peak of the season, the opera, the theater . . . and of course this person, whoever she is, must take it all in and you will be with her."

"Aunt Alice," she said.

She couldn't believe he hadn't met Alice at some time or another, but of course, despite Elliot and her haughty self-assurance, Alice never skated in the middle of the pond where the ice was thin, but always swept by on the edges, avoiding the possibility of striking up a friendship with some unsuitable person by mistake.

"But what about you?" said Eleanor. "There's so much to do here."

"Much to do? What have I to do compared to the glorious adventure you are about to have?"

"I am not sure I want to go," said Eleanor, thinking of Drury House and its inhabitants.

She wanted to go so desperately it made her feel ashamed.

"Not go! What rubbish."

Hardly a day had passed before there was a call from Sissy reminding her to get her passport immediately. "I haven't even answered her letter," said Eleanor, irritated that Sissy knew her so well.

"Go," said Jane. "I'd go in a minute if I could."

That night Eleanor phoned Sissy, who said, "Oh, good. I am so glad. Now she won't bother us. What would she do in Paris? I'm so glad you want to go."

"It's a lovely invitation," said Eleanor.

"Now don't worry that you'll have to be nurse-maiding all the time. You know she's half deaf, that's a bother, and she has to be reminded to take her pills, and she is slowing down. When she rests you can shop and if she doesn't feel like going to the dining room, you can go alone. Just order up a tray, and, who knows, you might meet someone pleasant."

Of course Sissy would meet someone, a man surely, and chances were he would be rich and unattached and she would spend the rest of her life tormenting Will and boring the rest of them about her wonderful conquest in Paris.

"Now, for heaven's sakes, Eleanor," concluded Sissy, "buy some decent clothes." And then Sissy hurried on to say, "You are so lovely. You have natural beauty that doesn't seem to need makeup. Just buy some basics, you know, something smart and something glittery. Do it for me."

Eleanor drove to Springfield that weekend and spent over five hundred dollars in Forbes and Wallace, trying on things that were smart, but not glittery. She substituted silky for glittery and came home feeling incredibly liberated. She had actually spent money, lots of money, on herself. It gave her a heady feeling, as if she had transgressed and denied her parents, who must surely have instilled in her the fear (almost amounting to sin) of overspending.

However, there it was, in bags and boxes on the backseat of the car, and as she turned in at the gates and drove through the pines, she decided to stop at Dave's and tell him her plans.

Dave's house had been the McMillan House when she and Jane were little girls, and was so familiar it seemed natural to turn into the drive and pull up at the back door. She and Jane had spent a good many afternoons in the McMillan House with her mother and Mrs.

McMillan, who sat and sewed and talked until teatime, when Mrs. McMillan went into the kitchen to make cinnamon toast and tea and their mother put down her mending and crossed the room and sat down beside Mrs. McMillan, Sr., who was tied into her chair and spent the days gazing out the window. Mrs. McMillan, her daughter-in-law, always told Jane and Eleanor that they could talk to the elder Mrs. McMillan, even though she wouldn't understand them because she was so old and tired she couldn't even sit up in her chair, and she assured them that the old lady didn't mind being tied into her chair, which was a rocker. "Oh, she loves to rock," the younger Mrs. McMillan would say. "She thinks she's still in India, where she and her husband were missionaries. I dare say she even thinks there is someone at the back of her chair fanning her."

Their mother never criticized the younger Mrs. McMillan, but when she went out to the kitchen Grace would sit down beside the elder Mrs. McMillan and hold her hand, which was twisted and swollen with arthritis, and say, "How are you, Mother McMillan? Are you comfortable? Aren't the birds at the feeder beautiful?"

Old Mrs. McMillan never spoke, but when their mother sat beside her, talking about the birds and what was growing in the garden and how many quarts of tomatoes she had canned, Mrs. McMillan turned her head toward Grace and listened. The rocking chair stopped rocking and when the tea came and their mother went back to her own chair she had to take her free hand and slowly and forcefully open old Mrs. McMillan's claw of a hand because the old woman didn't want to let go.

"She understands me," Grace would say to their father. "I wish there was some way I could help."

But there wasn't.

The house had been painted gray with white trim since Dave had lived there. As Eleanor drew up at the back, she noticed a motorbike parked in the garage. She didn't know he had a motorbike. There were probably a lot of things she didn't know about Dave.

She ran up the back steps and stood on the porch rapping on the door, but nobody came. She could hear music, probably the Texaco Saturday afternoon opera, and she tried again.

When the door finally opened she came face-to-face with Peg. She had never met Peg before, but she didn't doubt that she was meeting her now because Peg looked as startled to see her as Eleanor felt. Swinging open the door, Peg said, "Hi. I'm Peg Edwards.

I bet you didn't expect to find me here?"

Eleanor hadn't expected anything. She and Dave were barely friends, she had obviously chosen the wrong time and said so.

"No, no," said Peg. "I'm sure he'd want to see you," and she turned and crossed the kitchen and went into the hall and shouted up the stairs, "You have a visitor, Dave!" Then she walked back to Eleanor and Eleanor could see every ounce of flesh on her body just by the way her jeans hugged her hips and the way her breasts shook under the gray wool of her sweater.

"I'll come another time. Tell him it wasn't important," and she turned to leave, but there he was at the kitchen door, barefooted, tousled, shirt open, decently covered, but indecently exposed.

"Don't go," he said, "come in and have a glass of wine, come and see Salomae presented with John the Baptist's head."

"I can't stay," she said. "I just wanted to tell you I'm going to London in March."

"Lucky you," said Peg, snuggling up to Dave.

"I want to hear all about it," said Dave. "I'll call you later."

"Fine," said Eleanor.

But it wasn't fine. He had been officially separated for over a year. That ought to mean something, but apparently it didn't if they still went to bed together. She didn't doubt that's where they'd been. Well, she thought, that settles it. It doesn't matter to me what he does or who he's with or where he goes. I am going to England.

Meanwhile, in Cambridge, Alice opened her eyes to a beautiful morning. The weather was incredible for January, with only a sifting of snow and bright, clear days that filled her with a feeling of vitality. She sat up in bed and composed herself as Mrs. Briggs raised the window shades.

"Here we are," said Mrs. Briggs cheerfully, settling the tray on Alice's lap. "I've brought you a nice boiled egg this morning."

Alice sighed softly, and said, "Thank you, Mrs. Briggs." She had never been able to convince Mrs. Briggs that all she wanted in the morning was coffee. One must keep the upper hand, she reminded herself, and Mrs. Briggs's insubordination aggravated her.

Mrs. Briggs was now straightening things on the top of the dressing table, but she paused and turning to Alice said, "What was that?"

"I said," replied Alice loudly, "thank you for the egg. You mustn't do it again. I should not eat eggs in the morning."

"Can't be helped," said Mrs. Briggs, who

was deaf herself. "My legs aren't what they used to be. It's the stairs. You've got a nice lot of mail this morning."

"I see that I have."

"Pardon?"

"Thank you," shouted Alice, nodding and smiling as she picked up her mail. Poor Mrs. Briggs, she thought, as she watched her hobble across the room. Mrs. Briggs, squat and shapeless, wore a print housedress and an apron. Her stockings sagged, the swollen flesh of her ankles lapped over the tops of her laced brown Oxfords, and it wouldn't have surprised Alice to know that Mrs. Briggs still wore a corset. I ought to find someone else, thought Alice, but help was hard to find and Mrs. Briggs had been very loyal. Whenever Sissy complained about her, Alice said, "But darling, poor Mrs. Briggs has nothing but her Social Security. She needs me." It also crossed Alice's mind, now and then, that she had never had anyone work for her who asked so little in the way of compensation. That was surely worth something.

She took up her mail, scanning postmarks and handwriting. Unfamiliar handwriting meant that someone's children had written to inform her of their mother's death, or some other catastrophe of age, and she was glad to recognize John's familiar scrawl. Ah, she thought, what does he want? and then it occurred to her that Grace usually wrote and she said aloud, "I hope there's nothing wrong."

As one of his last official acts, aside from teaching, as an employee of the school, John had written to ask Alice for money, and momentarily she was amused to think that anyone thought she was in a position to contribute significantly to Harrison, although she did now and always would support the annual giving there. Sometimes she felt dunned to death because Harvard, Amherst, and Vassar kept her on their lists. It crossed her mind that a small gift to Harrison would mean a great deal more to the school than a small gift to Harvard, but the trouble was she didn't have any idea what her assets were. Ned tended to all of that, thank heavens. This was a dodge she had been using for years, a helpless denial of matters financial, and she knew perfectly well that Ned would cover anything.

What a lovely day, she thought, glancing out and noticing that the moisture in the tree-tops visible from her window was glittering with frost. Shining like diamonds, she thought, and then, for some unaccountable reason, this made her think of Sissy's wedding day.

For a long time she had worried about Sissy. Of course she wished Sissy might be happy, but, more importantly, she wanted to be able to feel that she had made the right choice. She could remember her own feelings on that day as they had all paraded over to the chapel, the breeze catching Sissy's gown so that it billowed up around her as she hurried along, wind-driven and diaphanous.

Her own thoughts came back to her exactly. Sissy may think she's unhappy now, Alice had thought, but someday she'll thank me.

Just then the phone rang, and when Alice picked it up and said hello, Sissy asked, "Are you awake?"

Of course she was awake, she had just said hello, but Alice replied, "Yes, dear, I'm awake."

"Guess what. Eleanor called last night and said she'd love to go."

"Go where?"

"Mother! To London."

"Oh, I'm so glad. Won't we have a good time. Of course I remember, but I was distracted. Uncle John has written asking for money for Harrison and it was just occurring to me that it would be nice to give something as a memorial for Harold."

"That's a good idea," said Sissy, "I'll talk to Ned about it, but I called for a reason. Now that it's settled and you're going I think you need some new clothes."

Sissy, whose chief interest in life was shopping, was always providing Alice with new clothes, and Alice said, "But, darling, you've given me so much."

"I know it, but I like to do it. Besides, it will be cold in England."

"It's cold everywhere in March."

"I want you to have a new coat. Now don't say no, Mother. You can call it your birthday present. I'll have Jordan Marsh send out a selection. What about a new fur coat. Your poor old Persian lamb looks chewed up."

"It's perfectly good," said Alice.

"I'll send out three and you must take one."

"It's lovely of you, dear. Such an extravagant thing for you and Ned to do, but do you think I shall be able to keep Eleanor entertained? Her life is so drab and when I think of Jane . . ."

How had the conversation taken such a turn? They had been talking about coats and now suddenly they were dwelling on sorrows. "Eleanor will entertain herself," said Sissy. "After all, life goes on. We can't everlastingly moan about the past. Call me when the coats come. Bye now." And Sissy hung up.

13

Sissy chose three coats for Alice, all exquisite, but Alice had no trouble choosing the one she wanted. The sable was too extravagant. It might be suitable for London, but it was too showy for a woman her age from Boston. The sealskin was undoubtedly smart and sleek, but sealskin made a woman look aggressive, Alice thought, and she decided on the mink, which was lustrous and elegant. A woman in mink looked cherished.

When she phoned Sissy, Sissy said, "Oh, good, that was my favorite, too. A woman looks rich in mink. You will look elegant."

"That's what I thought too, darling. Thank you. What am I to do with the others?"

"I'll call the store and they'll send someone around for them. Probably today, so stay at home for a while."

"I will, and thank you again, both of you."

In mid-March Eleanor took the train to Boston the day before the flight and arrived at Sissy's in Wellesley via the Barringer limo. She was very excited. When Sissy saw her, she said, "What a nice coat. Blue is certainly your color." Was it possible Sissy had forgotten helping her find and buy it?

"Leave your bags there," commanded Sissy. "James will take them up. Let's have tea. Isn't it a horrid day. I hope you won't have to take off in a downpour. You'd think Mother was going to the moon, but it's her first flight and she's in a dither. . . . It's yours too, I almost forgot. Let's have a cup of tea."

"I'd love that," said Eleanor.

As they sat, sipping and talking, Eleanor almost felt herself already transported to the Savoy in London. She found herself imagining all sorts of things as she tried to listen to Sissy. As usual, Sissy had something odd to say. This time she was rattling on about wanting to paint again and her idea for a studio in Chatham.

"The thing is," said Sissy, "I haven't painted in years. I used to love to paint. Self-expression is very important to a woman. I'm convinced of it. There is a perfect place for a studio in the garage apartment in Chatham. Of course it needs remodeling. It will take a little time, and I know I will never be able to paint like Jane. . . . And by the way, how is Jane? How are your mother and Uncle John?"

Eleanor noted that Sissy didn't ask for Will, which meant that either she had stopped caring for him or had seen him recently. "They're all fine," she said. "Jane is . . ." What could she say about Jane, who seemed to grow more frail by the minute? She wished, oh, what did she wish? She wished they could start all over again. Bring Harold back for Jane, bring Charles for her. Let Sissy have Will . . .

"I suppose Jane doesn't get any better," said Sissy. "How could she? You must bring her something nice from England. And another thing, don't let Mother push you around. She thinks it is still 1921 in England. That's when she and my father went over and swilled gin and tea and stayed at the Savoy, and bought a set of Wedgwood, service for twelve of course. She'll find lots of changes, I expect."

When Sissy and Eleanor picked up Alice in the morning, she was wearing her mink and had two silk scarves knotted at her throat and hanging in streamers to her waist. She looked very smart and rich. She carried a leather pouch and poor Mrs. Briggs, flushed and panting, hobbled down the steps with one of the bags. James went for the rest, and, when Eleanor looked back as the limousine began to move, she saw Mrs. Briggs at the front door waving. Mrs. Briggs was surely glad to see the last of them, Eleanor thought, imagining the fun she would have drinking Aunt Alice's tea and splashing on her cologne and letting the dust accumulate all over the house.

When they had boarded the plane at last and were seated, Aunt Alice took a deep breath and said, "I am going to have claustrophobia. I can't breathe. What can I do with my coat? I had no idea it would be so cramped. I should never have come."

The old Aunt Alice would have treated this as a lark. One little peek through the curtains behind them would have revealed the coach seats and given her the feeling of being among the rich and privileged, and then she would have felt better.

Eleanor, whose seat was on the aisle, stood up and helped Alice shed her coat and, instead of stuffing it into one of the overhead cabinets, she folded it carefully and put it on an empty seat.

"Somebody is bound to sit on it," said Alice.

"Look," said Eleanor, "we're beginning to move."

This was an illusion. Some other vehicle was moving. When they really did begin to move the plane shuddered, the propellers roared, and the runway flowed away beneath them like a rushing stream.

"What is that awful racket," said Alice. "Are we going to have to listen to it all the way to London? What is all this bumping?"

"We'll get used to it, I should think," said Eleanor, who wondered uneasily if the plane sounded the way it was supposed to sound. Will or Charles would have known.

Eventually they were airborne, and when Aunt Alice was sure they were as safe as anyone in an airplane could be, she settled down with a magazine, pausing every five minutes or so to tell Eleanor what she remembered about her first crossing of the Atlantic.

"Oh, my dear, the dining rooms! The incredible displays of fresh fruits. Beluga caviar, champagne. We were so carefree. We had nothing to do but eat and sleep and walk the deck. We encountered the most fascinating people. Russians, for the most part, counts and princesses, who had escaped with nothing but the clothes on their backs and their jewels sewed into the hems of their dresses and the cuffs of their trousers."

Eleanor yawned. She was growing sleepy. It had something to do with the drone of the engines, the rushing of the wind as the plane labored its way across the ocean.

She didn't open her eyes again until they began their descent over Shannon.

When they were, at last, safe in their room at the Savoy, Aunt Alice recovered sufficiently to order tea, cress sandwiches, lemon tarts, and hot scones with strawberry preserves. It was actually breakfast time in Boston, but in London it was teatime. It would do nicely until they were bathed and rested and ready for dinner, but they surprised themselves by sleeping through until the next day.

By the time they had been in London for a few days, Aunt Alice began to grow restless. They had seen a play, visited Westminster, had tea at Brown's, been to Convent Garden. For Eleanor the days were passing too rapidly. There was still the Tower of London, St. Paul's, Parliament, the Speaker's Corner, more plays, Buckingham Palace, and the changing of the guard.

"Gracious, darling," said Aunt Alice, "do you really want to stand out there in the rain and watch soldiers dressed in red and black trade places at the gate? Bundle up. Your mother will be very cross with me if I let you catch cold."

The following day they toured Harrods and had lunch at Fortnums, where Alice had a case of shortbread shipped to Fresh Pond Park. It was packed in tin boxes and on the lid was a photograph of a Scotch warrior in his dress kilt and regalia.

"Who are they for?" asked Eleanor, and Alice said carelessly, "Oh, the children and friends, poor Mrs. Briggs and you must take some for Jane and your mother and the old ogre in the library."

"He's not an ogre and thank you very much, Aunt Alice."

"You're welcome, and will you once and for all call me Alice? When you say 'aunt' it makes me feel a hundred years old. Now run along and get a cab and go to the tower. I've seen it once and I don't need to see it again."

By the time Eleanor got back to the hotel it was getting late and she found Alice talking on the phone. Her face was flushed and her tone animated as she said, "Sally, darling, how many years has it been? Of course I'll come. Tomorrow? That would be lovely. Three Chimneys in Abingdon," she said. "Two doors from St. James's."

She put down the phone and said, "That was my old friend Sally Richmond. She married an Englishman in 1918 during the war. The Richmonds were very wealthy. I did hear the crash took most of it, but Sally escaped. She's asked us for tea tomorrow, but you needn't come unless you want to."

Eleanor wouldn't have missed it for the

world, and she had promised Sissy to look after her mother and she said, "I'd love to go. It sounds quite romantic."

"Well, then, you must come. It will be an adventure. We take the train from Victoria to Dorking and then a taxi to Sally. People said at the time that she had made a splendid marriage. Would you mind going back for the weekend if we're invited?"

"Of course not," said Eleanor.

Alice was nearly dressed for dinner and was taking great pains with her hair, which, in the damp of London, had gone rather limp. "What did you see?" she asked.

"The room where Sir Walter Raleigh was imprisoned for so long and the room the little princes occupied."

"Barbaric," said Alice. And then with a sigh, "That's the best I can do. At least it's still on my head and my head is on my neck."

The following afternoon they set out at two and by the time they reached Abingdon Alice was fluttering visibly. "St. James's," she called to the driver, "two doors down, or three. I can't remember. It's called Three Chimneys."

"Here you are, mum," he said, pulling up to a stone cottage that was nearly hidden behind a hedge of cedars. From the road it seemed a small, modest place and Alice said,

"I don't believe this is right. She said Three Chimneys and I see only two."

"This is right, mum, but I'll wait until you're in the door."

From the walk Eleanor could see what looked like a beautiful garden, brick enclosed, with a wide-arched entrance. Yellow flowers were in bloom, daffodils probably, and perhaps tulips, and she decided she would explore after tea and leave Alice to her old friend.

Alice was still muttering when they rang the bell, but when the door swung open she cried out, "Sally, darling, how wonderful to see you!"

"How lovely of you to come. I haven't seen a soul from home all winter."

"This is my friend Eleanor Hammond."

"How do you do," said Eleanor. "It's nice of you to include me."

"Come in, come in," said Sally, ushering them into a large living room with french doors opening toward the garden. There were framed photographs on every tabletop in the room, some handsome oriental rugs, and comfortable chairs. Sally said, "I am a little short-handed this afternoon, but I didn't think you'd mind."

Later, as they drove back to the Savoy, Alice would say to Eleanor that she imagined Sally had help only now and then. Poor Sally. The house was so small. However, as they settled down with the tea tray that seemed to have materialized while their backs were turned, Alice said, "What a dear, charming place, Sally. And you've been here all these years. Tell me about the family?"

"My husband died six years ago. Perhaps you knew that?"

"I didn't," said Alice, "and I'm so sorry."

"He was a wonderful man."

"What was his profession?"

Sally laughed and said, "He always called himself a farmer. What he really did was manage the estate."

"I'm sure you miss him greatly," said Alice, pegging Sally as the wife of an estate manager, which was not bad, of course, but not what she had expected.

"And children?"

"Oh, my, yes," said Sally, and she rose and crossed the room and came back with a family portrait showing her son, Randolph, and his wife and their four children.

"Oh, lovely," said Alice. "I hope they live nearby."

"They do," said Sally. "Perhaps someone will pop in while you're here."

As soon as she felt she could excuse herself, Eleanor asked if she might explore the garden.

"Of course you may, but do be careful. We've had so much rain there are lots of muddy places."

Eleanor said she would be careful and as she stepped out through the french doors she heard Alice say, "My beloved son, Harold, was killed in the war, but I do have Cornelia and her little boy. She married Ned Barringer. Perhaps you remember the Barringers?"

"The name seems familiar," said Sally.

And then the doors swung shut and Eleanor was free. She lifted her face to the sky, where clouds flew before the wind, and took a deep, deep breath. The garden would be incredible before long, but it was pretty now. There was a man in rubber boots raking under the bushes that stood along the brick wall, and when she spoke to him he gave her a startled look and touched his cap.

"Do you mind if I look around?"

"Look all you like, miss," he said, resuming his raking.

Glancing around, she spotted a great house in the distance, rising, like a castle in fairyland, above the trees that stood around it. "What a beautiful house," she said. "Who lives there?"

"The family, miss," said the gardener. "That is Lord Melville's house."

"And who is Lord Melville?"

"Her Ladyship's son."

"Oh, I see," said Eleanor.

"Her Ladyship moved down to the small house when Lord Melville died. She wouldn't stay in the big house without him, miss," and the gardener sounded so moved by this there was no mistaking who "Her Ladyship" was, or who had once occupied the big house.

What will Aunt Alice think when I tell her? thought Eleanor in exultation. If Alice knew who Sally was and if they were invited for a weekend, it would surely be a triumph. And yet as she thought it through, she decided it would probably be better not to mention it. If Her Ladyship had wanted them to know she would have made it clear, and then there would be the awkward business of wrangling an invitation. Even when they were flying home at the end of their two weeks and Alice remarked, as the plane hovered over Boston, that she felt sorry for poor Sally, who had grown up in an enormous house, even then Eleanor kept silent.

She did say, "But I thought Three Chimneys was charming." And Aunt Alice replied, "Oh, it was, darling, but so plain. I don't think there would have been anyplace for her to put us if she had asked us to stay."

"Perhaps not," said Eleanor. "But I loved the Savoy. What could have been nicer?"

"Nothing," said Alice. "It was splendid."

14

Jane died in November, escaping at last from a web of tubes and bottles and leaving behind an impression of sweetness that lingered like lavender in closed drawers. During the fall, as she slipped away from them, they began to adjust to the loss they would feel later, but when it came they were not prepared at all. To Eleanor, Jane had become a candle, flickering as the room darkened and the day ran its somber course until the flame became a glow and then a pinprick of light, and, at last, nothing more. Unless, perhaps, you could accept that Jane had become a silence too, in which the ringing of bells seemed to throb unheard.

As soon as friends and neighbors knew of their loss, there was a general outpouring of sympathy and sadness. It seemed to Grace that they were repeating those terrible days when people realized that Jane was very sick. Not just sore-throat, bad-chest sick, but deathly sick, with something there was no help or cure for. Thus Jane's death became the final act in the tragedy that was her life.

Among the first to appear was Doug Parsons. Not knowing what to bring, he appeared with a bottle of scotch, which he slipped to Eleanor at the door.

"This helps me through dark times," he said. "Just put it away for whoever needs it." And then he went in to John's study, where they sat and talked for almost an hour on the problems currently besetting preparatory schools and the part they were destined to play in a changing world.

When he confronted Eleanor again as he made his departure, he took both her hands in his and, holding them tightly, he said, "May flights of angels sing her to her rest. For she surely deserves it," he said in a gruff voice, and then he bolted down the steps and across the lawn.

Sissy and Alice came for the funeral, arriving at the chapel and joining the family there and at the house afterwards. Both wore black, both wore furs and carried the soft-grained leather bags that were the mark of a well-dressed woman, so that they seemed by their very appearance to enrich the occasion, as though the two of them arriving in a chauffeured limousine testified to all assembled that this was an event of consequence, that persons of wealth and power cared, that Jane was cherished and that her grieving family deserved support.

Afterwards, at the house, Grace's friends served coffee and cake, and Alice moved through the group, saying to strangers, "I am Alice Dwire. So good of you to come. How we will miss Jane. She was such a beautiful child."

Wilson had come alone. Val wouldn't leave the baby, he said, and she didn't think this was the time to bring Allison, but how wrong she was. A baby in the house would have balanced their loss as nothing else could have.

Wilson stood at the door with his father, greeting people who spoke of a Jane they had rarely seen in low voices. Then he went along into the dining room, where Grace, with flushed cheeks and shining eyes, poured coffee with hands that shook and talked quite naturally of her daughter, saying to most of those who came to the table, "I wish you'd just step into Jane's room and look at her paintings and sketches. They're on the bed. . . ." She waved her hand carelessly. "Well . . . all around the room," she said. "We tried to persuade her to make a book of them, but she was never satisfied."

Then, with a little gasp and turning aside, Grace said to anyone near her, "Let me give you a cup of coffee. It's such a cold day. I wouldn't be surprised if we had snow."

"Darling Grace," said Alice at last, when people were beginning to leave, "let someone else pour and you come sit with me for a while. I want to know all about that precious baby. Where are your pictures? I've brought some of Matthew. . . . He and Allison aren't too far apart, are they? Isn't that curious and wouldn't it be fun to see them together?" Then, taking Grace's arm, Alice led her into the living room, where they settled down together on the sofa in front of the fire.

Across the room Eleanor was talking to the Webbers, who were retiring in June. They were buying a house in Northridge, a tiny place that they would add to. She tried to listen. She could see Dave Edwards talking with her father, who nodded soberly, and she wondered what they were talking about. Dave and his wife were now divorced and he didn't look particularly happy. She had hoped she and Dave might have consoled each other in their state of marital endings, but there had never been more between them than a shared cup of tea. Suddenly she realized that the Webbers were still talking to her, and she said, "I'm so sorry, I missed that. What did you say?"

"We'll talk later, dear," said Margaret Webber. "It's time we left."

"Thank you for coming," said Eleanor at the door, and then, as they disappeared, she was finally free to join her father and Dave.

"It was good of you to come," she said.

"I'm sorry not to have come more often," he said. "Life has surely been difficult for all of you."

"Come again soon," she said.

Sissy and Wilson, who had been huddling together most of the afternoon talking, presumably, of the old days, had now joined the party and stood together in the front hall, speaking to people as they departed. "Yes, we'll miss her," said Will, and this sounded false to Eleanor, who knew how seldom Will came home.

The crowd was thinning out. In a minute there would be no one left but the women in the kitchen and the one or two old men who lingered with their father, hats in hand and reluctant to leave.

"Oh, God," said Sissy. "I feel so sad. Yesterday it was tennis rackets and sneakers and now today . . . isn't there anything to drink?" she asked desperately, looking hopefully around and then saying, "I suppose not. I suppose it's the same old 'no drink, no smoke' rule."

She clasped her hands together as though, in desperation, she felt the need of support and had no one there to draw it from except herself. Sissy suddenly looked drawn and thin, her pale-faced, dark-eyed beauty fading, and for some reason this touched Eleanor, who said, "People do drink and there are smoking parlors for students who think they can't live without it, but Mother and Daddy —"

"Oh, I know," said Sissy impatiently, glancing around restlessly and saying, "First Harold and then your Charles and now Jane. Where will it end?" And, turning to Wilson, she said, "I want to go for a walk. Take me for a walk, Will. I can't stand it here any longer."

"I ought to go," said Will, looking at his watch.

"You don't have to go," said Sissy. "I want to go for a walk. I can't stand it here. Look at them," and she waved her hand at their mothers. "Baby pictures," she said. "Please Will, just across to the chapel."

"Don't go tonight, Will," said Eleanor. "Can't you stay over just one night?"

The thought of being alone with her mother and father was almost too much for Eleanor to bear. What was there for her to do? The women in the kitchen were doing the dishes. There wouldn't be anything left to do but to put out the leftover food, sit down, bow their heads for the blessing, slip their napkins out of the napkin rings, and eat silently. Her mother would say again that people were kind, that they were fortunate to have such friends. Her father would agree. He would say that he missed Jane and that he was thankful she hadn't seemed to suffer at the end. And what would she say? wondered Eleanor, looking at Wilson and begging him silently to stay over.

"I have a full day tomorrow," he said, "I told Val I'd be back."

Eleanor nodded. She wasn't surprised. She knew Will was weak, that he couldn't bear unpleasantness. How often had he visited in the past few years, since Charles's death, or during the long, empty days of Jane's last illness?

"God," said Sissy in disgust. "Do what you want to do. I'm going out." She pulled her coat from the closet and opened the door and Will, without a backward glance, followed.

As Eleanor watched them disappear into the shadows, she knew that they were still lovers. She supposed she had always known that, although she felt it was none of her business, but why wasn't it? It would account for so many things. No wonder Val was half-crazy with jealousy. How many times had he been away needlessly when Val had needed help with Allison?

She turned back to the fire and the remainder of the family, and her father, who saw them disappear down the drive, said, "They won't be gone long. It's getting cold and the chapel's locked."

"Where is Sissy going?" called out Aunt Alice, belatedly anxious and then, grasping what John had said, she remarked, "The chapel locked? Why is the chapel locked?"

She went on in dismay. The chapel was never locked. How could that be? Why would anyone lock a chapel and separate the sinners from their only refuge?

"True, true," John murmured vaguely, "but boys can be destructive all the same."

This didn't seem to bother him particularly, or at least he gave no evidence of its validity. Boys had always been destructive, and there was no longer the respect for property that there had been in the old days. But, after all, it was the tradition of faith that mattered, and he thought of the wonderful men of Harrison and Andover and Choate and Exeter and Mount Hermon, ranked in the pulpits of their various chapels, all of them like ships' captains, piloting their schools safely over the shoals of sin and into the wide world beyond, where a dedication to worthy values would negate the baseness of life, and worse, the purposeless wandering of the uncommitted.

As long as those good and loyal men were revered and supported by trustees who were faithful to their founders, all would be well.

John remained at the door to his study waiting for some response to this, but none came. Grace and Alice had turned back to the fire and were murmuring about things, family, he supposed. The problem of the schools he had mentioned hadn't touched them, for they seemed to have accepted his view on such matters. But what he had said and what he felt to be true were two different things. The changes at Harrison and elsewhere shook him at the foundations of his being, despite his protestations to the opposite. Daily chapel had shrunk to one assembly a week and students now had no idea what vespers were. The dining hall was staffed with food-service people, meals were catered, trucked in, and served cafeteria-style. Milk and water pitchers had disappeared, and milk and water, as well as coffee, tea, and cola drinks, were dispensed from steel cylinders into plastic cups. No one said grace. Some faculty members still took their meals with the students, but as there was no assigned seating, there was no community and fellowship at table. There was, however, a lot of shoving and loud voices and roll throwing. I won't be sorry to retire, John thought. He had outlived his usefulness here, he felt.

And, to be truthful, he had also ceased to regard the trustees of Harrison, and their counterparts elsewhere, as infallible. They were busy men with heavy responsibilities who met four or five times a year to consider what their schools lacked and needed and how to achieve what they deemed was most pressing. Fifty years ago the trustees took for granted the need for a strong moral position in everything. With Christianity as its base, they were free to make school policy. Now, with changing times and a more cosmopolitan student body, no one seemed sure what was basic to the continued vitality and dedication of the school. Retirement, unwelcome as it might be, loomed as a possible escape, thought John.

Glancing across the room, he saw Sissy and Will leaving for their walk. A funny time to go for a walk, he thought. It was already getting dark and he thought he remembered hearing Wilson say that he needed to get back tonight. Something about Val and the baby. He couldn't remember what. Things were not going well for Will, and John wished they were closer. Not that they weren't on good terms. They were, but Will kept things to himself.

Eleanor was doing something in the kitchen. He could hear the sound of running water and the soft clink of silver and china. It had always been reassuring to him to hear the sounds of women's work in progress. Even Jane had hummed as she painted, bumped her wheelchair over the hump in the floor where they had added a ramp that connected the living room to her bedroom, and talked to the cat. The afghan that had covered her legs lay neatly folded in the seat of her chair. Her workbasket had been put on the window seat. Such reminders pained him, and he envied the men and women of the past who had believed in eternal life. Their conviction that Jane would have already been there, safely tucked into heaven as she waited for them to join her, was something he might hope for, but as it was he thought mostly about what her life had been. If she could have been well. If she could have run and laughed and played with her own children. If only there could have been more good days and good times.

But such had not been the case.

For a while after Jane's death, they simply moved through the days, doing what they could. The disposal of her possessions, her clothes, her needlepoint, her paints and books, the gifts she had been given through the years, her correspondence, was something Grace couldn't face.

"We can't take it with us, Grace," said John.

"Where are we going, John?" she asked wearily and he said, "We're going to retire," he replied.

Grace didn't like to talk about retirement. She would think of it when she had to, she told Eleanor. "When your father finally makes up his mind," she said.

Eventually things eased and the commonplace took precedence once more. One morning Grace looked up from the piece of toast she was buttering and said, "Today is the twenty-first. The shortest day of the year." And then, reaching for the jam, she said, "Now the days will be getting longer."

Will and Val came home for Christmas and for the first time Val let John hold his granddaughter. They were thinking about a house, Will said, and John replied that he thought it was a good thing to do. "We'll all be on the move," he said.

And then, with the coming of a new year Grace began to resume a social life. She was tired of that "big, empty house," she said, but what she meant was that she couldn't bear the loss of Jane's company and Jane's need of her. When Sally Thomas called and asked her to come to Literary at her house in February, Grace said yes. She had always liked Literary, but she was surprised at how much she enjoyed the meeting. Perhaps it was the sociability that she so enjoyed, she thought afterward. After all, she and Jane had survived on literature, but now, here she was among a welcoming group of women who understood her suffering and loss. This was like a rare elixir in her decimated life, a solace and consolation.

But things had changed in all those lost years, and some things were disturbing. There seemed to be so many young wives on campus and, while they seemed like nice girls, there was something strident and aggressive about them that disturbed her. They had a new vocabulary. They "focused" on "issues" and "rights." No one simply sewed for the naked and destitute of the world. Drives were arranged, lectures and courses were given, and intense people talked about cultural background of the alien needy. She was not sorry that retirement was coming.

Eleanor decided to upgrade her resume and signed up for a course in Library Science at UMass in the summer. On the strength of this, Doug Parsons shuffled into her cubbyhole of an office in the library one morning and said, "Well, well. So you're going to summer school. If you plan to work for your degree I would be inclined to put your name forward for librarian when I retire."

His announcement astonished her, and she blurted out, "Oh, but you can't retire."

"My dear," he said, beaming with pleasure, "of course I can retire. I am expected to retire. I am forced to retire and I do not view it as entirely unbeneficial. I intend to spend my few remaining years in riotous living."

The idea of Doug Parsons doing anything that could be described as riotous struck Eleanor as being absurd and she had the grace not to laugh. "Thank you," she said.

So this is the way life unfolds, she thought as she cataloged new books. Doors opened and closed. Students came and went. Days became weeks. What had been raw grief at the time of Jane's death was now softening. She passed Dave Edwards on the campus and he spoke. She went to see Sissy in Wellesley one weekend and foolishly unburdened herself. "I'll never marry again," she said. "No one ever appears that I could be interested in. Nothing ever happens."

"Nothing ever happens unless you make it happen," said Sissy. "Believe me, Eleanor. I know."

15

Sometime after Jane's death Eleanor realized that something odd had happened to her. When she looked in the mirror she saw her mother. Brushing her hair and putting on lipstick helped, but as she went down the back stairs and into the warm kitchen, where Grace was stirring hot cereal, their two persons seemed to fuse, and Eleanor heard herself speaking in her mother's voice, saying, "What a beautiful day. Isn't that a pair of cardinals at the feeder?"

The cheerful voice, the hopeful observation. She had become her mother, taking on the role naturally. How had this happened? But of course she knew. It had happened when Jane died and her father took up the ramps, storing them in the garage in the event of another wheelchair, when the best of Jane's paintings were framed and others put into folios that were kept in a chest in the front hall and taken out to show visitors who asked to see them. That's when it had happened.

Eleanor picked up the milk pitcher and sugar bowl and put them on the dining table, then the toaster and their napkins, rolled carefully and inserted in the carved ivory rings.

"Thank you, dear," said Grace, bringing in the coffee and calling, "John, breakfast is ready," in a tired voice. She sat patiently behind the coffeepot until he appeared and sat down and said, "God bless this food to our use and us to thy faithful service, Lord. Amen." And then, snapping open his napkin and laying it across his lap, he said, "Where's my coffee, Mother?"

He and Eleanor spoke in cheerful voices, but Grace had used every decibel of cheer that would ever be hers to command in the long years of Jane's illness, and now she said very little about anything. Overnight they had all become old. Her father was now sixty-four, her mother was fifty-nine, and she was on the near side of thirty. People said, "Things will improve. It takes a long time. After all, you don't erase twenty years of suffering in a minute." Words painted the familiar picture of a desert bounded by illness.

Curiously, she found that the things people mentioned, the loss, the void, the pain, scarcely entered her thoughts. It was the host of deadening practices that supported them and in so doing eroded life: the folded napkins in the sideboard drawer, the double boiler of oatmeal, sheets changed on Monday, the ever unanswerable question, "What shall we have for dinner?" She wondered if Charles's mother and father attempted to put their sorrow aside for such questions. Somehow she doubted it.

What would she do if she couldn't escape to the library? she wondered. Coming up the hill at dusk, surrounded by students panting toward their dorms, shouting to one another as they made their way toward meat loaf and scalloped potatoes in the dining hall, Eleanor plodded along in her old polo coat and wondered if any of the family would ever come alive again.

And then one day in January it was announced that a new wing was going to be added to the library, a visual-aids wing, honoring Dr. Parsons. She was glad Doug was to be honored, he deserved it, and she made a cake and took it for coffee time in his office.

"A cake," he said, "for me. A whole cake?"

"Yes," she said, "and I hope it's fit to eat. I haven't made a cake in years." It was just what her mother might have said, she realized in dismay.

The cake was discovered by any number of people. According to Doug, it did noble service, and she knew that he had asked Dave to come and try it because she had heard him on the phone. In his bumbling old bachelor way, he may have wished to see two friends united in a life dedicated to knowledge and literature, but Dave was busy. She had a feeling Dave would always be busy, divorced or not.

Now and then Eleanor thought about England, where she had felt wonderfully alive. What would be better than to honeymoon in England? she thought, but she wasn't eager to marry anyone at the moment. At least she wasn't ready to think about marrying anyone. She would probably go on at the library, taking early retirement because there was Charles's money to fall back on. Suppose she retired when she was forty-five. Would she be honored by a shelf in the stacks called the Eleanor Hammond Collection? At fifty-five would she be asked to officiate at the dedication of a rare book room, and at sixty-five would some artistic alum perhaps be commissioned to paint her portrait, which would be hung over one of the fireplaces in the reading room? Probably nothing as grand as that, but maybe a party for the faculty with coffee and fruit punch at which she would be presented with a first edition of *Uncle Tom's Cabin*.

She came up the stairs from a basement lab

(to be replaced with the Parsons Wing) where students who had the money for materials could develop their own film, and she bumped into Dave Edwards.

"Sorry," she said, looking up.

"My fault," he replied. "I didn't see you."

"That's all right," she said, "nobody does."

He gave her a sharp look and she smiled. Let no one say, she thought, that poor Eleanor Hammond . . . who? You know, the librarian, that mousy person, has no sense of humor.

"Poor Eleanor," he said, grinning at her, "why so down?"

"I am not down," she replied.

"Good. Tell your father I'll be around to see him soon. I didn't realize he was retiring in June."

"I'm not sure he realizes it either."

"Ah," he said, "so that's the way it is," and he consulted his watch, a round steel thing on a stretchy band that ought to belong to an engineer with a weathered face.

"It's about time to lock up," he said. "Mind if I walk along and have a word with your father today?"

"Fine," she said.

They walked up the hill in a throng of students. Boys overloaded with books stumbled along, putting distance between themselves and their last class, jostling, shouting, barking obscenities, and then nodding self-consciously at Dave and Eleanor as they brushed past, muttering "Sir," and "Pardon," and disappearing through dorm doors that swung and slammed at regular intervals.

"The days are getting longer," she said, although it hardly seemed so. Shadows lay like discarded rags on the dingy snow, through which dead grass was emerging. I sound like my mother, she thought.

"Yes," he replied. "We'll be putting our clocks ahead before we know it."

Was it possible he sounded like his father? she wondered with a small shock of recognition, and she looked at him closely, saw that he was hunched against the cold, his Harris tweed jacket too light for the weather and his scarf hanging limp and useless around his neck. As they came into the yard she could see her father's desk light and, pausing at the door, she said, "You'll have to stay for tea. They'll insist."

"Fine," he said.

As they entered, Grace emerged from the kitchen. "Oh," she said in surprise, "company."

"You remember Dean Edwards, Mother."

"Of course I remember you, Dave. Come in."

"He wants to see Daddy."

"I have the kettle on," said Grace happily as she led them into the study calling out, "Company, John," raising her voice only a little because she didn't wholly believe in his deafness and she often wondered if it was simply that he had grown inattentive. Frequently Grace thought that if this were true it might be deliberate, and now and then she even spoke sharply to him.

In the kitchen she set up the tea cart, taking down her Spode pot and china cups. "Fix a plate of cookies, Eleanor," she said as she sliced a lemon and filled the milk jug.

"Lemon or milk?" asked Grace, looking around with a bright smile as she poured. The rattle of cups and spoons, the snapping fire, the sudden burst of conversation brought life into the room. Eleanor hardly needed to listen to her mother or note the unusual heartiness in her father's voice to feel uplifted. A new face and a new voice halted momentarily their sad plunge toward oblivion, for it seemed to Eleanor that her father's approaching retirement had rendered him helpless. He seemed to shed vitality as a balding man sheds hair and, daily, animation faded in her mother.

Suddenly her father left his chair to tend the fire. Ordinarily indifferent to showers of sparks, he now took up the poker and pushed the logs together. Jauntily knocking a pine-cone toward the blaze and settling the screen securely, he sat down with a contented sigh. Turning to Grace, he said, "Dave wants to know if I think Alice might be interested in making a significant gift to the school. What's your reaction to that?"

"It seems to me," said Grace, "that I remember your writing just such a letter some time ago."

"So I did," he said. "I suppose I should have followed up. The question before us, however, is this: Does Alice have enough money to make a significant gift to the school, or does she not?"

"I should put in here," said Dave, "that Mrs. Dwire has always supported the annual fund and the Dwire scholarship fund. At one time in the past she was invited to contribute meaningfully to the development fund. She never responded to this."

"I don't know what she might think about it, or if she has money of her own," said Grace, stirring her tea vigorously. What, after all, did she *really* know about Alice? she wondered, remembering all the impositions of the past, and she said, "Has Alice any money?"

"People seem to think so," said Dave. He leaned forward to take another cookie. Peg never made cookies. She usually bought enough Girl Scout cookies to stock a tea room.

"Well," said Grace, "there is Sissy, but of course it's Ned's money."

"One can always ask," said Eleanor.

"In that case," said Dave to John, "would you mind broaching the subject again? There is a feeling that a request from you would be stronger than another plea from the trustees."

John laughed. "Alice would be more impressed if the trustees, individually, showered her with attention. What do you think, Eleanor?"

Eleanor thought if Aunt Alice could buy something spectacular and present it to the headmaster of Harrison at commencement, that she might be tempted to do so. A new organ for the chapel, perhaps, given in memory of Elliot Dwire, although the present organ was played more and more seldom.

"I've no idea," she said.

"Well, if anything occurs to you, let me know. Thanks for the tea, Mrs. Richards."

"Come anytime," Grace said, accompanying him into the front hall. "My, it's dark," she remarked. "Here it is, almost February. The days ought to be getting longer."

Dave wound his scarf twice around his neck while her father continued discussing what little he knew of Alice Dwire's finances, and Eleanor touched his arm. "We're going to

277

make him late for dinner, Daddy," she said.

"Eat here, my boy," replied her father heartily.

"Another time. Thanks."

Eleanor followed him onto the porch, hugging herself and shivering. "It's cold," she said.

"Better go in . . . and thanks for the tea."

"Anytime."

He started down the steps and she called after him, "I doubt she has any real money, but you never know."

Standing under the porch light, she looked small and girlish and it occurred to him that she must be having a thin time. "How about dinner sometime?" he asked.

She nodded. "Fine," she replied.

As he went down the drive the chapel clock began to strike. Six o'clock. In the distance she saw the post lights that marked the walk to the dining hall. If she watched long enough she would see him pass under them as he went rapidly up the hill to supper. What would it be tonight — sausage and baked potatoes or shepherd's pie? — and she imagined him in the cafeteria line, serving himself beets and canned corn, sitting down finally at a table where nine boys were already pushing things around on their plates and growling about the size of each other's desserts. She could remember when meals were served to students who were required to wear coats and ties. In those days the married faculty were invited for special events like Thanksgiving. She could remember the clamor of boys pushing toward assigned tables, the dinner bell, the utter silence as the headmaster rose to give the blessing. Then there was the scuffle to be seated and the passing of vegetable dishes around the table. As the meal progressed, her father always found the time to speak to each boy by name.

Shivering and upset as the ghost of her past materialized before her, she went into the house and closed the door. In the kitchen her mother put the teacups and saucers in the sink.

In the study her father sat at his desk.

In the dining room Eleanor opened the sideboard drawer and took out knives and forks for supper.

16

Eleanor didn't mark on the calendar when Dave first asked her for dinner, but she remembered the date anyway. It was during exams, that terrible time of year when it usually snowed, radiators banged, the wind blew new snow in clouds of fine powder that whirled around her with stinging force, sanded roads froze overnight. People who didn't know how to drive on icy roads ended up in the ditch.

Now they had dinner occasionally, spending conversation time on such entrancing stuff as the projected addition to the library. Dave rarely gave her much time to think about it. When the mood was right he called. If the mood was right, she accepted.

The phone was ringing as she came into the house that afternoon, and, as she pulled off her boots and hung up her coat, she heard Grace calling her.

"It's for you," said Grace. "I think it's Dave."

Eleanor took the receiver and said hello and he replied, "How would you feel about Kelly's for dinner tonight?"

Kelly's was a quiet, steamy place where the fried clams were good and the booths private. Kelly's was a habit that had, over the years, become a tradition with faculty who retired to Northridge and celebrated the fact at Kelly's.

"We'll do better than that another time, but I have a stack of papers to read tonight."

"That is one thing I'm spared," she said, "but I sympathize. Kelly's it is."

She put down the phone and went into the kitchen. "That was Dave. He's asked me out."

"Tonight?" said Grace. "Oh dear, we're having pot roast for dinner. Wouldn't you like to ask him here tonight and go out another night? It's such a bad night. The radio says it's turning icy."

"We'll be all right," said Eleanor. "I'm going to take a quick shower and if he comes early let Daddy entertain him."

"It's so cold," Grace said. "Do you think you ought to take a shower when you'll be going out so soon?"

"I won't wash my hair. Would that make you feel better?"

"Yes," said Grace.

She was half-dressed when he arrived, but she didn't hurry. He never gave her much warning. It was diminishing, she thought, as though she were always an afterthought. But that was forgetting Peg. She still blushed when she thought of stopping unannounced and finding Peg at home. If she had known what Peg had meant to him . . . but she didn't. For all she knew Dave saw Peg regularly, but she hoped not.

She pulled on a blue turtleneck and stepped into her skirt, shook her head, and gave her hair a quick brush. She had heard the bell ring when he arrived and now, as she came down the stairs, she heard Dave say, "I don't mean to put you on the spot. I don't believe in hounding people to give to the school."

"Not at all," said her father. "As a matter of fact, to get anything significant from Mrs. Dwire would require hounding. I haven't pursued things, but to tell the truth there has been so much going on. . . ."

So much going on . . . Eleanor was amazed. What had been going on? Breakfast, lunch, dinner. Who had called or come by? No one that she knew of. Pulling on her coat, she went into the study, interrupting what might otherwise become a long conversation. "I'm ready," she said.

"It's getting icy," he replied.

★ ★ ★

Settled in a booth, they talked of usual things. Exams were over and he was relieved. At the library there were more new books to catalog than any one person could be expected to handle. And now, more pressing, they discussed what specials had been scribbled in chalk on a piece of slate that hung over the bar. Early conditioning had taught Eleanor to take the special, whatever it was. Tonight it was corned beef and cabbage or sirloin tips with mushrooms.

"What to drink," said Dave, "wine, beer, or booze?"

"I'd like a glass of sherry," she said.

"And a beer for me."

"Light or dark?" asked the waitress.

"Dark."

"Domestic or —"

"Domestic," he replied.

"Well," said Dave, "that takes care of that. What do you see that you'd like? How about the prime rib? That's usually good."

"What are we celebrating? Think of it — prime rib on a Wednesday."

"Have it," he said. "I am currently solvent."

"You're beginning to know me almost too well."

"I know more about you than you might think."

"Really," she said. "And I know too little about you."

"What would you like to know?" he asked, taking his beer from the waitress before she poured it and put a head on it. "Fire away," he said.

She smiled and said, "Eventually."

"Eventually what?"

"Eventually I will know more about you."

"Meanwhile, how are things going?" he asked.

She shrugged. "More or less as usual."

The waitress brought their salads and a choice of dressings in a stainless compartmented dish. "French, thousand island or blue cheese?" she asked.

They both took the blue cheese and watched as she dribbled it around on the top of a pile of lettuce garnished with some slivers of tomato.

The waitress turned away and Eleanor said, "And what is it exactly that you think you know about me?"

"Well," he said, "do you remember when you first came to see me about a job? Before I even had time to offer you a chair you said, 'My mother recommends a spot in the library or the alumni office.' "

"And what's so funny about that?"

" 'My mother,' " he said. "There you were

in need of a job and, I presume, wanting a job, and you said, 'My Mother.' You sounded ten years old. I wanted to put my arms around you on the spot. I phoned Doug and didn't get much encouragement from him, but he changed his tune before you'd been there a week."

He laughed and she blushed. She wouldn't tell him that she had found him attractive instantly and had been dismayed to realize that she could feel that way about anyone just then. "Well why didn't you?" she asked.

"Why didn't I what?" he said.

"Put your arms around me and comfort me and take me out?"

"I planned to, sooner or later," he said.

"But you didn't."

"Well, you know," he said. "There was Peg, things weren't settled. I was embarrassed the day you stopped in." He shrugged.

"It's just as well," she said. "We both needed time."

"Time has passed," he said. "Now what . . ."

She sighed. "So many things," she said. "All the changes that are coming. Mother and Daddy have got to move in June and they haven't done anything about a house. They won't be able to find anything in Northridge and they haven't money enough to get what they'd like to have."

"Well," he said, "there's one thing you have to remember. Nobody gets rich teaching. There are trade-offs, of course — housing, utilities, things they haven't had to think about for years. . . ."

"I know," she said, "but it seems to be such a shame."

"It's a fact of life," he said roughly, taking her hands and holding them tightly, holding her hands so tightly they began to hurt, and for the first time in months she was feeling something.

In bed at night she had often wondered if she would ever feel anything again or if she would go on forever devoid of feeling. What could make her care again? But now Dave's hands crushing hers filled her with emotion and she said, "I know. I know all about faculty housing and salaries and growing up in a beautiful house that will never belong to the family. I know about all that."

He nodded and his grip eased. "All right," he said, "I had to say it. And now we can start where we should have started a year ago, two years ago. What a waste."

"But not too late," she said. "Never too late."

17

One brisk day in February, John and Grace drove across the river to Northridge. The sun on the snow was dazzling and all the charms of a New England village were on display. Large, square, white houses with ells and barns stood well back from Main Street. Trees lined the street, and standing in the village green was a granite marker engraved with the particulars of an Indian attack at that spot that ended with the burning of the first settlement there. There seemed to be everything to recommend Northridge for retirement, including the fact that many former faculty at Harrison had resettled there and even gone so far as to buy lots in the Green Meadow Cemetery.

Grace wasn't sure what she wanted in a house, having a scaled-down version of Drury House in mind, and she sat in the car and looked helplessly around and wondered which house John had chosen.

"Now, Mother," he said. "Don't expect too

much. It's a small house but it's well built and there's not much on the market in our range. It was built in 1936, I think, before the war when good materials were available."

"If you like it, I'll like it," said Grace.

John sighed. He wasn't sure this was true and, when he turned down School Street, which was perpendicular to Main, he sensed by the little intake of breath and stiffening of spine that Grace was not pleased. He turned into the drive, which had been plowed, and said, "Now just remember, we don't have to take it."

It was a white clapboard half cape with dormer windows front and back. Black shutters graced the windows and the front entrance. Although there was snow on the field behind the house, the gravel drive was muddy and the flagstones on the front stoop were smeared by the boots of househunters. It was the kind of house friends called sweet, or charming, and others called a box.

"Well," said John. "Here it is."

School Street houses were built on narrow lots that slanted toward the river. There were sleds leaning against the back entries of the houses, and John supposed that in the summer it would be bicycles. Bushes grew too close for comfort around the foundations of most of the houses, all in need of pruning.

"Which one is it?" asked Grace.

"Number Eighteen," he said. "Do you want to go in?"

Grace, who didn't like the house or the street or the realtor's sign or the sleds and bushes, managed not to say anything.

"I've got the key," said John.

"We're here," said Grace. "We might as well."

"There isn't much of anything in our price range," said John. "We'll just take a quick look. It may not be so bad."

The following afternoon they went back and this time they took Eleanor with them. She had listened to them discussing it and wondered why they bothered to show it, but as they came slowly down School Street her mother said, "Look at the sun on the snow, John. Isn't that beautiful? The sky looks as though the whole world is on fire."

"I like a western view," said her father. "I didn't notice that yesterday."

As they started up the walk, which had been spread with loose gravel, Eleanor said hopefully, "It is small, but you won't be needing as much room."

"You don't like it," said Grace.

"I'm not going to live in it. If you and

Daddy like it, I like it. I just need to get used to it."

As they went slowly up the path to the front door her mother said, "You can see the possibilities. There seems to be an asparagus bed and a rock garden on the other side. All it needs is a little weeding."

Grace's tone suggested they would spend the summer on their knees, happily pulling weeds out of the rock garden and from among the asparagus ferns.

Eleanor couldn't see any possibilities. It was a narrow, sloping lot with a tangle of grapevines drooping from rusty wires stretched between two rotting fence posts at the back. Bushy lilacs with base roots as thick and gnarled as the contorted arthritic fingers of the very old grew halfway across the drive. A gargantuan pine dominated the front lawn, its bulk obstructing the sun and its rusty needles smothering the grass.

She followed them up the uneven gravel walk to the front door, where her father struggled with the lock. The plate and handle of the fixture had been worn to the base metal and the key scraped as it was forced to turn.

"Easily mended," he muttered. "They'll have to do something about it."

The empty rooms inside were frigid. As they walked through the house commenting on the dimensions of the rooms and the patterns of the wallpaper, which was either striped or flowered, Eleanor was reminded of staff houses at Harrison. It was possible, she reflected, to make such houses bright and welcoming, but never open and gracious like faculty residences. She heard herself exclaiming in a high, artificial voice about the abundant kitchen cabinets and the fireplace that was framed with terra-cotta tile.

Their footsteps echoed as they passed from room to room, into the kitchen, and back up the narrow inner hall to the front again. Climbing a flight of steep stairs, they prowled in and out of two under-the-eaves bedrooms and looked down on the world from narrow dormers, while Grace talked about furniture and curtains and John thumped the walls.

Downstairs again, he moved about, rapping the plaster and making notes in a small spiral notebook. He was looking for studs he said, measuring for shelves, trying to explore all the possibilities Grace was so confident existed, although it seemed to Eleanor that as his fist pounded on the walls of this, his final abode, he was simply pounding in despair, wondering whether he might discover a way out.

"You know, Daddy," she said in an undertone, "even if you've signed a contract there might be some way of getting out of it. I do have Charles's insurance. I'd be glad to put it in the pot."

"No," he said abruptly. "There's nothing else available. We need a smaller house . . . at our age . . . we have to consider upkeep and heating. It suits us well enough."

Going into the kitchen, Eleanor found her mother standing at the sink, gazing across the yard. It will be better, thought Eleanor fiercely, when there are dishes in the sink and a teakettle on the stove.

"I always like a kitchen sink where I can see to the back," said Grace.

"I do too," said Eleanor.

"I think we can fit the kitchen table in all right. Over there."

"I should think so, and there is the back porch."

"Yes," said her mother vaguely, remembering a time when she would have given almost anything for a screened porch on which to have their meals in the summer. How little it mattered now. She turned around, her eyes blank with resignation and her expression bleak. "There's no pantry," she said.

"I know," replied Eleanor.

Later that week Dave phoned her to ask about a book.

"It's just come in," she said. "I'm fixing a cup of tea. It's freezing here, a pipe has burst somewhere, I suppose. Come and join me."

The kettle was whistling by the time he appeared and water steamed from the spout as she poured it out. "We haven't lemon or milk, but plenty of sugar."

"Sugar's fine," he said. "Tell me about the house."

"It's a terrible house," she replied. "The lot is narrow and the people across the street have junk all over the yard. The lawn is so uneven it will be hard to mow and there's no downstairs bedroom or bath."

She nursed her mug in her two hands and thought that it was a mean house. Her parents, who had always lived graciously, with the lawn mowed by the campus crew, would feel deprived. They would have to sell half of their furniture or let the Salvation Army take it away.

"You don't get rich teaching," Dave said. "Retirement income is low, but you grew up in a palace compared to many. They've lived well. You can't say they haven't known what to expect."

She nodded.

"I'm telling you," he said urgently, leaning forward and taking her hands in his, "anyone who marries a teacher can forget about money."

His insistence suddenly began to seem ludicrous. He knew she was aware of all this. How could he imagine she didn't know about campus life? She had never really known any other way, and yet the urgency in his voice touched her. After all, they had played this scene before at Kelly's. Wasn't he sure whom he was talking to? What would it take to make him realize she understood? It was campus life, like the compound life of missionaries, like the isolated lives lived by people shut up in castles. She burst out, "I know. I know all about faculty salaries and growing up in a beautiful house that will never belong to the family. I know all that."

He nodded and his grip eased.

"That was one of the problems, wasn't it?" she asked. "Peg didn't like campus life. She didn't want to live on the reservation."

"Partly."

"I've been spoiled," she said. "I like a big old house even when the radiators bang and the furnace won't work. You're absolutely right. They have always known what to look forward to."

She shivered. "It's cold down here. Will it ever get warm? What a miserable spring."

"Believe me," he said, leaning toward her,

"they have always known what to expect. It may even be a relief to them to live in a smaller place. Less to heat, fewer windows to wash."

"You're right. I know you are. It's just that we're so used to Drury House."

"I know," he said, "and what about you?"

"I'll go into school housing, I suppose, and one of these days I'll be able to ask you over for dinner."

"I won't refuse."

"You'd better not."

18

During the time his parents were buying the Northridge house, Wilson and Val were looking for a house in Connecticut. They had an agent in Darien, and on Saturdays they would get into the car and drive up the Connecticut Turnpike to consult Frank Phipps of Fairview Realty and look at what he had to show them. To date they had seen and rejected a half-Cape on an acre of unmowed grass, a three-story Victorian with a wraparound front porch, and a countless number of small houses all flanked by narrow lawns and carpets with breezeways. They had made a half a dozen trips and were beginning to think that there was no point looking in Darien unless they could put twice as much into a house when Mr. Phipps called Wilson one day in March.

"Frank Phipps here," he said. "I hope you're coming out this weekend. I've got the place you want."

"We hadn't planned to," said Wilson.

"This one won't be on the market long. I thought of you first and let me tell you, it will go fast."

"I see."

"It has everything you want. Three bedrooms, a nice neighborhood, a beautiful yard. It's convenient to schools, there's a new shopping center opening soon just three miles down the road. It's not far from the station, it's brick, it's on town water and sewer . . ."

They went out on Saturday and signed a contract. It had all the things Mr. Phipps said it had and one more besides. It had a fallout shelter.

"When this house was built five years ago a lot of people wanted them. People don't much want them now, but at the time most people thought it was a good idea," he said, dismissing the atom bomb, the possibility of an attack, the chances of a nuclear disaster, Russia, the Holocaust, and anything else that might upset them and spoil his sale.

Wilson, who hadn't seen a furnace since he'd lived at home, inspected the new furnace (another of Mr. Phipps's pluses) as though he actually knew what to look for, but Val went over to the fallout shelter and switched on the light.

"But wouldn't the electricity go out if there was an attack?" she asked.

"There's a generator in there somewhere," said Mr. Phipps, adding cheerfully, "I'll tell you what some people do, they use them for wine cellars."

Mr. Phipps's tone suggested that it might be possible, even pleasurable, to struggle through a nuclear attack imprisoned in one's own wine cellar, but neither Val nor Wilson was paying much attention to Mr. Phipps. Each of them was thinking how a house would change their lives. For Val it was the possibility of living like real people, with neighbors and a school down the street where Allison could go. It was a whole new chorus of sounds replacing the ever present undertone of New York traffic, the wail of sirens, and the scream of brakes.

For Will it was a solution to his troubles. He could simply stay in town late, meet Sissy as usual, and take a late train home. God, he thought, doesn't the air smell good out here, and he put out his hand and reached for Val's and for the first time in months they smiled at each other.

"Not bad," he said.

"Not bad," she replied.

The thought of moving acted like a tonic on Val, who began at once to sort and pack the remnants of their life together in the city. She had things left over from college hanging at the back of her closet, baby things stuffed into grocery bags for disposal. She was ashamed to offer them to the church, so she called the Salvation Army and as they disappeared with bags and boxes of clean, but stained, underwear and outgrown or out-of-style things, she felt as though she was coming out of hibernation, shedding her skin, and exposing herself to the light and warmth of the sun. It will be different, she thought. It's got to be.

While she was scrambling around trying to sort books and records, Mr. Phipps in Darien was trying to put together the jigsaw puzzle of a loan. "A thirty-year mortgage," he told Will jubilantly over the phone, and Will groaned. He would be sixty-seven before it was paid off, but he was beyond caring about long-range problems, and he thought grimly that a move of this sort ought to solve problems, not compound them. At least Val appeared to be satisfied.

Sissy knew all about the move to Darien, and couldn't see why Will thought it would make things easier for them both. How could she move to Chatham while he moved to Darien and consider it an improvement? Most of this had transpired when she was in Paris with Ned. If she had been on the scene, she could have persuaded Will to wait for a raise and then upgrade his housing in the city, but she hadn't been, and now she and Ned had plans for Vienna. What impossible thing would Will do while she was gone? Well, she thought, we'll be together tonight. That ought to help.

They were to meet at their usual place, and while she waited she ordered a martini. She didn't mind waiting. She liked to sit and sip and look around and remember all the happy times they had had here. Everyone knew them and greeted them when they came in, but no one knew who they actually were. There was something exciting about that, thought Sissy, but lately meeting this way hadn't been as thrilling as it used to be. She didn't know why. Will was always in a bad mood these days, and he had begun to talk about divorce again. What sort of person would buy a new house for his wife and talk about divorce at the same time?

They had always talked about divorce. After Matthew was born she would have bundled him up and rushed off to Reno, or to wherever Will was, and she wouldn't have cared if she was divorced or not, just as long as they could be together.

That was before Val. When he married Val things seemed hopeless, and they would have been if it weren't for Ned's money. All that money that she hadn't cared about suddenly began to do things for her. She bought whatever she wanted. She would just say, "Charge it," and whatever it was was charged and delivered. There was an advantage in being known. Wherever they went in Paris people made room for them, greeted them, waiters and drivers and clerks and hotel managers. And then, when she and Will were together, they were alone. They could do anything they wanted to do, just as long as they were careful not to be recognized.

Where is he? she wondered. Why is he so late again?

And suddenly, there he was, his cheek brushing hers, his smile, his greeting the same as always. What would she do if he ever left her?

The waiter may not have known Will's name, but he knew what Wilson wanted to drink. It was there almost as Will sat down, and Will took it and swallowed it raw.

"Darling," Sissy said, "you gulped that. Has it been an awful day?"

"So-so," he replied. "You didn't sound very keen on coming."

"I always want to come," she said, reaching across the table and drawing his hand to her face, where she caressed it and kissed it and said, "Don't be cross. Things will work out.

Chatham's not so far and it will be nicer. Ned never wants to go to the Cape anymore. Or is it Vienna you're upset about? It's just a trip, just two weeks and I want to go, and besides we're not leaving for a few more weeks."

"There's always something," he said. "I'm getting too old to play this sort of game. What is it going to be like five years from now? Ten years from now? Will we still be ducking around corners and eating in some offbeat place because someone might spot us and ring the bell?"

"It's going to get better," said Sissy. "Everyone's going to be more settled. Val and Allison are going to be happy in Darien. She won't mind if you don't come home on time."

"She minds now," he said grimly, "if you think she doesn't know about us, you're mistaken. It's like poison in her."

"Then divorce her. It would solve at least half our problems."

"How? What about a divorce for you, too?"

"I don't have your kind of problem, Will. Ned is years older than I am. I don't think it ever occurs to him to wonder what I do. Why should I get a divorce when I'm free to do as I please? Divorce is so messy. I have everything I want now, except you, but we do see each other and I love you so much. One of these days you and I will go on trips and when the time comes I'll have the money to pay for it. Ned can't live forever, and —"

"My God," Will said, "do you sit and count your money and hope he dies soon? That really gets to me."

"Well," said Sissy, "money isn't everything, but it comes close. Of course I don't wish him dead and I'd hate to see him suffer, but it's stupid not to look ahead and think about things."

"Let's eat," said Will abruptly.

"Good," said Sissy. "Let's not talk about things like that. It makes me feel creepy. Let's just go home and make love and forget all about everything and everybody."

19

March seemed to slide right past April into May. Now and then Dave called Eleanor and they went out for dinner or to a movie. They were growing used to each other. They sat side by side in the movies, holding hands, and sometimes, in tense or heartbreaking scenes, she didn't realize until afterward that her hand ached from holding his so tightly. He didn't comment, but he noted it all the same because it told him how she felt, what moved her, and what she could care about. He wanted to kiss her long before he did, but when they finally got around to it, it seemed natural and sweet and promising.

Sometimes she saw him daily, sometimes not. Often he would say that he meant to call sooner, but had been stampeded by end-of-the-year problems.

"I'm not surprised," Eleanor replied. "Traffic in the library has been a bit thick. Exams usually do it."

"It's always this way," he said morosely. "Who am I going to have to flunk? Who isn't going to make the college of his choice? What little bastard is going to skip out after lights-out and get caught with a beer in the Blue Light? I've been in this rut too long," he said, "I might as well quit."

"What would you do then?"

"I might resume laboring on my doctor-ate."

"That sounds all right."

"I would if I had the energy. I am rapidly becoming an old fogey."

"So you are," she said, but of course he wasn't and wouldn't be for at least another thirty years.

"Thank you," he said, "I asked for that. How about dinner tonight?"

"Fine," she said. "I'd like to."

"How are things with the house shaping up?"

"Slowly," she said, "but it looks unavoid-able, I'm afraid. I begin to think they like it."

"We'll talk about it later," he said.

Grace already had the table set.

"I should have called," said Eleanor. "Dave and I are going out."

"That's nice," said Grace. "Why don't you

ask him here sometime?"

"I will. I have."

"I know. You like to be alone. I can remember. Have a lovely time and while you're with him ask him if he wants to come over and look at Daddy's books. We can't move them all. Of course the library should take some of them. What do you think?"

"Doug's mentioned it. Just tell Daddy to take what he wants and leave the rest on the shelves. Then we can all make a dive for them."

They hadn't been to Kelly's for some time, but it suited them tonight. The booths offered privacy of a sort. The lights were dim, candles flickered on the tables, even the specials looked good.

"You're tired," he said.

"Yes, aren't you?"

"I suppose they've dumped the surprise send-off for Doug on you."

"Not really. The Ladies' Lit has taken over. My job seems to be to see that Doug acts surprised."

"Ah, the little plots and subplots of the campus world," he said.

"The longer you hang around the less trivial it becomes."

"Here comes the Friday special," he replied.

"Looks good," she said. "We can't always take prime rib. What would we have to look forward to if we did?"

"This for instance," he said, reaching across the table and taking her hands in his. "I want you to move in with me," he said. "How many times must I ask you? Please," he implored.

"Your sleeve is in the gravy," she said, "and so is mine."

"Oh, God," he moaned, letting her go. "Who cares? I am a lonely man. I want you. What's this about an apartment in Music Hall. Have you ever seen one of those overflow places?"

"It's only temporary."

"Come live with me."

"I can't. Even if I wanted to I couldn't," she said. "What would people say? We'd both be fired, probably. I was here before cards, before cigarettes, before booze, before sex. The feelings still run deep. My parents would be devastated."

"I think you're too sensitive about the past. The world is changing. We can say we're engaged. We can be engaged. We can be married if that's what you want."

And she did, but not this way. She wanted to be loved and cherished again. That was what she wanted.

★ ★ ★

It was dark when they returned. She could see a light in her father's study and another in the kitchen. He was sorting books, her mother was packing dishes. There were already boxes on the back porch, taped up and labeled: PUNCH BOWL AND TWO DOZEN CUPS, PLATTERS, JELLY JARS. Packed boxes that contained the remnants of a lifetime of events that might not come again. How many more parties would that punch bowl service, how much jelly would Grace seal for just the two of them?

"Come in?" Eleanor asked.

"Not tonight." But Dave took her in his arms and began to kiss her, light kisses and then suddenly kisses that revealed his desperate need.

"Please," he murmured, "please."

But she wasn't ready and she opened the car door and went quickly up the path away from him.

And then suddenly it was June. One week the campus was flooded with parents and alumni, and by the next the dormitories were deserted. The library went on its summer schedule, and Eleanor took time to help her parents pack. Doug was officially retired, but he wasn't ready to move and he prowled aimlessly through the stacks in case something of

308

importance had been overlooked.

As she worked at home it seemed impossible her parents could move into a smaller house and yet as time passed and things were discarded, order took over.

Both of her parents were tired. John, now retired, worked without comment, but Grace would hold up something and say, "Remember when you and Jane wore these?" Other times she wondered out loud: Whose was this? Did Eleanor think it was Will's and, if so, would he want it now?

"No," Eleanor said, quite sure Will would not want whatever it was.

On the day they moved, Eleanor went to the new house to direct the movers, while John and Grace went one last time through the rooms of Drury House.

"Now, Mother," said John, "no looking back."

"I know it," she said, but she felt as though she were being physically torn away from all that was dear to her. Their footsteps echoed in the empty house, and it seemed to Grace that even after they were gone there would be sounds in the rooms. The imprint of their life here went too deep to be simply swept away, vacuumed away, carried away by the movers, and she began to cry. She could actually hear the sound of children on the stairs, water running, doors slamming, and she turned to John and put her arms up like a child and gasped, "I can't bear it."

He held her close and stroked her back and murmured platitudes, but it was comforting and she took the handkerchief he offered and mopped at her face. But when he said, "There now, Mother . . ." she suddenly stiffened, and, looking up at him, she said, "I don't want to be called mother anymore. I was mother here, but over there I am going to be Grace." Then, because she was afraid she might have hurt his feelings, she began to sniffle again.

"All right, Grace," said John, "quit your bawling. We've got a lot to do before night."

The movers finished at the new house around three, and by five the bed was made and enough dishes unpacked to make a meal possible. Friends from both sides of the river dropped in, bringing food and flowers and viewing the chaos sympathetically.

When the movers eased out of the drive, Grace called Eleanor and asked her to come for supper. "There's so much here," she said, but all Eleanor wanted was a shower. "There's enough here," she said, "I'll just stay at home."

She had said "at home" without thinking. It had probably hurt her mother, but perhaps Drury House would always be home to all of them. Now she had to check things at the library and then, perhaps, she could settle down for the night.

Driving slowly up the hill later, she felt sad and exhausted. The house, in the early shadows of evening, looked large and graceless. Even the lilacs at the back drooped with the weight of blooms that were as limp and heavy as overripe fruit, and the house, with its dormers and chimneys, seemed angular and threatening in its forsaken state.

All the same, when she opened the door and stepped in and found things in good order, considering the absence of furniture, she began to feel differently. The campus crew would come in later, after she moved, and clean up the remains, salvaging some and taking the rest to the dump. Her mother had said over and over again during the past weeks that she certainly didn't want "them" talking about "us" when "they" came, "they" being the new residents. Grace had heard too many remarks in the past about faculty who had left unbelievable messes, even to the disgraceful point of spoiling vegetables and half-empty jars in the refrigerator.

On her way home Eleanor had stopped at the post office and found a letter from Val in the box. She would read it later. She put it on the kitchen counter, shed her jacket, and began to go through the house, one room at a time.

She didn't bother with the attic because her father had told her they would take care of that. She had never liked the attic, although on a rainy day it was ideal for hide-and-seek, being dark and scary with spider webs hanging in the corners and swarms of dead flies trapped on the sills between the screens and the windows. She made sure the attic door was locked and proceeded along the hall to her parents' room, which, at first, appeared to be empty. Opening the closet, she found several boxes neatly tied and labeled for the Morgan Memorial. She hadn't thought about the Morgan Memorial in a long time. She could remember her mother dropping in old clothes that were faded, buttonless, and holey. Her mother would say, "When there is absolutely no more wear in something, put it in the Morgan Memorial. They take anything."

"Rags?" she asked. "Even rags?"

"Rags can be torn up and made into rugs. Rags can be processed and turned into paper."

I must remember to put my rags in a special box, Eleanor told herself sternly.

All of the upstairs rooms were cleared except for a few remains that her parents had sorted and labeled SALVATION ARMY, MORGAN MEMORIAL, and DUMP. In the sewing room she found her mother's old dress form, head-less, limbless, the matronly torso of a forty-year-old woman stiff on its pedestal. Even without head, arms, and legs it seemed ready to make a statement of some sort, justifying its existence, she supposed. It was obviously not ready to surrender itself to destruction, although her mother had tied a tag around its neck that said DUMP. Wouldn't it be more merciful to put it in a bonfire? wondered Eleanor with a shudder, for that struck her as being almost like murder.

Suddenly she heard someone pounding on the back door. The sound seemed to echo through the house, and as she went down the stairs she thought she heard glass rattling and pots and pans clanging. It was only Dave.

"Well," he said, "just as I thought. Nothing for supper."

"Neither crust nor bone," she said. "Come in."

"I came to take you to dinner. How about it?"

"Tonight?"

"Yes, of course tonight."

For an instant she was tempted to say, "Let's eat here." There were cans of things and the fridge was half full, but the house was so bare and empty.

"Give me ten minutes to clean up," she said,

"and have a beer. I saw one in the fridge."

It was dark when he brought her home and when they turned up the drive she saw that even the house was dark. She hadn't thought of leaving a light. They had always been there with the house lights on and usually the sound of music on the radio.

"How stupid," she said, "not a light in the place. Keep your headlights on until I get the door unlocked," and she ran up the path to the back door, knocked over a milk bottle that crashed at her feet, and began to fumble with the key.

She turned to wave and smiled blindly into the glare of headlights, and suddenly there he was. "Not so fast," he said, "what's your hurry?"

"If you could see what I have to do you wouldn't ask."

"I'll help."

"Another time," she said. "I enjoyed myself greatly. Thanks."

"Think nothing of it," he said.

"I did, really. Thanks so much."

She was aching and tired and wished she could start over again, say something flippant, put him to work, touch him, smile. And then suddenly his arms were around her and he bent down and kissed her, a light kiss, almost too gentle to endure, and she felt herself shivering.

"Why are you shaking?" he asked. "Don't you think I'm entitled to one kiss?"

"Yes."

"And one for the road?"

"One more," she murmured and her hands found their way around him, and his lips on hers carried a more definite message, so that when they broke away she might have said, "Come in, it's not late," but she held back. The time was coming, but not yet.

That night she went to work in the kitchen. Even the top shelves had been scrubbed and here again things were in neatly labeled boxes. Which would it be here? Morgan Memorial or dump? But this time another recipient was provided. The Girl Scouts would take anything that still worked or held water. *Give them a ring,* Grace had scribbled on her note, *they will come and get it. And,* Grace had added, *everything useless goes to the MM.*

"Dear God," said Eleanor, "thank you again for the Morgan Memorial."

Before she turned out her light, she read Val's letter. They were moved, wrote Val. She could walk Allison to school. They had nice neighbors. Will hadn't been out of town for some time.

Did that mean, wondered Eleanor, that things were better or worse? She sighed and turned off the light. June bugs, attracted by the light, pinged against the screens. She probably wouldn't sleep. She would lie there and wonder why Val and Will continued to live together. How many years had Sissy been at the vortex of their troubles? What did the move to Darien really mean? Why was Will so easily manipulated? Was he weak and selfish? Or did they expect too much of him?

Only her parents and Aunt Alice appeared to be capable of managing their own lives, but of course they had reached the point of resignation long ago. Whatever unsatisfied longings they might have had must now be buried under private mountains of inescapable memories.

Until now Eleanor had seen that as her allotment in life. Was she, too, destined to be crushed by memories? she had worried. But now she had other things to think about, and just across campus Dave might be turning off his light, too.

20

Eleanor's last thought as she fell asleep was that she must try to give her parents more attention than usual. The dismantling of her own room was enough to make her realize what a wrenching experience this must be for them. Of course there were several old campus friends now living in Northridge and surely they would seek each other out for mutual commiseration if nothing else. The McIntyres came to mind. They had been missionaries in China and had come to Harrison in 1939. For a long time the McIntyres didn't play card games of any sort. Sherry, or anything else alcoholic, had never touched their lips, said Mamie McIntyre. But retirement had mellowed them, and it was said that they were avid bridge players now. She hoped retirement would have the same benign effect on her parents.

I am so tired, she thought, and then she didn't think anything else at all until the phone rang the next morning and she started up in alarm.

"Is that you, Eleanor?" asked her mother. "You sound hoarse."

"I'm fine, Mother."

"I know it's only seven, but I wanted to catch you before you got to the library."

"Is everything all right?"

"More or less," said her mother, "but I wish you'd come over here later on if you can. Your father's knocking a hole in the house."

Oh, my God, thought Eleanor, who immediately visualized her father, white-haired and frantic, battering down a wall in his desperation to escape. If this was his reaction after one night in the house, what would happen next? she thought in despair.

"What kind of a hole, Mother?" she asked calmly.

"He's taking out a window. It's not as bad as it sounds and I suppose if he wants to make a door where a window is now that's his business, but he's doing it by himself and he's planning to add a room and a bath to the house. He's coming down the stairs now so I'll have to hang up, but —"

Her mother's voice was remarkably strong, thought Eleanor, as though all the tubes and wheels of her body were working well, a new and reassuring development. Eleanor could hear her now speaking firmly to her father.

"Eleanor!" barked her father. "Is that you?"

"Yes."

"We need a downstairs bedroom and bath. The lot's big enough, there won't be any trouble over a permit. Don't pay any attention to your mother. She'll thank me this winter."

Her mother interrupted from the upstairs phone. "He's doing it all himself," she said indignantly. "We don't need it. If it's not his back it will be his heart."

"Never mind that now," said Eleanor. "I'll be over as soon as I can."

Grace had barely finished talking with Eleanor when the phone rang. It was Alice.

"Grace, darling," said Alice. "How are you? Your letter is just here and I wanted to catch you before you got away for the day."

Where on earth would we be going, thought Grace, but she said, "How good to hear your voice."

"I was just thinking about you and what a long time it's been since I have heard from you and suddenly, in the mail, came your letter. I didn't realize John was ready for retirement."

"Things have been hectic here," said Grace.

"Well, I should think so. And you're living

in Northridge, that pretty little town with the wide Main Street and the churches."

"Yes," said Grace.

"Bring me up to date, dear," said Alice. "How is Eleanor and what about Will and his family?"

"All's well," said Grace. "Val and Will have just moved into a house in Darien. Eleanor will go into school housing. She's still in the library but I think I mentioned that in my letter."

"You must tell her that Sissy spends most of her time in Chatham and will want her to come for a visit this summer. Ned has built her a studio there and she is painting."

"I didn't know she painted."

"Nothing like Jane, of course. Jane's work is really beautiful. Sissy does more what I would call dabbling."

"That sounds like fun."

"I suppose it is, but I'd prefer she'd spend more time with Ned and the children. Of course they are going to Vienna soon, so she hasn't cut herself off entirely."

"It all sounds lovely," said Grace.

"Is John there?" asked Alice. "Did you know he'd written me about making a gift to the school?"

"Yes," said Grace.

"Tell him I am thinking of a memorial for

Harold. Of course I haven't any money, but I think Ned would be interested, for Sissy's sake, of course."

"That would be marvelous. I'll tell him," said Grace, "and love to Sissy."

"Thanks. I won't be seeing her until the first of the week. This is one of her New York weekends. They have a place on Park Avenue . . . but, of course, you know all about that."

Grace knew there was an apartment somewhere, but she said, "Thank you for calling. It's lovely to hear your voice."

"Tell John I'll let him know about the money and do stay well. Bye, bye."

That morning Ned and Sissy sat at opposite ends of the table in the breakfast room, a small, pleasant room that overlooked the garden, which was now a mass of blooms.

Sissy poured their coffee and Ned looked up from the paper. "The Brandons will be in town this weekend," he said. "They want us to have dinner with them at the Ritz tomorrow."

"I'm sorry," she said, "but I'm going down to Chatham today and I won't be home until Sunday."

"I thought you were going to New York today," he said, and Sissy, who was close to the edge, said quickly, "that's next weekend."

"There's nothing pressing in Chatham, and I want you here."

There was to her. She had a date with the builder and Will was coming down. She was boxed in on all sides, and she said, "I don't like the Brandons. They're years older than I am."

"That's your misfortune."

"Tell them I'm sick. Tell them anything you like."

"I ask very little of you, Cornelia."

She rang for more coffee as she tried to think of an out. She hadn't seen Will in weeks. Damn, she thought.

At that moment Ned's eggs appeared. He always had two poached eggs in the morning, two opaque lumps placed on crustless triangles of thin toast, and she watched with distaste as he cut into them, precisely quartering each egg with his knife and fork. Inasmuch as Ned never troubled her at night anymore, it was not Ned who revolted her, but Ned's habits, his eggs, his pink and white skin, his close-shaven cheeks, his small shoes, always shined, his short, manicured fingernails with their perfect white moons. He was a little man, and as he grew older he became smaller and more dapper, whiter, a short man with a small paunch who wore dark suits and starched white shirts and silk ties.

"You know how much Chatham means to me," said Sissy. "I haven't had any place or any time to paint in years. I've never had a real studio."

Sissy sighed. It probably wasn't worth a scene. She would have to get in touch with Will, but that would be easy enough to do.

"All right, Ned," she said, and then to get as much mileage out of it as possible, she added, "Just for you."

It was a lost weekend in Wellesley. After behaving with all the charm she could summon, and enduring Mary Brandon's inane monologues rhapsodizing her two grandchildren, who were potty trained at one and reading at four, Sissy felt entitled to a reward, and as soon as the Brandons left, she called Will. "I'm sorry about the weekend," she said, "they were deadly people, but they're gone and I've got to see you. We're leaving so soon. Can't we make it tomorrow, darling? I've missed you so terribly."

"Where?" he asked.

"In New York."

"I might be able to manage that," he said. "Chatham is out for the present."

"We'll work that out later," said Sissy, "and I'll see you tomorrow?"

"Right," said Will.

As usual she was there ahead of him and, as she sat there sipping a martini, she tried to think what she could say that he would not misunderstand. The last time they had been together everything seemed to go wrong and she wanted to make up.

When he finally appeared she waved and smiled and said, "Darling, I was afraid you were going to stand me up."

"Sorry," he said, "I couldn't get a cab."

"You really should get a driver, Will."

She is impossible, he thought. Where was he going to get the money for a car and driver, particularly now when he had just taken on a thirty-year mortgage?

"All set for Vienna?" he asked.

"More or less. I never know what to take for Matthew."

"It must be a terrible problem," he said, "and to think you've just gone through the ordeal of Paris."

"That's hateful," she said.

"Sorry. How long will you be gone?"

"Only two weeks. I told you that, Will."

"It must be nice to be married to a rich man."

"What's the matter with you? You know I have to be nice to Ned."

His drink came and he gulped it.

"Are you hungry?" she asked.

"Not particularly," he replied. "I have never been to Vienna," he said slowly. "I will probably never go to Vienna. However, there is a Vienna, Virginia, on the outskirts of our nation's capital. I might manage that someday."

"Oh, Will," she said. "Don't."

"Don't what?"

"Don't talk that way. Don't you think we ought to order?"

"Fine," he said, "you order."

She ordered filet of sole and salad and black coffee. She wondered what was the matter. Will had never been so . . . but, on the other hand, Will had been difficult for weeks now. Every time she tried to make him understand that she had to humor Ned more, he said hateful things. As though he thought she wanted to be nice to Ned. He ought to be able to see it from her side. Why had she gone along all these years if not to have the kind of life that would make it possible for them to meet and make love, and what about him and Val? He could have divorced her years ago. Why hadn't he?

They ate slowly. The wine was good, but as he sat there drinking Will was aware that he had had too much. He didn't feel like talking. Talking with Sissy had become like being the bat board at the tennis courts. He was the board and she served. He was tired of hearing about her studio and Paris and now Vienna. He was bored with Miss Purse and how wonderful she was with Matthew. Miss Purse had seen Paris with them and now she would see Vienna.

"Darling," said Sissy, "you've barely touched your dinner."

"Sorry," he said. "I'm tired. It's been a hellish week."

"I'm afraid we can't go to the apartment," said Sissy, "but don't worry, darling, I have a hotel. I am actually supposed to be in Philadelphia with one of my Vassar pals, who hasn't lived there in three years, as a matter of fact."

"It's all right," he said. "I'm not feeling up to par tonight anyway."

Dammit, thought Sissy, he's doing this on purpose. There's no pleasing him. But she smiled and said, "I understand, darling. Sometimes life is just too much." As she said this she had a funny feeling that she had said it all before, and then, suddenly, she realized that she was talking to him the same way she talked to Ned. Humoring him, coaxing him, trying to please him when what she really wanted was someone to please her.

"Let's go," he said abruptly, dropping two fifties on the table, and, lurching to his feet, he grabbed her wrist and pulled her along.

"Stop it, Will," she said, "you're hurting me."

But he held on to her and she stumbled after him, trying to look as though she were perfectly willing to be dragged offstage, and, in the entry, content to struggle with her own coat while he fumbled with his.

Outside the balmy day had turned to rain and a playful breeze had now become a gust that drove the rain under the canopy where they stood.

"This is terrible," said Sissy, hopping up and down as the rain drenched her feet. "Don't you see a cab? You can't just stand there. For heaven's sake, go out in the street and flag one."

"Patience," Wilson said, "patience, Cornelia," and he rammed his hands into his pockets and stood rocking back and forth as he glanced up and down the street. Eventually someone would pull in for the start of their evening and then he and Sissy would be able to finish theirs.

When a cab finally drew up, he held the door for her and helped her in. "I'll let you go this time," he said. "If I don't see you again before you get off, have a good time."

He sounded so final she almost grabbed his arm and begged him to come with her, but she could see that he was soaked and he looked tired. She could always count on Will, couldn't she? All she had to do was smile and reach for his hand. Now she smiled and, brushing her hair back with her hand, she said, "I know I look awful. Next time will be better. We're both tired." She leaned forward and kissed him. "There, darling," she said. "Take care of yourself."

He stood, watching the cab thread its way down the street, and then he turned in the opposite direction. Turning up his collar, he began to walk more rapidly, heading up the street toward the lighted avenue, taking long strides and breathing deeply. He passed a boutique and saw a mannequin in a slinky black dress with a piece of fur slung over its shoulder. It made him think of Sissy and the sort of outfit she liked, and it occurred to him that after all this time he knew pretty well what Sissy liked and what she wanted.

Right now she wanted to go to Vienna, but she wanted it on her terms.

She wanted to spend time in Chatham and stay for as long as it suited her to stay; to paint if she felt like painting; to come and go to New York and other places she had become accustomed to, when the mood struck;

and to see him when she felt like seeing him.

He reached the corner and paused to glance at his watch. There were still people passing along purposefully, but here and there, in shadowed doorways and around corners, there were loiterers, those who drifted in the margins.

Was he one of these? Someone destined to live on the edge of things, neither here nor there, bending always to accommodate the life-styles and wishes of others? Whom, but Allison, could he call his own? What did Val want from him and what had Sissy ever given him? How many years had he wasted trying to do the best he could for each of them and what now was to be his reward?

Suddenly he saw an empty cab turn in his direction and without a moment's hesitation, he stepped into the middle of the street to hail it. There seemed to be only one place left to him and, fleetingly, it seemed odd to him that he hadn't realized this sooner.

By God, he thought, it's not too late and with a little bit of luck I can catch the last train for Darien and be home for the weekend.

21

Eleanor left Drury House for the last time one hot day in June, and as she backed down the drive a part of her felt the pain of it as keenly as though she had suffered an injury, while another part of her tingled with excitement. Her car was crammed with clothes and lamps and pictures, things she didn't want to leave for the building crew who had stripped the house and taken off before her.

She had wanted to be last and alone. The idea of breaking down and shedding tears seemed foolish, but however she felt, she wanted to be alone.

"Can you understand that?" she asked Dave. To her parents she said, "I'll let you know."

Reaching the bottom of the drive she stopped the car and gazed back at the house. It's a nice house, she thought, substantial, pleasing, a well-built house, a family house. A good house, but she was glad to be leaving it. It was time to put away the past and think about the future. There had been too much sadness here, but perhaps that wasn't to be blamed on the house. Still, Drury House was the scene of their suffering, she would be glad to leave it behind.

The truck with her furniture was backed up to the basement entrance of Music Hall, where an elevator, big enough to accommodate a piano, was already half loaded with her possessions. A paint crew was working at one end of the building. They had finished painting in her apartment the day before and left the windows open. Now late afternoon sun poured into the room and all of the screens, which had been left unhooked, had invited the attention of flies and mosquitoes.

As the men staggered up the hall with the ponderous, overstuffed mahogany-legged chairs and sofa, she stood in the middle of the room trying to decide where to put them. As it turned out there was only one place big enough to take the sofa and the other monsters of the past. The sight of them squatting uncomfortably in the small room was depressing. Slipcovers might improve them, but she wished she could simply send them off to the Salvation Army and buy something new. Lord, it's depressing, she thought. She had brought Drury House with her, right into

Music Hall, and she gave up trying to direct traffic and went from window to window hooking screens and pulling down window shades.

Someone had filled the ice trays in the refrigerator and she made some ice water and collapsed on the sofa, sinking into deep plush that had never seemed so thick and woolly before. Perhaps Aunt Alice had been right when she told her to come back to Boston to teach at Chambers again. If she had done that she might now be living in an apartment in Cambridge with blond Danish furniture and a Jordan Marsh wardrobe in her closet.

The men were finally finished. She heard the last rattle and bang of the service elevator and then suddenly it was silent. Not knowing what to do next, she went into the bedroom and hunted for a towel and shampoo, her bathrobe and hair dryer, and then she took a shower. Shampoo foamed over her shoulders and water hitting the sides of the metal shower stall roared in her ears. She felt as though she was standing naked under a waterfall. Perhaps she could stay there for a long time, at least long enough for the furniture and the walls to fight it out among themselves for space in the small rooms.

When she finished she felt better and, pulling on her robe, she stood at the window toweling her hair and thinking. From her bedroom window she could see the chapel on the bluff above the athletic field. Time went so fast it wouldn't be long before the trees on the hillside would be red and gold, the air crisp with fall and trees in the orchard heavy with apples. Boys singly and in groups would be crossing campus, kicking soccer balls, shouting, rushing to class, flooding toward the dining hall. There would be frost in the morning, fog in the valley, pumpkins on doorsteps, cider, open fires, a world she loved, and all of it quickening as the term advanced toward Christmas.

She plugged in the hair dryer and waved it over her hair, blowing it into waves and curls, and it was some time before she realized there was someone at the door. Opening the door a crack, she saw Dave, flowers in one hand and a bottle of champagne in the other. Clutching her robe together and shaking her hair away from her face she said, "Everything's a mess and it's sweltering. Come in. Are the flowers for me? And what about the bottle? Oh, you wonderful man," and she flung the door open and let him in.

As she backed away, stumbling over a foot stool that hadn't decided where it belonged, he reached out and caught her and as he pulled her into his arms he saw a white edge of breast and curve of waist, and taking a deep breath he said, "So that's what's been hiding underneath those skirts and sweaters."

By then he had glimpsed leg and thigh and glancing down he saw a slim pale foot, narrow and childlike. "Not to mention sensible shoes," he added. "What is it about academe that compels women to hide their best features under a layer of —"

"I know," she interrupted, "drab, ancient, good, basic clothes."

"Ah, but the unmasking."

"The heat has gone to your head," she said.

"Don't change," he said, "sit down and tell me what you'd like to do about dinner."

"I would like to go somewhere air-conditioned and have a huge salad."

"And a chilled bottle, and what else?"

"Let me dress."

He eased her down beside him, careful not to rearrange her costume although he was tempted to rip it off. What did she want? he wondered. Peg had never wanted any nonsense. She was direct and physical for the time required, but she didn't want cuddling and small talk. Peg had been good in bed, eager and lusty if it suited her, which, toward the end, it rarely did. After the terrible jolt of her leaving it had taken him a while to realize it was not entirely him, it was her convictions that women were deprived, legally, financially, every way, that had taken her away from him, and by then it was too late to try again.

Eleanor's hair was soft and fragrant, still damp. He leaned toward her and suddenly they were kissing in a way they had not kissed before.

Pulling away, she gasped, "I've got to get dressed."

"Why? Why do you have to dress?"

"I just do. I can't go anywhere looking like this," she said desperately because she suddenly wanted him to pull off her robe and ravish her.

His arms tightened around her. "I won't hurt you. That's the last thing I want. I don't want to hurt you."

"I know," she said. "I don't know. I'm —"

"You talk too much," he said, stroking her hair.

"I know."

"I suppose you want to be married. Is that it?"

"No," she said abruptly. "If I wanted to be married I'd say so. I don't want to take advantage of you, make you feel you have to marry me. You know."

He laughed. "Go ahead. Take advantage

of me," and he pulled her closer and began to kiss her again.

Oh the wonder of it, she thought, giving in, letting him lead the way, and then, suddenly pushing him away she stood up, clutching her robe across her heaving breasts. She backed away from him, bumping into a carton of books, muttered, "Damn," and continued, "Of course I want to be married. I want children. I want a home. I want to marry somebody who loves me, and I will love him. And I want to know about Peg and tell you about Charles. What is the use in getting married if they are part of the package?"

She was panting now and sat down suddenly, glared at him, and said, "I hate this furniture. I have lived my life with it. They were good to let me have it and I am supposed to be making do, but I want something new. Something that is mine, not somebody else's. I don't want to marry you and sleep in the bed Peg slept in. I don't care if that sounds funny. It's the way I feel."

"Peg didn't sleep in my bed, not since we came here. She slept on a futon on the floor. She said it would keep her from getting round shouldered in her old age."

"Did it?"

He laughed. "I wouldn't know. It is my considered opinion that Peg will go through life as rigid as a broomstick because she doesn't know how to give and take."

"What does that mean?"

"It means she doesn't give. She takes."

"I guess I more or less knew that, but do you think it's fair to divorce a woman just because she thinks women get the short end of the stick? Was she a good cook? Did she keep you in clean socks? Was she good in bed?"

"She was a passable cook and I suppose the laundry got done. Yes, she was good in bed, if I remember correctly."

"How good?"

"Jesus," he said irritably, "you are like all women. I did not like her futon. I did not like her rigid body even when it was demanding attention. I must have been in love with her once, but by the time we were divorced I wasn't even angry with her anymore. If I had wanted to sleep on the futon seven nights a week I could have, but I didn't want to. I was living with a stranger. I don't want that to happen again."

He looked at his watch. "Well," he said, "bed first or bed later or bed not at all?"

"Don't you want to know about Charles?"

"If you want to tell me."

"I loved him. If he were here now I would still love him. We didn't have time to take up causes, but even if we had I wouldn't have wanted to take the time."

"I see."

"He was wonderful in bed. When he was killed I thought I would never want to go to bed with another man."

"I see."

"But when it's been good you are so aware of what you've lost. Not just a warm body in a bed, but someone to be close to. Someone you could always talk to and someone who would always understand."

"You want a lot," he said, reaching for a cigarette. All this talk. What did it amount to? There must be some way to wipe the slate and start over again.

"I don't like cigarette smoke," said Eleanor.

"There, you see," he said, "we are not meant for each other."

Rising, he crossed to the window, where he stood watching the shadows yawn toward dusk.

She knew then that he had been hurt in more ways than she had. If they married she would have been blessed with two good husbands while he had lost one wife bitterly and wondered now what he could hope for with another. She crossed to the window, put her arms around him, and leaned against his back. "I would love you too," she said. "There is

always room for more love in one's life . . .
but bitterness? Never."

He stood quite still.

"Please," she said, "please tell me you love
me."

"I love you," he said, without turning. "I
want you to marry me."

"And you will love me forever and ever?"

"Yes. And you will worship the ground I
walk on."

"And you will give me children before it's
too late."

"And you will give me comfort and understanding."

"Yes."

And then, at last, he turned and held her
tightly while they listened to the chapel clock
strike seven and saw the bright light of afternoon soften to gray. He leaned down and
kissed her gently, kissed her forehead, her
face, her lips, her throat, and she, reaching
up to put her face against his, said, "Wouldn't
it be a good idea to go to bed now, and then,
perhaps, later too?"

22

A week later, when Eleanor groped her way back from the Elysium Fields, where she and Dave had been living in discreet rapture, they had settled on Thanksgiving for the wedding. Neither of them wanted a wedding, as such, but they wanted to be married and if the school or her parents discovered that they were already sleeping together, they might be obliged to move the day forward.

"Suppose we're tired of each other by then?" she said to his bare shoulder, and he, basking in the glory of sharing her bed and her body, mumbled, "Rubbish."

"I think we should go over to Northridge this weekend and alert Mother and Daddy," she said.

And he nodded and kissed her throat and gave other positive evidence of agreement.

Grace was delighted and said promptly, "We'll have the reception here," and she went immediately to her desk and rummaged around until she found a piece of paper and then she began to make a guest list.

John thumped Dave on the back and kissed Eleanor and said, "Splendid."

Grace stopped scribbling and, looking up, said to no one in particular, "We really ought to have engraved invitations this time. Do you think there's time to order?"

"Of course there's time," said Eleanor, "but that's not what we want. All we want is to go to the chapel with witnesses."

"Well, of course we'll have witnesses, dear," said her mother. "We will all be witnesses. I mean for the others, the guests."

"I thought, I mean *we* thought, it would be nice to have just family and special friends. Dave's parents will drive down from Maine, and we both have one or two college friends near enough to consider it. I thought we would phone people here and write notes to the others."

"Oh," said Grace, and she looked at John, who nodded and said, "She's the boss, Grace. Whatever they want to do is fine with me."

"Well," said Grace briskly, "we must have a cake and coffee, and nuts and sandwiches. It will be cold by Thanksgiving so we can have a fire and we could decorate with greens and poinsettias. Who would you want to invite, dear?"

"Oh, you know," said Eleanor carelessly because her thoughts were years away, when she and Jane had been little girls and her mother would go to weddings and bring home tiny boxes of wedding cake tied with white ribbon, which they would put under their pillows at night. Jane used to say . . . but what did it matter now? She put her mind to the task at hand and said, "Doug Parsons, of course."

"He's buying a house here in town. Did you know?" said Grace, writing his name on her paper. "We'll have to have him in for supper, John." And then she turned back to Eleanor and said, "Go on."

"I'll have to get my address book," said Eleanor. "Let's not worry about it now."

"How about Alice and Sissy," said Grace.

"Of course," said Eleanor. "We couldn't have a wedding without them, could we?"

But, as it happened, they were going to have to, because when Alice replied to Grace's note she wrote, *I can't bear it. I am going to miss another wedding. Sissy too and we are both heartbroken.*

Grace was reading this aloud, and when she read the word *heartbroken* Grace looked up and shook her head and said, "How absurd Alice is."

"Go on," said Eleanor. "Why can't they come?"

Grace began again with *we are both heart-broken* and continued, *Cornelia has invited me to go to Florida with them for Thanksgiving. It will be their last visit to the Palm Beach house — Ned says Palm Beach is getting too crowded for comfort.*

Grace paused and said, "I can't imagine such a thing."

"Go on," said John. "Finish it."

Well, it can't be helped I suppose but I am terribly disappointed. Give Eleanor a hug for me and have a happy time. Eleanor is very special to me, you know. I often think back to her Cambridge days when she was with me at Fresh Pond Park, and I have the happiest memory of our trip to London. I am sending her a little package addressed to you for safe keeping. It is not the ordinary sort of wedding gift, but something just for her. I want her to have something of mine that she can keep forever or until she has a little girl of her own to pass it on to.

"Oh dear," said Grace, jumping up. "It came just this morning. I nearly forgot it," and she went to the mantel and reached behind the clock. "I can't imagine what it is," she said, "but it's addressed to you, dear."

Eleanor turned the box slowly in her hands. She had imagined a piece of china, or furniture, books, or even a second-best fur jacket that had been replaced by Sissy's mink.

"Open it," said Grace. "What do you suppose it could be in a box that size?"

It was an old and faded jeweler's box, big enough for pearls, but it was not pearls. It was a ring accompanied by a note and Aunt Alice's card. Eleanor looked at it carefully then handed it to her mother. It was an old-fashioned ring, a red stone surrounded by diamonds, or perhaps rhinestones, and she wondered if the note would be illuminating or just another of Aunt Alice's vagaries.

Dear Eleanor, Aunt Alice had written. *This is just for you. You have been a second daughter to me and I want you to have this ring that I have cherished since Elliot bought it for me in Paris on our wedding trip. He told me it was a ruby with diamonds and I've no reason to doubt him, but that is not the reason I have treasured it. It represented all our hopes and plans, many of which I have experienced through the lives of our children and friends. May you be blessed with all the good things I have had. Think of it as a token, a part, a remembrance, your share of my estate. For all your kindness to me you surely deserve a portion . . .*

Eleanor stopped reading. She could feel herself beginning to cry and she didn't want to cry. It was a lovely gift, whatever its value. It was more than a token, it was a giving of self and she was grateful.

Don't be silly, she told herself taking a deep breath and looking up, but no one was looking at her. They were all inspecting the ring.

Grace had put it on her finger and was admiring it.

"Look at it," said Grace. "It's quite lovely. I'm surprised at Alice, but then, of course, she didn't have to pay for it, did she?"

John frowned at her and shook his head, and Grace passed it to Dave, who took Eleanor's hand and led her to the window where, in the sunlight, they could see the sparkling circle of diamonds and the radiance of the ruby. He lifted her hand and kissed it.

"There," he said. "It's beautiful. You are beautiful. I hadn't expected to marry a woman of substance. I was willing to take you, penniless as you are. Mind you remember that."

"I do so pledge," said Eleanor. "For as long as I live."